intimidation

intimidation

Wanda L. Dyson

BARBOUR
PUBLISHING

ISBN 1-59310-244-5

Cover design by UDG DesignWorks

This book is a work of fiction. Names, characters, places, and incidents are either products of the author's imagination or used fictitiously. Any similarity to actual people, organizations, and/or events is purely coincidental.

For more information about Wanda L. Dyson, please access the author's Web site at the following Internet address: www.WandaDyson.com

Published by Barbour Publishing, Inc., P.O. Box 719, Uhrichsville, OH 44683, www.barbourbooks.com

Our mission is to publish and distribute inspirational products offering exceptional value and biblical encouragement to the masses.

 Member of the
Evangelical Christian
Publishers Association

Printed in the United States of America.
5 4 3 2 1

dedication

Christi. . .you know all the reasons why.
And to my Father. . .for loving me the way You do.

acknowledgments

Thanks to all the wonderful people at Locks of Love, ACFW, Rehoboth Ministries, and the Frederick County Christian Writer's Group.

A very special thanks to Roger Ruel for all his expertise, writers Kendra Parson and Candy Spears for all the brainstorming, and Margie Vawter for her labor of love in editing this series.

And to my daughter Jayme for being so patient and helpful while I was recuperating from surgery and then spending so many hours holed up in my office trying to write through the pain. I love you, baby girl.

prologue

Revenge is best served cold.

Well, if that were true, then this was going to be a gourmet's prizewinning dream.

Buttoning his collar against the night's cold wind, Archie thrust the shovel into the dirt and stepped on it, pushing the blade deeper before tipping back the handle, lifting it out, and tossing the soil to his left.

He wasn't thrilled with being out here in the woods at two in the morning, but when someone was willing to pay the kind of money he was making on this job, he'd have braved a blizzard to get this grave done.

It wasn't often he bothered with thoughts of quitting the business and buying a place in the islands, living the easy life. . . but with this kind of money—well, who wouldn't be dreaming of white sand and blue water?

Dead leaves rustled around him, and a lesser man might have been casting wary glances over his shoulder and jumping at shadows. Not Archie. If anyone were foolish enough to be out here, then there would be two bodies in this grave.

After dumping another pile of dirt, he looked over at the .44 sitting within easy reach. It was one of his favorite pieces, completely fitted with a scope and a silencer.

Once he aimed it at something, it was dead.

Off in the distance, a dog started howling. Poor animal. What kind of people would leave a dog out on a night like tonight? By morning, the temperature would be hovering around thirty-five degrees. Why do people get sweet little animals and then toss them out to freeze or suffer through cold rains?

Those people should be chained outside all night so they could see what it was like for their poor dog. Or shot.

Archie entertained himself with thoughts of heading over to find the dog after he'd finished the grave. He'd let the dog loose, then sneak into the house and shoot the owners while they slept.

He wouldn't, of course. He couldn't afford to have the police investigating some meaningless murder and tromping all through these woods looking for possible clues and finding this grave.

Oh no. That would not be a good thing. This grave was reserved for someone very special. And his research confirmed that she was indeed a very special lady. It was unfortunate she was married to an FBI agent who had stuck his nose into someone's business and now that someone was going to strike back.

His instructions were clear. Take the woman, but keep her alive until her husband came through with the disk. Then he was to kill them both and turn the disk over.

He couldn't help wondering what was on that disk. *Must be pretty important to be worth the lives of an FBI agent and his wife.*

Grinning, Archie slammed the shovel down into the ground with renewed strength. Maybe he'd have to take a look at what was on that disk before he turned it over to the man who hired him. Who was to know? And maybe, just maybe, it would be worth a few million to someone.

The clouds parted, and a sliver of moonlight touched on the grave, revealing the cold, black depth.

Almost deep enough.

How long would it take her to die once he sealed the grave? Five minutes? She could hold her breath for maybe three or four, and then the panic would set in. She'd want to scream and yell and claw her way out, but in the end, the black shroud of death would claim her.

What would her last thoughts be? Would she still be fighting death? Or would she surrender to the inevitable and spend her last moment or two thinking about her husband and children?

Too bad he would never be able to find out.

Oh, he could probably put a tape recorder down there with her and come back later to find out if she was screaming or praying or begging. But once he buried her, he wouldn't ever come close to this spot again.

That's how you got caught. And Archie didn't plan on ever getting caught.

You never look back. You never go back. You never think back.

Do the job and walk away.

Then keep on walking.

chapter 1

I need your badge." Chief Harris stared down at his desk, avoiding JJ's eyes. "And your gun."

"I don't believe this." JJ had been struggling to keep his temper under control ever since he'd been called into the chief's office and saw his union representative sitting there. He had suspected this might be coming down, but now that it was, he wasn't prepared for it at all. He yanked his badge from his belt. "It was a good shoot. The kid was robbing the store!"

The kid in question had been a nineteen-year-old with an empty gun and gang colors. The problems for JJ were that he was off duty when he'd entered the store, interrupting a robbery in progress, and that the kid's gun was empty—something he couldn't possibly have known when the kid swung it around and aimed it at him.

"You know how this works. You're on leave until the investigation is complete." Harris lifted his head and eyed JJ's gun, a silent reminder.

JJ yanked the gun from his shoulder holster and slammed it down next to his badge. "This is wrong, and you know it.

I'm not some trigger-jumping rookie. The kid had a gun. He aimed it at me. There was no way in the world I could have known it was empty."

"And did you identify yourself as a police officer? Did you tell him to drop the gun?"

The union representative, a short, thin man in his midforties, coughed, looking pointedly at Harris. "Chief," he said, a warning note in his voice.

JJ tried to stomp down on the urge to punch his fist through a wall. "The kid turned, raised the gun, and aimed it at my face. Tell me something, Chief. You think if that gun *had* been loaded, I would have had time to finish saying *all that* before he pulled the trigger?"

"Lieutenant Johnson," the rep interjected.

"We'll never know, will we?" Harris took JJ's gun and badge, opened a desk drawer, and tossed them in. "This is temporary, Johnson. You know the routine. You'll still collect your paycheck."

"I'm not concerned about my pay!"

"Lieutenant." The rep spoke a little louder. JJ continued to ignore him.

"I have cases I'm working. I have a job to do. Some kid decides to rob a store, and the police officer who stopped it from happening is shoved out the door and sent home. This is—"

"Enough!" Harris cut him off, half rising out of his chair, his bulk shifting. "Go home. Take a vacation. Get drunk. Sleep late. I don't care what you do, but do it somewhere else."

"But—"

"We're done here, Detective. Go home."

JJ spun on the balls of his feet and stalked out of the office, slamming the door behind him. Everyone in the bull pen stopped what they were doing and looked up at him. He glared. They slowly lowered their heads and went back to their work.

"Lieutenant."

JJ whirled around and glared at the rep. "Not now."

"We need to talk."

"Make an appointment with my secretary. I'm on leave."

JJ shoved the door open to his office, muttering under his breath.

His partner, Matt, stood up. "I take it he put you on leave."

JJ grabbed his coat off the rack, knocking it over in the process. He stepped over it, resisting the urge to kick it across the room. "You're in charge. I'm outta here."

"JJ, you know this is procedure and it's only temporary."

"And pigs fly with purple wings." He jammed his arms into his coat sleeves. "I did my job. End of story. Now some family is screaming about their precious little boy being dead, and my neck goes on the chopping block. They should have taught their precious little boy that robbing a store can get you killed."

There was no point taking his outrage out on his best friend, but he was beyond being reasonable. He slammed the office door with even more force than he had the chief's, and headed for the stairs.

You do your job, put your life on the line, dodge bullets and killers and death, and try to keep the town safe. And what happens when you actually succeed? Stripped of authority, stripped of badge and gun, stripped of dignity, and sent home to wait for the idiots in the Internal Affairs Division to finish their *investigation*.

He wanted to tell them what they could do with their investigation.

His Jeep chirped as he punched the keyless remote, turning

off the alarm and unlocking the doors. As soon as he climbed in, he pulled out his cell phone and dialed. While it was ringing, he started the engine.

"This is Zoe Shefford. I can't take your call at the moment. Leave a message, and I'll call you back. Have a blessed day."

Have a blessed day indeed! "Yeah, it's me. Call me." He snapped his phone shut and tossed it to the console between the seats. Then, taking a deep breath, he backed his Jeep out of the parking space. Now what was he supposed to do with his life?

◆　◆　◆

Amanda Marie Bevere had been born on a rainy spring day with very little fuss. She'd been causing a commotion ever since. Her eight-month-old brother, Cody, however, was a quiet, happy baby who demanded very little aside from love and care. And it was a good thing, too, because Mandy was a walking, talking hurricane of activity.

The activity at the moment appeared to be coating her face with her mother's makeup, dressing up in one of Lisbeth's dresses, and carrying a scarf that trailed behind her in a most dramatic fashion.

Donnie bit his lip to keep from laughing as his daughter fluttered the scarf.

" 'Scuse me," Mandy said, her nose in the air. "Has my limmothene arrived yet?"

"Amanda." Lisbeth groaned as she set her paintbrush down and climbed to her feet. "What have you done?"

Unruffled, Mandy began to wave her scarf. "I am sooo late. Call my driver."

Lifting her daughter to her hip, Lisbeth shrugged an apology in Donnie's direction as he continued to work on painting the dining room wall. "I'll be right back. Time to clean up our little glamour girl here."

"Daddy, I'm bootiful, huh?"

Donnie's face twisted with the effort not to laugh. "You certainly are, Mandy Bear. The most beautiful one of all."

His daughter fluttered the scarf in farewell as Lisbeth carried her out of the room. "Who needs to go out for entertainment with a child like her around the house?"

"What was that?" Lisbeth's voice drifted back into the room.

"Nothing, dear," he shouted back to her, allowing himself the luxury of laughing now that the child was gone. Heaven knew Mandy needed no encouragement.

A few minutes later, Lisbeth was back, looking a little flustered. "Have you seen the infant Tylenol?"

Donnie shook his head as he set his paintbrush down. "No, why?"

"Cody is feverish."

"Where's Mandy?"

"I left her in the bathroom when I heard the baby crying."

Donnie grabbed a rag and proceeded to wipe the paint from his hands as he headed upstairs. "I'll clean up Mandy while you take care of Cody."

For once, Mandy had decided to be obedient. Donnie found her perched on the edge of the bathtub, right where his wife had left her. And she hadn't broken or spilled anything while left alone.

Donnie picked her up and set her on the counter next to the sink, wet a washrag, and began to clean her face.

A few minutes later, Lisbeth appeared in the doorway. "Thank you for getting her cleaned up."

"No problem. How's Cody?"

"Sleeping." She put her fists on her hips and turned her attention to Mandy. "Now. What to do with you, young lady. You broke the rules. You know what that means, don't you?"

Mandy dropped her head again, doing a fair job of looking chastised.

Donnie pursed his lips, struggling not to smile. How his wife managed this day after day was beyond him. The child was so precious and so irrepressible.

"Oh, I think you deserve more than just a few tears, Amanda Marie. Since you can't respect other people's things, I guess you can't respect your own, either."

Tears came in earnest now as Mandy twisted her fingers together. "Mommy, I sorry. I sorry. I won't do it again. I won't."

"You told me that last week when you got into my jewelry box." Lisbeth walked away.

Mandy hiccuped pitifully as she struggled to get down off the counter. Donnie picked her up and set her down. She raced out of the room after her mother, pleading. "I sorry, Mommy. I lub you."

Donnie took a deep breath, straightened the bathroom, and thanked God he had the easier job of chasing criminals.

By the time he'd cleaned the bathroom and slipped back downstairs to finish up in the dining room, Lisbeth was standing in the hallway, arms crossed. "Coward."

Donnie threw his hands in the air. "Guilty as charged. Why do you think I buy you anything you want on Mother's Day? I know what you have to deal with." He pulled her into an embrace and kissed her forehead. "What is our daughter doing now?"

"Curled up on her bed, crying her heart out."

Donnie flinched. "I'm sorry."

Lisbeth smiled—one of those crooked little smiles that let him know she was going to torment him and enjoy every second of it. "You'll pay dearly. I want Damon's ribs for dinner."

"Let me clean up the paint, and I'll call in the order and go pick them up." He was getting off light, and he knew it. One look at his daughter's face filled with tears and misery and he would have given the child anything to make her smile. *Yep. Coward.* No backbone at all. If Mandy grew up to be a wonderful, giving, caring woman, it would all be due to Lisbeth's discipline.

"Donnie?" Lisbeth appeared in the doorway leading to the kitchen. "Your phone is ringing."

Donnie set the can of paint down and hurried to answer the phone in his basement office. The phone in the basement was strictly for his coworkers to call him. None of them knew he was married, and he was determined to keep it that way. He may not be very good at facing down his daughter's misery, but he was very determined to keep his family safe. The fewer people who knew he had a family, the less chance someone on the wrong side of the law would use them to get back at him.

"Bevere."

"Don." It was his partner, Jack Fleming. "You watching the news?"

"No, why?"

"Someone leaked the news that several high-level al-Qaeda

prisoners are being brought up from Gitmo for trial. The press is all over this. So much for sneaking them in."

◆　　◆　　◆

. . .and then his dad would come through the door, dressed in a suit and tie, with a big smile and would throw open his arm and sweep Justin up in a bone-crushing hug. "I've been trying to find you for years. I'm so sorry you've had it so rough, but all that's going to change now. I have a big, fine house with a big yard, and you can have your own room, and I'll sign you up for little league, and I'll even coach your team if you want, and we'll go on vacations to places like Disney. . .

A high, sharp voice cut through his daydreams.

"You don't know nothin', old woman. You don't know what it's like for me, strugglin'. . ."

"Strugglin' to what? Find another man to take care of you and your drug habit?"

"It ain't like that!"

Ignoring the fact that one shoelace was untied, Justin slowly crawled out from under the back porch. His mother was back again! Peace and quiet were over. It had lasted all of seven months this time. But as always, she would come sweeping in, screaming and yelling, and upset his grandma and smack him around. When she found some money, she'd disappear without a word.

Days would pass before he and his grandma believed she was gone again. They would tiptoe around, expecting her to come storming in at any moment, but slowly things would get back to normal. Little by little, his grandma would smile again.

"I just need a few dollars to tide me over till I find another job. Why do you have to give me such a hard time?"

" 'Cause I know you, Tamella. You jes' gonna use it to buy more drugs."

Licking his lips, Justin pushed his glasses further up his nose and slowly crept up the porch and into the kitchen.

"Jes' give me a twenty. That's all I need. I know you have it."

Justin eased into the living room. His grandma was standing in the middle of the room, fists on her hips bunching her apron at her waist. "What I have is little enough to support myself and your son! When was the last time you bought anything for that boy? School clothes? Food? Took him to a doctor?"

His mom was pacing, picking at threads on her stained sweatshirt. "I jes' need a break, that's all. I was doin' good on that job till that jerk decided he had to cut back and said I had to go. He shoulda fired Pauline, not me, but she follows him around like a puppy. It's sickening!"

"In other words, she showed up for work every day, didn't stay out all night doin' Lord knows what, and was respectful to her boss. I know the story, Tamella. You don't half work and then blame everyone else when they fire you for it."

There was a moment of silence. Justin held his breath as his mother caught sight of him and turned her full attention in his direction. "Justin Shay! You get yourself over here before I drag you over."

Grandma stepped in front of him. "You leave that boy alone, Tamella Shay! You ain't takin' him out of this house!"

"I just need a few dollars. Twenty. If you can't see your way to help me, I jes' don't see how I can leave my little boy here."

Cautiously, Justin crept closer to his grandma, clinging to her apron strings.

"I ain't givin' you nothing for no more drugs. That boy needs his momma, and he don't need one who's too high to even know his name." She reached behind her and moved Justin aside. "Go to your room, Justin."

His mother reached out and pushed his grandma. "Don't you send him outta here!"

He rushed forward, pushing his mother away. "Don't hurt Grandma!"

Tamella Shay smacked Justin across the head, knocking him to his knees. His grandma wrapped her arms around him and pulled him up against her rail-thin body. "You best leave here now, Tamella, a'fore I call the po–lice."

"Just remember, he's my child, and I can take him any time I want."

As the screen door slammed, his grandma started to rock him, murmuring the Lord's Prayer out of habit. "We must keep praying for your momma, sweet Justin. She's hurtin' mighty bad."

Justin tipped his head back and looked up at his grandma through his tears. She was a tall woman, five-ten in her stockin' feet, she'd told him once, and so skinny she looked sick. She had long gray hair she kept braided and tucked under a turban, with big, dark eyes that rarely smiled anymore. Even at him. "She hurt us, too, Grandma."

"I know, baby. I know."

But it wasn't the smack against the head that had him crying. That didn't really hurt. She'd hit him harder plenty of times. No, it was the threat of taking him away from his grandma. His mother would do it; he knew she would. And if she took him away, who would take care of Grandma?

chapter 2

Y eah, it's me. Call me."
    Zoe frowned as she saved the message on her cell phone and then dropped her phone into her purse. JJ. And he sounded like he was having a bad day. Well, he was just going to have to wait.

She pulled open the door to the salon and stepped in. Light rock music filled the room from speakers in the ceiling, just loud enough to cover most of the numerous conversations going on through the room. The smell of chemicals, sprays, shampoos, conditioners, dyes, and nail polish filled the air like a familiar perfume—comforting in its own strange way.

"Daria busy?"

The young girl behind the receptionist's desk had short, spiked hair, tipped in bright red; fingernails tipped in purple; and lips that were almost as black as the abundance of eyeliner that nearly obscured the young woman's eyes. "She's not taking appointments today. Can I schedule you with someone else?"

"I'm not here to have my hair done."

Zoe strolled on past the desk and headed through the

shop, acknowledging a few of the greetings she received from stylists who recognized her. Beyond the shampoo area, she pushed aside the curtain and stepped into the narrow hallway that led past the storage room to Daria's office. She was surprised to find Daria's door nearly closed. It was unlike her friend to be buried back in her office on a busy day, and less like her to shut out the sights and sounds of the shop.

Zoe knocked softly and eased the door open. "Daria?"

There was no response, but that didn't stop her. She was on a mission. Daria's sister had called her this morning and told her that Daria had sold the photography studio, was barely running the salon, and had retreated from the family completely. The family was hoping Zoe could achieve what no one in Daria's family had been able to do—get her to open up and talk about whatever it was that was sinking her in depression before the woman lost everything she owned.

"Daria?" Zoe stepped into the office. It was a disaster. Papers strewn everywhere, coffee cups piled up on every flat surface, trash can overflowing, files stacked on the floor. Oh yeah, Daria was definitely in trouble. Either that, or the place had been ravaged by someone only interested in destruction.

Then she saw her best friend sitting slumped down in the chair behind her desk, staring at the wall. No makeup, wrinkled clothes, her hair flat and lifeless. This was even worse than she thought.

Unbuttoning her coat, Zoe stepped over a box of conditioner. "If Daria won't come to the friend, the friend must come to Daria."

"I'm busy."

"Yeah, I can see that." Shrugging out of her coat, Zoe folded it over her arm, shoved a stack of towels off the only other chair in the room and sat down. "You want to tell me why you sold the studio?"

"I'm too busy to handle it anymore. Running one business is enough for anyone. I was an idiot to think I could run two."

"You were doing just fine until. . ." The words lodged in her throat.

Daria turned then, her eyes so bleak with despair it sent shivers down Zoe's back. "Until that poor excuse for a human being killed my DeAnne."

"I know it's been hard for you, Daria. She was your niece and your goddaughter. But she's gone, and she'd be crushed to see you like this."

Daria turned away, swiveling her chair around to present her back to Zoe. "Go away, Zoe. You don't understand."

"You know better than that. I lost my sister, Amy. Remember her? She was my twin. And I spent years trying to deal with her murder, and you spent years trying to help me deal with it, so don't tell me I don't understand."

"Just go, Zoe."

"No."

Daria spun around, fury mixing with misery. "I don't want you here; don't you get it? I don't want anyone here."

"Yeah, I get it." Zoe kept her voice soft. "You want to turn in on yourself, push everyone away, and wallow in your misery. DeAnne died. Her parents are dealing with it. They're mourning and moving on while you—"

Daria jerked to her feet. Considering she barely topped five-foot-one, it wasn't particularly threatening to Zoe. "You don't have any idea! I don't care if they've mourned and moved on! DeAnne was special! I loved her!"

"So did her parents, Daria. Noreen and Frank lost their

daughter. Hannah lost her sister."

With a sudden sweep of her hand, Daria cleared her desk. Zoe jumped back as everything went flying. "DeAnne was not Noreen's daughter! She was mine!"

Crumbling to her knees, Daria bent over, sobbing. "DeAnne was *my daughter*."

When the Department of Homeland Security was established, many agents in the FBI immediately volunteered to work exclusively on finding and stopping terrorists in the United States. Two such agents were Rick Harrelson and Neil Lagasse. Ambitious, intelligent, and dedicated, neither had been with the FBI longer than five years, so they both saw the handwriting on the wall—more action, more money, and more glory. It had been an easy decision and one they hadn't regretted for a moment—not until Neil had blown the surveillance of a suspected terrorist by the name of Assar el-Hajid.

They had been watching the guy for weeks. Day in and day out. Mindless, endless surveillance. Rick had gone for food, and Neil, after four hours at the window and a pot and a half of coffee, had slipped away for two minutes to use the john. Two lousy minutes, and his boss chose that moment to stop in and check things out. And Assar chose that moment to hightail it out of the house he had been holed up in across the street. Assar had vanished—along with money, guns, and a possible dirty bomb.

Now Assar was somewhere in the country, hiding out in some Muslim neighborhood, going to a local mosque, and planning who knew what while Neil was lucky to still have a job.

Now that job was tenuous at best.

Neil popped another stick of nicotine gum in his mouth and winced at the taste. What he'd give for a cigarette, even if it were politically incorrect. There were just some things in life a man shouldn't have to give up just because other people didn't like it.

Of course, the number one person who didn't like it was his partner, Rick. The guy had literally been driving Neil crazy to get rid of the so-called nasty habit that stank up the car.

He still couldn't believe he was actually trying to quit. Of course, he was as cranky as a mare in season, but he wasn't going to apologize for it. If Rick wanted a nice-smelling car, he would have to put up with the attitude.

Now his wife didn't care one way or another. All she asked was that he smoke outside and that he brush his teeth before he kissed her. It worked for him. But then, he didn't spend nearly as much time with Carmen as he did with Rick.

Rick hung up the phone and leaned back in his chair. "That was Jamal. He said word on the street is that someone is looking to put a contract out on a federal judge."

Neil forgot all about his smoking woes and sat up straighter. "Any idea which one?"

"Walter Kessler."

"Whoa." Judge Kessler was getting ready to preside over one of three trials—all involving al-Qaeda terrorists. The question now was, was the hit being contracted because of that? Were terrorists behind this? "Does Jamal have any idea who the hit man is?"

"No. But he'll let us know if he hears anything else."

Neil spit his gum into the trash can. "All things con- sidered, you know there's only a handful of men who could handle this kind of job."

His partner slowly rotated his coffee cup. "Bevere's got pretty extensive files on most of the known assassins we need to look at. We need to get our hands on them."

"This is a pretty high profile case we got here. I think that trumps anything he's got going on."

Rick picked up his mug, took a sip, and then set it down. He smiled. "We're supposed to play nice in this new era of cooperation."

"I'm going to play nice. I'm going to say please right after I tell him he has no choice but to hand them over."

Tugging at his tie, Neil stared at his partner. "We need to nail this one, Rick."

◆　　◆　　◆

JJ was in a foul mood. He knew it, but it didn't stop him from sulking at the table while Matt and Matt's wife, Paula, tried unsuccessfully to work him out of his funk. He glanced at his watch again. Zoe was late, and that wasn't helping his frame of mind either.

"She'll be here," Paula offered softly, along with a smile that didn't quite show through her eyes or the tight lines bracketed around her forehead.

"She's late again. Guess she had more important things to do."

Paula rolled her eyes. "Stop it, JJ. She told you she was dealing with a problem and would be here as soon as she could."

"And pigs fly with yellow wings." JJ picked up his glass. "I lost my job today. I think that trumps some file she may need to make sure is locked up at the office, or some last-minute decision over paint colors for her dining room."

"You didn't lose your job." Matt set his glass down with a shade more force than was necessary, his infinite patience finally at an end. "It's procedure. You'll be back to work in a week or so."

JJ had a caustic reply right on the tip of his tongue, but Zoe was rushing up to their table, shedding her coat, offering up apologies, and leaning in to kiss JJ's cheek as she dropped down in the chair. Immediately, their waiter came over to take her drink order.

"Just water, please. With lemon." She adjusted her coat over the back of her chair. "This has been the day from hell. How are you, Paula? You're looking wonderful."

JJ sat there, grinding his teeth, waiting for her to move around the table, making pleasant conversation with Matt and Paula, and finally get around to asking him how his day was. He couldn't wait.

It was nearly five minutes, but she did finally turn to him. "You don't look like you're in a very good mood."

"I lost my job today."

She looked like the bottom had dropped out of her chair—her mouth fell open, her eyes widened, her body stiffened. "What?"

"He didn't lose his job. He's on paid leave."

For once, JJ wished Matt would drop off the face of the earth. He wanted sympathy, and he deserved to get it from someone!

"Why?" Zoe turned back to him. "Why would they do that to you?"

"I shot a robber last night. The parents are screaming foul, so the department is hanging me out to dry."

Matt gave him a hard look and then turned to Zoe. "He shot an unarmed teenager who was robbing a convenience store. Procedure when an off-duty officer uses his weapon, and especially in a case where the victim was essentially unarmed—"

"He had a gun!"

"—is that Internal Affairs goes over the case just to make sure there was nothing illegal about the shooting. During this investigation, the officer is put on administrative leave, with full pay. When it's over, they go back to work. End of story."

"I'm not some rookie, and I resent them treating me like I was!"

Zoe stared at him for a long moment and then reached over and took his hand. "Of course you're not a rookie. I'm positive they're just trying to make sure you aren't accused of anything you didn't do."

This wasn't quite the sympathy he was looking for, and for some reason, it seemed as though maybe she was even placating him. "You don't get it, do you?"

"I do, Josiah. You're not going to work tomorrow, your actions are being second-guessed, and your judgment is being questioned. You have an excellent record, and suddenly they're treating you as though you were wet behind the ears and green as spring."

He'd listened carefully this time, and he picked it up. Not a trace of sympathy to be found. She was just stroking him, getting him to calm down.

"You don't get it. What is it with you people? I thought you were my friends." He stood up, tossing his napkin down on the table. "Excuse me. I'm outta here."

"JJ." Zoe sprang to her feet. "Don't do this. Not tonight."

"Oh. Not *tonight*. Let me go tell the chief to put this off another day or two so you won't be inconvenienced."

"That's not it, JJ. I am sorry you're going through this. I know this isn't easy for you."

He saw the frustration mirrored in her eyes, but in her case, she was just frustrated with him.

"Isn't easy?" He choked down the urge to scream as loud as he could. "Isn't easy? This is my job we're talking about! My life's work! And they toss me aside like it's nothing. Easy?"

Zoe reached out and took his hand, but he pulled away and picked up his coat.

"Call me when you have time to make me a priority in your life."

◆　◆　◆

"Would someone like to explain what just happened here?" Stunned, Zoe dropped down heavily in her chair.

Paula tore a roll apart and started to butter it. "Well, it goes something like this. A man's job is everything to him. Defines him. More so JJ than most men I know. And now they are investigating something he did that in his eyes was right. His ego is deflated, and his woman, who is supposed to fall all over herself to let him know she feels devastated for him, just brushed it off as a temporary thing that means nothing."

"But it *is* a temporary thing that means nothing. He'll be cleared."

"You know that. I know that. Matt knows that. And I think somewhere deep inside, JJ knows that, but it doesn't take away from the fact that right now he's hurting, and no one is acknowledging that it's okay for him to hurt."

Zoe turned to Matt. He shrugged. "What she said."

"Of all days for this to happen." She sighed heavily as she stood up and slipped back into her coat. "I've been running all day, putting out emotional fires, and I'm tired of tiptoeing around people's feelings."

"Walk softly or leave him alone to deal with this by himself," Matt offered.

"I'll walk softly. I'm not going to abandon him now. He's been left to deal with too much alone as it is." She picked up her purse and slung it over her shoulder. "Sorry, you two. Another night."

She hurried out of the restaurant, hoping to catch JJ in the parking lot. She wasn't that lucky. His Jeep was gone.

JJ was one of the most intense people she'd ever met. Standing just over six feet, he had pale green eyes; thick, unruly black hair; broad shoulders; and a face constructed of those full, off-centered features that reminded her of a brawler—right down to the crooked nose broken in a fight. And he used that intensity to his benefit, coming across as intimidating and unapproachable.

He didn't intimidate her in the least. And never had. Which was probably one reason why he was attracted to her.

She drove straight to his house, knowing that if she didn't, it would only make things worse, but her mind kept drifting back to her best friend. Daria had collapsed in Zoe's arms and cried for the better part of an hour, trying in between sobs to explain how her family had talked her into giving up DeAnne and letting Noreen raise the baby as her own.

"I was just sixteen, and Noreen was married and trying to have children; and the doctors were telling her she might not be able to have children." A sniffle and a hiccup. "They were relentless. Noreen was married and could afford to raise a child. I still had to finish school. I'd ruin my life. No one would want to marry me. The child deserved more. On and on, until I finally agreed."

"But I don't remember you ever being pregnant, and I've known you since we were in eighth grade!"

Daria had sniffled again, wiping her nose, her eyes, and her cheeks. "Noreen and Frank were living in Columbus. Remember when I went out there to spend the summer and ended up staying until Christmas?"

"Oh yeah. Now I remember. You came back saying Noreen had a baby and you stayed on to help her."

"DeAnne. My baby. I came back home a couple weeks after she was born."

Zoe had taken Daria's hand and held it. "And here I teased you about putting on a few pounds while you were visiting your sister."

"All these years, I watched my sister raise my daughter, and I couldn't say a word. And now she's gone, and I still can't say a word. They act like I have no right to grieve." Daria had lifted a tear-streaked face. "I have a right, don't I?"

Zoe had wrapped her arms around her friend and held her close. "You have every right. Every right in the world."

All those years of knowing Daria and never knowing the truth. You think you know someone better than they know themselves, and you end up finding out they're hiding some deep secret. But Daria had finally gotten it out. All the pain of not being a mother, of not being able to help plan the funeral. Of grieving for a niece and a goddaughter, but not being able to grieve for a daughter.

Zoe wasn't foolish enough to think Daria was over it. The healing would take a long time, but she knew Daria had taken a turn in the road today, so she was hopeful things would start to get better.

Now to deal with JJ.

But when she pulled up in front of his house, the driveway was empty and the windows dark. He hadn't come home.

She sat there for a moment, drumming her fingers on the steering wheel, trying to determine if she could have beaten him home. Not likely.

So where was he?

Zoe pulled out her cell phone and called him, but his voice mail picked up right away. His phone was turned off. Headlights suddenly blinded her. JJ?

But the car pulled up next to her and lowered the window. She narrowed her eyes, trying to see the face behind the wheel. Then she hit the power button for her window. It was one of JJ's fellow detectives, Gerry Otis.

"Gerry?"

"Hi, Zoe." He drew his fingers through his thinning hair. "I gather JJ's not here?"

"No. I was looking for him myself. Is something wrong?"

Gerry blew out a heavy breath, turning to stare out the windshield of his car. "Yeah. You could say that. Any idea where he might have gone?"

"Maybe his parents'. I was going to try there next."

Gerry shook his head and looked back over at her. "I just came from there. He's not there. And his dad knows to call me if he does show up."

Shivers of apprehension ran down her spine. "What's going on, Gerry?"

He ran his fingers through his hair again, mussing it even more. "The press is going to crucify JJ. The kid he shot? Straight A student. Never been in a gang in his life. Never been in any trouble at all. His dad split a year or so ago. His mother has been supporting him and his four sisters. She took sick a couple weeks ago. Lost her job. Too sick to get out of bed. He was desperate to get money for medicine for her and food for his little sisters."

Zoe slumped back in her seat. "Oh no."

"The press is all over this, painting the kid a saint and JJ a saint killer. The kid is dead, his mother is on her deathbed, and four little girls will be attending two funerals. You get the drift."

"JJ will be devastated."

"He'll be lucky if they don't get him dismissed from his job."

Zoe stared at Gerry in disbelief. "Lose his job? But it was a mistake. An honest mistake!"

Gerry shook his head and spit out the window to the pavement below. "Won't matter. The politicians will need a scapegoat to go down for this. Someone has to pay, and the press wants JJ's head. They'll get it. The chief. The mayor. They'll be all too glad to toss JJ overboard to make this all go away fast."

chapter 3

A rchie rubbed the soft cloth down the barrel of the gun, admiring the way the light from the gooseneck lamp reflected off the blue barrel. He set it down and reached for the can of gun oil. The strong pungent smell of Hoppe's oil greeted him like an old friend.

A professional took care of his equipment, and Archie Kemp considered himself every ounce the professional. Even if it was as a professional killer.

Whether it was cleaning his guns, or weighing each cartridge separately to ensure maximum load and consistency, or loading the clips, he always wore surgical gloves. He'd known too many killers who had been nailed for something as stupid as a fingerprint on a shell casing. He made sure that nothing was ever left to chance.

Archie's head jerked up at the sound of a car pulling into the driveway. No, not a car. The van. Kitty was back. He pulled off his gloves and tossed them down as he headed for the garage.

She had already backed the van into the garage and was shutting the bay door when he joined her. He leaned over and kissed her pretty little redhead. "Any problems?"

Kitty shook her head, sending red curls bouncing as she wrapped her arms around his neck. "None. There were a couple of times I thought he had made me, but I played it smart."

"That's why I love you, Kitty. You're as smart as I am."

Smart, pretty, and as loyal a partner as he'd ever found in this life. When he'd met her, she'd been a seventeen-year-old runaway working the streets. He'd only planned on paying her for a couple of hours of her time and sending her on her way, but something had sparked between them right from the start. He kept her all night. The next day, he'd offered to buy her from her pimp, but the punk had been unreasonable.

And stupid. The pimp hadn't realized whom he was dealing with. What Archie Kemp wanted, Archie Kemp got. A small-time street pimp was no obstacle. The pimp died for his stupidity, and Archie got Kitty.

Nine years later, she was still here. She'd had plenty of opportunities to walk away and disappear out of his life, but she never had. She loved him, she said. He couldn't honestly say he loved her—he wasn't sure he could love anything or anyone—but what he felt for Kitty was as close to love as he was liable to get. It worked for him.

Kitty reached up and stroked his cheek. "The fact that I'm smart *and* I know how to take *real* good care of my man."

He laughed again and tipped his head to kiss her hand. "Oh yeah. There *is* that, honey. There *is* that."

She pulled a notebook out of the monstrosity she called a purse and handed it to him. "I got his schedule, and the route he travels to and from work. Taking him out is going to be a piece of cake. The whole way from his house to work, he was talking on his cell phone."

Archie was no longer listening as she rambled. He was studying her notes. Streets, landmarks, times, and notations. People he'd met with, where he'd gone for lunch, what time he arrived at his office, and what time he left. It would all matter a great deal when the time came.

Finally, he closed the notebook with a smile. "Good job. I have to go out for a bit. I'll be back later."

Kitty's brows furrowed. "You don't want me to go with you?"

Archie shook his head as he climbed into the van. "I don't need you for this."

"And then he tells me he was just keeping the money safe in his account because he suspected someone in the company was embezzling." Dan Cordette laughed as he opened the restaurant door and held it for Zoe, then followed her outside. "This business gets crazier every year."

Smiling, Zoe glanced over at her boss as she wrapped her green wool scarf around her neck. Her reply froze on her lips as a dark feeling skittered up her spine. Her smile faded. Slowly, she began to look around, almost positive she was going to find some nearby lurking danger.

Mid-February in Monroe wasn't exactly tourist season for the small town nestled in the Appalachians just two hours from the nation's capital city. The weather was clear but cold, with the temperature hovering in the low forties. A few people meandered the walkways between stores and businesses, but more were hurrying from one destination to the other, tucked down deep in overcoats, mufflers, and scarves. No one seemed particularly interested in Zoe, and no one appeared to be up to no good.

"Something wrong?"

"I'm not sure. Just a bad feeling."

Dan tensed, cautiously glancing up and down the street. "If you were anyone else, I'd dismiss it. See anything?"

"No." Zoe tucked her hands deeper in her pockets and wished again that she were nestled in a warm building. "But something. . .it's like the sense of almost immediate danger, but I can't see where it's coming from or who it's directed at."

Could it be JJ? She'd waited for three hours, but JJ hadn't come home. He hadn't shown up at his parents' house, either. Matt hadn't heard from him. So where was he? How depressed was he? How hard was he taking this? It just wasn't like him to disappear and not answer his cell phone. Or take care of Zip, his golden retriever.

She'd gone over at seven this morning, and still not finding JJ at home, fed Zip and let him out.

Then she'd gone to her office for a meeting with her boss, and while she was waiting, called everyone she knew. No one had seen or heard from JJ.

So was this feeling she was getting centered on him? That didn't feel right either. This was about someone else. *But who?*

Her cell phone rang with a little jingle that told her it was JJ. She grabbed her phone and flipped it open. "Where the devil are you? Everyone is worried sick!"

"Everyone? Or you?"

"Everyone *and* me. Are you okay?"

There was a pause that had her taking a deep breath. Dan had stopped walking and stepped away to stare at something in a store window, giving her a little privacy.

"I'm okay, Zoe. I just needed some time to think. I've got a lot on my mind."

"I'm sure you do. I took care of Zip this morning."

"Thanks."

She heard the roar of an eighteen-wheeler through the phone. "Are you out near the interstate?"

"I'm on the interstate."

"Are you headed back?"

Another heavy pause. "Yeah."

"JJ, I'm sorry about last night. I had no idea it—"

"Don't. It wasn't your fault really."

She glanced over at Dan who gave her a quick smile of encouragement. Talking to JJ was sometimes like pulling eyeteeth. What was it about men that made them so reluctant to talk about what they were feeling? How hard was it for them to admit they were scared or hurt or angry? Okay, forget the angry part. JJ had no problem expressing himself when he was angry.

"Look, I'll be home in about an hour. We need to talk. Can you meet me there at the house?"

What was it about those words "we need to talk" that always set a woman's heart to pounding in her chest?

"I'll be there."

He hung up without responding. Closing her phone, she slipped it back into her purse. "He wants to talk."

"Doesn't mean what you think it means, Zoe."

"How do you know what I'm thinking?" She huddled deeper into her coat as they crossed the street.

"Because all women think that when a man calls and says he wants to talk, it means something dire."

"What else could it mean?"

"That he's done thinking, or that he's nearly done working this out and just wants to tell you what he figured out. Or that he can't figure it out and is ready to see what ideas you might have."

Zoe nearly rolled her eyes. "Well, why couldn't he ask me what I thought last night?"

They walked through the parking lot and stopped next to Zoe's car. "Because he hadn't thought it out for himself yet. Men don't ask for advice until they're sure they can't work it out for themselves, and they aren't inclined to sit around and just *discuss* things the way women will. It's a man thing."

As she climbed into her car, she felt that dark finger of dread run down her spine again.

What is it, Lord?

◆ ◆ ◆

Jack Fleming was surprised to find the office was nearly empty. Being an FBI agent was a 24/7 job, which meant that most of the agents—himself included—paid little attention to the fact it was a Saturday. Criminals worked seven days a week, and so did he.

His partner, however, was not at his desk, poring over files. Not totally surprising. Donnie Bevere was a dedicated agent, but there was always at least one day a week when Donnie was unavailable. *Ah, to be a young, good-looking single man again.*

Nah. Jack sank down in his chair and scooted up to his desk. No way would he want to go through all that again. He'd leave it for the young Donnies of the world. He was quite happy with his Diane, thank you very much. There may not be much in the way of razzle-dazzle and fireworks anymore, but he didn't have to be anyone but himself. It was comfortable. Secure. Familiar.

At his age, familiar was good.

He picked up his letter opener, a gift from Diane on one of his birthdays, and turned over the stack of mail on his desk. For the next few minutes, he went from envelope to envelope, trashing some, reading others. The fax machine a few feet away sputtered and hummed with an incoming report while phones around the room rang from time to time. Some were answered; some were not.

He slipped the white sheet of paper from the envelope and shook it open.

Beware! Your wife will soon die.

It took a second for Jack's mind to wrap around the typed words. Then his heart lurched in his chest, and he dropped the letter, grabbing the phone. His fingers stumbled across the number pad, and he had to stop twice and dial again, but finally he heard Diane's voice, bright and chipper, on the other end.

"Hello?"

"Diane? Are you okay?"

She laughed. "Well, of course I am. You've only been gone an hour. Give me a chance to miss you."

He ignored her lighthearted humor. "I want you to lock the doors, and you don't let anyone in, you hear me? *No one.* I'll be home in a few minutes."

"What in the world are you talking about, Jack?"

"Just do it! I'll explain when I get there!"

Justin ignored the cold that nipped his fingers as he hunched down in his jacket. He'd outgrown it last winter, but there was no money to buy him a new one. Just as there was no money for mittens. He did have a stocking hat, but it was one he'd found several months earlier. It didn't matter if it was second-hand. It kept his head warm as he trudged through the woods near his house, shuffling his sneakers through the thin layer of remaining snow and dead leaves.

He was on his way to his favorite thinking place. It wasn't much—just a small makeshift tree house made from a sheet of plywood he'd dragged through the woods and placed carefully at a fork in the limbs of a big oak tree, some sheets of tattered plastic as a roof and walls, and a shoe box of little treasures he'd collected.

No one knew about this place—not even his grandma. It was special to him, all his own. He didn't have to share it with anyone. He could hide from the world here and no one could find him.

At least, he liked to think no one could find him here.

Reaching the tree at last, he climbed up the thick limbs and crawled through the plastic. Settling himself in the middle of the small space, he sighed heavily. His little space was as empty as his life.

His mother had come back this morning looking for money again. Her eyes had been red and her nose running like she had a bad cold. She had been shaking and angry. His mother had actually shoved his grandma down onto the sofa and grabbed her purse. After taking all the money Grandma had, his mother had run out, never even acknowledging what she had done.

As soon as the door had closed behind her, he'd run to his grandma's side. She had cried, even though she'd told him she was fine.

He didn't think she was fine at all. She'd been lying on the sofa all day like she was real tired. It scared him.

Opening the shoe box, he pulled out his last piece of bubble gum. He'd been saving it for a special occasion, but he needed it today—the fruity flavor, the struggle to chew it down to a soft mass, the delight of blowing the best bubbles when it was chewed down just perfect.

Just as he was about to pop it in his mouth, he heard a strange rustling sound. Silently, he crept to the edge of the platform and peered out through a tear in the plastic. It took him a few minutes to finally spot the man through the trees.

He was a well-dressed white man, which kind of surprised him. Well-dressed people didn't venture much in this area. It was too poor. Too dangerous.

But this man didn't look like danger scared him much at all. He didn't look to be very tall, but he was thick, like a pit bull, with a fat bumpy nose.

Justin didn't like this stranger in his woods. He didn't belong here. But the man seemed to know exactly what he was doing as he swept at a layer of ground cover.

Curious, Justin leaned forward a little, hoping to see what the man had hidden under the leaves.

A few minutes later, the man uncovered a big, deep square hole in the ground. It looked kinda like the hole they dug for Grandpa when he died. Why was it there?

Justin edged a little closer to the edge, trying to see what was down in the hole. His mind raced with ideas. Treasure? Money? Gold?

Suddenly, Justin heard the distinct crack of wood splintering. The floor beneath him shifted.

He gripped the plastic, struggling to save himself as the plywood began to give way.

◆　　◆　　◆

"What's wrong, Jack?"

Jack was buttoning his overcoat when Special Agent Lew Sherman arrived at Jack's desk. "Thanks for getting down here so fast." Jack picked up the letter and handed it to Lew. "This just came to me in the mail. I've called Diane and told her to stay put, but. . ."

Lew glanced over the letter. "We can run it for prints, but I doubt we'll find more than yours and mine on it. Where's the envelope?"

Jack picked it up and handed it to him. Lew turned it over and looked at it. Then he lifted his head. "This isn't addressed to you, Jack. It's addressed to Donnie."

"Donnie?" Jack snatched the envelope out of Lew's hand. "But it was in my stack of mail." Sure enough, it was addressed to Special Agent Donnie Bevere.

Lew smiled as he folded his arms across his chest. "You can relax now. Somebody's idea of a joke. Guess whoever wrote this doesn't know Hollywood Handsome is single."

Jack sighed heavily, dropping down into his chair. "I just had ten years shaved off my life."

"Call your wife before you shave twenty off hers."

"Yeah. I'll do that. Thanks, Lew. And I'm sorry to bring you all the way down here on a false alarm."

Lew shrugged. "I was just catching up on my files. Nothing I wasn't willing to leave for a few minutes for something more exciting." He slapped Jack softly on the arm. "Call your wife."

Jack reached for the phone as Lew strode away. "Diane? Yes, it's all right. I'm sorry I scared you. It was just bad information. Everything's fine."

Shaking his head, Jack tossed the letter into the trash.

"You feel like dinner out tonight? Maybe take in a movie?"

◆ ◆ ◆

Justin grabbed the tree limb as the plywood cracked and the corner broke off. He hung there, terrified, as the man looked over.

"Hey, you!"

Justin dropped to the ground and began running. The crashing behind him urged him to run even faster. It didn't even dawn on him that he was running in the opposite direction of home. All he could think of was escaping.

"Kid! I'm not going to hurt you! I just want to make sure you're okay!"

No. No. He would hurt me. Gotta run. Run as fast as I can. Have to hide. Hide from the bad man. Run. Run. Faster. Faster.

His sneakers slipped on wet leaves and slushy snow, but he kept darting between trees, crashing through the brush, terrified to look over his shoulder. The man could be right there.

Heart pounding, Justin jumped the small creek bed. His feet hit the other side and slid out from under him. One moment he was on his feet, the next he was sliding down into the creek. Into the freezing cold water.

A scream lodged in Justin's throat as he rolled over, expecting the man to be standing over him, maybe even with a gun in his hand.

The man wasn't there.

No sound of his voice. No sound of crashing footsteps.

He was alone.

Then suddenly he heard something off to his left. Without waiting to find out whether it was man or beast, wind or twig, he scrambled to his feet. He slipped and clawed his way up the creek bed and lurched forward into the brush.

Keep moving. Keep running. Run. Fast. Get away. Get away before the man found him.

A few moments later, he broke free of the woods and ran out on Ridge Road. He stopped for a second, doubled over while he fought to catch his breath.

"Hey, Justin!"

Justin raised his eyes to see his friend Robbie waving at him from across the street. "You better get home! Trouble now!"

Justin nodded and straightened, still breathing hard. Three blocks and he'd be home. After glancing over his shoulder, he started trotting down the street. No one was behind him.

Maybe the man was still lost in the woods. Justin knew those woods like the back of his hand. They were more familiar to him than most people's backyards.

He turned the corner to his street and skidded to a halt. An ambulance sat out in front of his house. The front door was propped open. Police and medical people were running to and from the house.

Something had happened to Grandma!

◆   ◆   ◆

The late afternoon sky was a gloomy gray, adding to JJ's overall mood. While the coffeemaker sputtered, sending the aroma of freshly brewing coffee into the air, he stood at the back door, watching Zip chase a squirrel down the length of the privacy fence. Dumb squirrel. He was on top of the fence. The dog was on the ground and couldn't reach the creature. Why was the squirrel running as if he was going to die within moments?

Zip ran along the fence, jumping every so often, barking continuously, always trying and always failing to catch the squirrel.

Fatigue pulled at JJ. Driving all night, trying to still the chaos in his mind, stressing over his job and reputation. Then there was this latest news.

The kid had not only been unarmed, he'd merely been a scared kid trying to save his family.

What if he'd taken one more second to look into the kid's eyes before pulling the trigger? Would he have seen fear and desperation? Pain? Would it have made a difference? People in fear will pull a trigger just as fast as one with evil intent.

Had there been some indication that JJ had missed? Some little instinct that he'd ignored in the heat of the moment? Had the kid's hands been shaking? He couldn't remember now. Couldn't remember the look in the kid's eyes. Couldn't remember if the kid had said anything to him when he turned and pointed the gun in JJ's direction. It had run together now in a blur.

He could only remember pulling the trigger. Seeing the kid's stunned look just seconds before he crumpled to the floor. Hearing the sound of the store employee's screech. Smelling the cordite, acrid and bitter, from the gun. Feeling the sense of relief that he was still alive.

If Zoe had been there, would she have gotten some strong

sense the kid was harmless? She had this inner knowing that baffled him.

When he'd first heard of Zoe Shefford and her abilities, it had rubbed his nerves raw. He didn't believe in the supernatural, and to him, it was all fake, a sleight of hand con. Little by little over the past year, working side by side with the woman, she'd not only forced him to rethink some of his convictions about the supernatural and about her as a person, but also about God.

He braced his hand on the door, staring out but looking in.

He remembered that first day of working together, leaving the Matthews' house, when he'd called her a decked out demagogue of deceit. He'd eaten those words so many times during the serial killer investigation, he'd choked on them. Zoe Shefford was sincere, honest, moral, and had one of the sweetest, most generous natures of any woman he'd ever met. If someone were in need or in trouble, she'd go so far as putting herself in the line of danger to help him. Another bone of contention between them. Her impulsiveness had nearly gotten her killed, not once but twice.

And it had forced him to admit that he'd fallen in love with her.

He'd always been attracted to a specific type of woman—tailored, demure, and soft-spoken, and apt to quietly look to him to run the show. Zoe was just the opposite, to the extreme. She wore long flowing skirts and dresses, flowery scarves and shawls, and layers of soft materials; spoke her mind; and never failed to challenge him every chance she got. Demure? The infamous Zoe Shefford was never going to fade into his shadow.

Lowering his head to the door, he absorbed the cool glass

through his temple and found that it actually felt good, easing the low throb.

He loved everything about Zoe, even when she was driving him crazy and riding his last nerve to the finish line.

Not that she knew it. He wasn't sure if it was fear of getting hurt or just his own obstinate way of maintaining some control over her, and he wasn't inclined to analyze it. He kept his feelings to himself and was content to just let the relationship be what it was.

He raised his head and rolled his neck, then began to knead the tight spot at the base of his skull.

To be honest, even though he'd grown to trust these instincts and feelings she got, he still wasn't comfortable with them. What do you do when you're a cop who prides himself on logic and good detective skills and someone says they feel a crime is about to be committed?

He used to roll his eyes and ignore them. Now, if that someone was Zoe, he tucked the information away and kept an eye on it, half expecting it to happen at any moment.

He sure could have used some of her instincts and feelings when he'd walked into the convenience store.

JJ heard the front door open, and knowing it was Zoe, steeled himself to stay where he was, watching the battle being waged in the backyard even as he ignored the strange little thump in his heart.

"Something interesting going on out there?"

JJ looked over his shoulder at Zoe and nodded. "Zip has thoroughly convinced this dumb squirrel that he's going to catch him, and the squirrel is *so* out of reach, it's not funny."

Zoe draped her coat over a kitchen chair and joined him at the window. His arm went around her waist as he pulled her close. "Watch them. The squirrel runs up and down the fence, at least three feet higher than Zip can reach, and he doesn't see how safe he is."

"We're all like that, JJ. We know bad things are out there, and we panic, trying to control everything around us, never realizing the Lord has placed us high in Him, just out of reach of being destroyed by whatever danger comes after us."

Time to change the subject. He released her and walked over to the counter, reaching for the coffeepot. "You want some?"

"Sure."

She was all air and light, breezy spring colors and graceful movements, and yet she blended with the dark greens and cherrywood accents of his kitchen as if it had been designed with her in mind.

He shook his head. Here he was, his job on the line, and he's thinking about the way her smile lights the place and makes it warm all at the same time.

Maybe he could understand these men who get laid off and lose their minds, after all.

After calling Zip in, they settled in the living room with their coffee. Zip circled a few times before dropping down in front of JJ's chair to snooze.

Zoe sat tucked in the corner of the couch, her feet folded under her, holding her mug with both hands. "You want to tell me what's going on inside that head of yours?"

"Not particularly."

She was wearing a long skirt in one of those soft flowery colors. Pink or rose or something. Why did she always have to look so soft and sweet—like some candy confection you just wanted to savor?

"I heard about the kid's family situation."

He knew she was trying to give him a gentle opening; but even though he'd asked her to come talk, he still felt the words crammed down inside, and he wasn't sure how to get them out. "I'm trying to make sense of it."

She sat there, coffee in hand, watching him over the top of her mug. Concern? Pity? Sympathy? He wasn't sure what he saw in her eyes. "It wasn't your fault, JJ. There's no way you could have known."

"It doesn't make this kid any less dead or his mother any less sick. And it doesn't make what I did any easier to live with."

He stood up quickly, too jumpy to sit still, and began to pace. "I keep second-guessing, and that's not doing me any good, but I can't seem to stop. I did my job, and I did it right, but the outcome was wrong."

"I don't know what to say to make this easier for you, JJ."

"I don't think there's anything you can say. I feel like everything is spinning out of control, and I don't know how to get it back."

Zoe set her cup down. "This might not be a bad time to turn to your heavenly Father and trust Him to see you through this."

"Don't push me, Zoe. I told you months ago: I'll go to church with you sometimes, I won't just dismiss religion out of hand, and I won't roll my eyes when you say something I can't quite accept; but I warned you not to cram this down my throat."

He saw the color fuse on her cheeks, and she dropped her eyes. That was unfair, and he knew it. She wasn't shoving anything. "I'm sorry. You're just trying to help me."

"You have nothing to apologize for. You're entitled to be a bit of a bear right now, but once I think you've rolled in your self-pity long enough, I'll start getting tough with you. Then watch out."

He couldn't help smiling a little. "Heaven help me."

Dropping down on the sofa next to her, he turned to look at her. "I didn't really call you over to talk about the case."

Zoe set her cup down and folded her hands in her lap. She looked apprehensive, and he wasn't sure why.

"I haven't been very fair to you. I mean, I've been fair, just not entirely. . . ."

Zip jumped to his feet, barking sharply as he ran for the front door. It startled JJ, cutting him off and making him jump. He jerked to his feet just as the doorbell rang. "Are we expecting anyone?"

"Not that I know of."

"Zip! Quiet!" Edging back the curtain, he looked out the front window, then dropped it quickly and stepped back.

"What is it?"

He turned to Zoe. "The press."

"Detective Johnson!" The doorbell rang again, and then someone pounded on the door, setting Zip off again. "Could we get a statement, please?"

"Not on your life," JJ said softly.

"What are you going to do, JJ?" Zoe asked.

"Sneak out the back?"

"You can only hide for just so long. You want me to get rid of him?"

"Then he'll say I'm hiding behind you. No thanks." JJ walked over to the door and flung it open, grabbing Zip by the collar. "No comment—and you have one minute to get off my property, or I'm letting the dogs loose."

Then he slammed the door closed in the reporter's face.

"I hate the press."

"I know the feeling. Want some more coffee?"

JJ followed her back to the kitchen. "I still have to tell you something important."

"So tell me."

Zoe's phone rang. She shot him an apologetic look as she pulled out her cell phone. "Hello?"

JJ strolled over to the kitchen door and gazed out. The sun was setting off to the west, deepening shadows in the yard, as well as in his mind.

He'd shot a boy who hadn't deserved to die. It had taken him hours to finally come to terms with that truth. He'd rationalized himself into focusing on the administrative leave, on the injustice of it, but there was no running from the cold facts. A desperate boy was dead, and if JJ had just taken a few seconds more to judge the situation, that boy might still be alive.

Zoe gave him a pointed look as she tucked her cell phone back in her purse. "JJ? Stop second-guessing yourself. You reacted to an armed robbery in progress. There was no way to know the boy's circumstances."

He saw the tears in her eyes. "What's wrong, honey?"

"I have to go to the hospital."

"What happened?"

"Daria. She was in an accident. Noreen thinks she may have tried to commit suicide."

◆　◆　◆

One second Justin was standing there, gaping, and the next, his feet were carrying him faster than he thought he could go, pounding pavement and up the front steps. He slammed into a police officer just inside the house.

"Whoa up, little man. Where's the fire?"

"Grandma! Where's my grandma?"

"She's pretty sick." The officer knelt down. "We have to take her to the hospital. Do you understand?"

Tears started streaming down Justin's face. Oh yes. He understood. His grandma had spoken to him many times of this moment. He just hadn't believed it could really happen. He thought she was just being a typical worrywart. But now the moment had arrived, and they were carrying her away.

Now he had to play this the way his grandma had drilled into his head time and time again. He had to be cool. He couldn't let them know anything. If they did, they would take him away, too.

Then the question came. "Do you live here with your grandmother? Where are your parents?"

"My mom's at work. She'll be home soon. We live down the street."

"You need to go tell your mom we're taking your grandmother to First Mercy for treatment. Can you do that?"

Justin nodded. "Can I see my grandma before she goes?"

Just then, the EMTs came through with the stretcher, his grandma tucked and strapped in. He ran over and touched her face. She looked at him, never saying a word, but it was there in her eyes. The warning. The plea.

"I know, Grandma. I'll be okay. I promise. I remember everything."

The panic in her eyes melted away, and then she was being carried through the door. Justin stood there for a moment, watching them load her into the ambulance.

He was on his own now. And if the police found out there was no adult to care for him, they would take him away from his grandma. That couldn't happen. He couldn't let it. He'd promised his grandma he would be here when she got back.

The police officer came to the door. "Do you want me to drive you home?"

Justin shook his head. "I'm just going to make sure everything's locked up, and then I'll go home and wait for Mom. Grandma made me promise that if anything ever happened, I'd water her plants and make sure the cat was fed."

The officer nodded, staring. Justin tried not to believe that the cop saw right through him. That he knew Justin was lying.

But then the officer turned and walked out the door. Justin heaved a sigh of relief.

But he'd be back. His grandma had warned him of that.

They'll come back if they think you're here. Maybe to see if you are. Maybe to make sure no one breaks in. Either way, you have to make sure no one ever sees you. You understand, Justin honey? If they find you, they'll take you away from me. I'll never see you again. They'll put you in one of them foster homes, and I'll never see you again.

Justin squared his shoulders. He just wanted to clean up and get something to eat. He was so tired and muddy and wet from running from that man, but it would have to wait. Right now, he had to make sure the policeman thought he had gone home.

Justin walked out, locking the front door behind him. Then with a quick wave to the police officer still sitting in his car writing something down, Justin starting jogging down the street, looking for all the world as if he had someplace to go and someone waiting for him.

chapter 4

Sunday, February 12

Archie paced from the living room to the kitchen, his thoughts moving faster than his bare feet as he mulled over this latest development. Who was the kid? And what had he seen?

It may be nothing to be concerned about, but Archie didn't like little surprises dropping out of trees. He had carefully covered up the grave and made sure it wouldn't be easily found in case the kid came back, but after waiting hours, there had been no sign of the little boy.

Maybe the kid had just been playing and oblivious to whatever Archie had been doing. Maybe. But maybes could turn dangerous.

If only he'd caught the kid. A quick snap of the neck and no more concerns.

It didn't work out that way. The little brat had been quick on his feet and obviously knew those woods well. It hadn't taken long before he disappeared completely.

Archie glanced up at the clock. Still over an hour before Kitty would be back with more surveillance information.

Time enough to go over the week's plans again.

He sat down on the sofa and started sorting through the detailed maps he'd drawn for the first hit. He had to make sure he had several options for getting away clean, just in case. It always paid to have options. He had to plan the time down to the very minute. Time to make the hit. Time to break the weapon down. Time to get to the car. Time to drive away.

If things went right, he could slip out of his job at lunch, make the hit, and be back at his desk before anyone knew anything had happened.

Smiling to himself, he leaned back, folding his arms behind his head. After this job, he could afford to disappear. Maybe set up operations down in the islands. Maybe head over to Europe and make a few new contacts. The world was his for the taking.

Maybe later this afternoon, he'd drive back out there to the woods and see if the kid showed up again.

What a shame it would be if a kid brought his world crashing down.

◆　◆　◆

"Coffee?" JJ held out a cardboard cup of hospital coffee under her nose.

"Thanks." It didn't matter to Zoe that it tasted terrible. Or that it was about the fourth cup in the past two hours. She needed something to do with her hands. Something to do with her mind. Or she'd go crazy.

Daria had been driving too fast. Lost control of the car. Slammed into a tree. Rolled into a ditch. Had been in surgery most of the night. And now. . .it was the wait and see game.

She was still unconscious.

Frank had taken Noreen home as soon as the doctor came out and reported that Daria had made it through surgery and would be in recovery for several hours. JJ had tried to convince Zoe to go home and rest as well, but she had refused.

Had Daria been trying to commit suicide? Or had it simply been an accident? There would be no answers until Daria woke up.

Had this been the sense of impending danger she'd felt yesterday? Maybe she should have prayed more about it. But so much had been going on and all she'd given it was a quick, cover-it-all prayer that she'd hoped would help. Now Daria was fighting for her life.

Maybe if Zoe had prayed longer or harder, this could have been avoided.

Father? Did I not do enough? Were You calling me to do more, and I got distracted? Did I let You down? Did I let my best friend down? Please don't let her die, Father. I need more time with her. She doesn't know You yet.

Suddenly, it washed over her again. That familiar sense of impending danger. She stiffened.

Pray, child.

For whom, Father? Closing her eyes, she bowed her head. It wasn't Daria she saw. It was another woman. And a grave.

Who, Father? Who is she?

Pray that her faith is strong. Pray that she trusts Me in the darkest hours. Pray that her family looks to Me and trusts Me with all that is to be.

"Miss Shefford?"

Zoe's head jerked up as the nurse spoke. "I'm sorry. I didn't mean to startle you. I just wanted you to know that you can visit with Miss Cicala for a few minutes if you like. She's resting comfortably, but she's not awake yet."

Zoe jumped to her feet. "That's okay. I just wanted to be able to see her."

Zoe took JJ's hand, gripping it tightly, as they entered Daria's room. Machines beeped and chirped—the only sign of activity as Daria lay, pale and motionless, in the bed.

Leaving JJ at the foot of the bed, Zoe moved to Daria's side, taking her friend's hand in hers. "What happened out there? Please tell me it was just an accident. You're going to be fine, you know. I just want you to get well quickly. We're all here for you. Noreen. Frank. Even JJ. We've been here all night. Noreen just went home to shower, and then she'll be back."

Daria showed no signs of having heard a word. Zoe couldn't help the tears that trickled down her face as she held onto her best friend. "You and me, we've been through so much together, kiddo. We'll get through this, too."

She reached up and combed her fingers through the few strands of Daria's hair that stuck out from under the bandages. Then she leaned down close to Daria's ear. "And God loves you, too, my friend. He's here, too. And He has so much for you yet in life. You think He took DeAnne from you, but He didn't. He's here to help you through all of this. Trust Him, Daria. Lean on Him, and let Him give you strength and peace."

The door opened, and the room was suddenly invaded by the sounds of the busy halls outside—people talking, wheels squeaking, trays clanking, phones ringing.

"Time's up, Miss Shefford. You can visit with her again later this afternoon."

Zoe nodded as she leaned down and kissed Daria's cool cheek. "We'll be back later, okay? You just rest for now."

◆   ◆   ◆

Justin slowly eased the closet door open and listened carefully. Other than the refrigerator hum and the tick of the clock in the hall, he didn't hear a thing. Rubbing the sleep from his eyes, he crawled out of the closet.

After the police had left the day before, Justin had returned here to the house, where he'd taken his bath and changed clothes. Dinner had been leftovers heated up in the microwave and eaten in the dark.

The loneliness was closing in on him. He wanted his grandma! How long would she be in the hospital? They'd never talked about how long something like this might last. If she wasn't home by tomorrow, he was going to try calling the hospital and see if he could talk to her.

Dragging a chair over to the counter, he climbed up and pulled a box of cereal down from the cabinet. After breakfast, he should be going to church, but how could he go without Grandma? People would ask where she was, wouldn't they? Then they'd get all concerned about who was taking care of him.

No, he better stay home.

He could watch one of those church programs on television. He didn't want God to think he was skipping out on Him or anything.

Then maybe later this afternoon, he'd go back to the tree fort and see about fixing it. There was some extra wood in the garage from where those guys fixed Grandma's back porch last summer. That should work.

After pouring the milk on his cereal, he sat down at the table and bowed his head. "Take care of Grandma, okay, God? Please? I need her. But you know that, don't you? And watch over me. And help my mom. And make Grandma come home quick. Thank You and amen."

Picking up his spoon, he dug into his Cheerios.

◆　　◆　　◆

Donnie held Cody in his arms as he followed Lisbeth out of the pew and down the aisle toward the door. Mandy, at her mother's side, smiled and called out to people as she fairly bounced, her Sunday school project grasped tightly in her little hands.

Every once in a while, she would turn her head and look at him, making sure her daddy was still there behind her, giving her the confidence to strut her stuff.

"Donnie. Lisbeth. Good to see you this morning." Pastor West smiled, reaching out to shake Donnie's hand. Then he bent over and grinned at Mandy. "And how are you this morning, young lady?"

"Blessed," Mandy replied with a wide smile. "Why'd that bad man throw Dan'el in with the lions? Everybody knows that lions eat people. Daddy told me so. Huh, Daddy?"

"Yes, Mandy." Donnie shrugged apologetically at the pastor. "Kids."

Pastor West merely chuckled. "It's not the first time someone didn't understand the point behind one of my sermons."

By the time Donnie finished talking to the pastor and joined Lisbeth out front, she was surrounded by four other ladies and was deep in conversation about their Bible study.

"With Cheryln out of town visiting her grandchildren, we can hold the meeting at my house," Janet was saying.

"That's fine." Lisbeth caught Donnie's eye and gave him that smile that let him know she'd be just a couple of minutes. He nodded and headed for the car with the kids.

"Hi, Don!"

Donnie turned to the little blond who spoke to him. Kathy? Kathryn? Karen? She was relatively new to the church, and they'd only met a couple of times, so he wasn't altogether sure of her name. "Good morning."

"You don't have any brothers at home just like you, do you?"

Donnie laughed, shaking his head. "Sorry. No such luck."

Smiling, she waved him off and went back to her conversation with the ladies. Donnie headed for the car.

Lisbeth caught up to him as he was buckling Cody into his car seat. "By the way, her name is Katy."

Donnie lifted Mandy into her seat as he looked over at his wife. "You know me so well, it's scary."

"I just know you well enough to know that when you can't remember someone's name, you get this little furrow between your brows." She opened the passenger door. "But it's hard for you to remember everyone. Especially Katy."

Donnie opened the back of the van. "Why especially Katy?"

"Because every time you've seen her, she's been wearing a different colored wig. I think the first time she came to services, she was a brunette. Then it was short blond. Then long black. Then she was a redhead. This week, long blond."

Lisbeth leaned over the seat as Donnie buckled Mandy into her seat. "How is anyone supposed to keep track?"

"She's just having fun. It's kind of refreshing." Lisbeth leaned over and smoothed Mandy's dress down. "She doesn't put on airs. What you see is what you get. The other women in the group are slowly warming up to her."

"I wouldn't think Katy would have a hard time fitting in. The women in the church have always been pretty friendly."

"Friendly, yes. Ready to embrace someone as outspoken and wacky as Katy? That takes a little more time. And Lorraine doesn't care for her at all."

Donnie shut the van's side door and circled the van. As soon as he got behind the wheel, he looked over at his wife. "Lorraine? I didn't think there was anyone Lorraine didn't like."

Lisbeth shrugged. "She treats Katy very nicely, but she told me in private there was just something about the woman she didn't care for."

Donnie put the key in the ignition. "That's quite surprising. Katy seems like a nice enough person."

"I think it's because Katy is always volunteering for everything. Lorraine thinks she's trying too hard to fit in."

"Well, that's kind of typical of a new believer. Trying to find out where in the body they fit."

"That's what I told Lorraine. Remember how I was when we first joined this church? I don't think there was a single committee I wasn't on."

"Having children cured you of that."

Lisbeth laughed as she leaned over and kissed Donnie on the cheek. "Having Mandy cured me. She was more than enough."

"More than enough what, Mommy?"

Lisbeth turned in her seat. "More than enough little girl to make any mommy happy."

Mandy's face scrunched for a second and then cleared with a smile. "Oh."

Donnie eased out of the parking lot. "Lorraine seemed a bit off today."

Lisbeth looked out the door window. "She's going through a hard time right now."

"With what?"

She looked back over at him. "I'm not really at liberty to say. Lorraine talked to me in confidence, and it's not something she'd appreciate other people knowing. Suffice it to say, things are little stressful for her right now, which is another reason I think someone as perky as Katy gets on her nerves."

"My nephew is dead. Marcus was a good boy and was just trying to save his family, and for that, he's dead. His mother is inconsolable. His sisters are devastated. That officer, or detective, or whatever they want to call him, needs to not only be removed from law enforcement, he needs to be charged with murder."

The uncle had center stage with the reporters while small photographs of the boy and JJ were tucked up in the corner of the screen. It was a picture taken of JJ months earlier during some press conference when he'd been angry with a reporter for asking some personal question.

JJ snorted with disgust as he turned from the television where reporters continued to throw out question after question—anything to keep the man talking. Anything to keep the momentum going.

A couple of people in the hospital waiting room eyed him closely, but no one said anything. Still, JJ felt as though he had already been judged and condemned. And no one had asked for his side of the story.

He leaned down and whispered in Zoe's ear. "I'm going to take a walk."

Zoe stood up, gathering her coat and purse. "Let's go."

Outside, the day was much the same as it had been for nearly a week—overcast, cold, and dreary. For once, JJ didn't mind.

"Don't let it get to you, JJ. If that man had been so concerned about his nephew's living situation, where was he when the boy needed help? He's just jumping on the bandwagon hoping for money and a chance in the spotlight."

"Even if it costs me my career." JJ jammed his hands down inside his pockets and wished he'd remembered to grab his gloves when he'd left the house.

"For some people, it's all about what they want and never mind what it costs someone else." She tucked her hand around his arm and leaned against him. "Whatever happens, JJ, it will end up being the best thing for you in the long run."

"I wish I could believe that."

"I wish you could, too."

JJ let silence dominate for a few minutes while he organized his thoughts. Finally, he turned to Zoe. "How can you be so sure God is concerned about you personally? That He cares about your job or your friends or your plans for the week?"

"Because He created us for one reason, JJ. Fellowship. He used to walk in the Garden of Eden every day to hang out with Adam and Eve. To talk to them. Laugh with them. He made sure they had everything they needed in life—food, companionship, and shelter. He gave them every good thing and warned them of the bad things. That tells me He cares."

She wrapped her scarf around her neck. "When Jesus

came to earth, He pointed the people to God, but not as the God of Moses, a God so remote they feared even saying His name, but a God they were told to call *Father*. The scriptures say we have fellowship with the Father, through Jesus, by the power of the Holy Spirit. Fellowship, JJ. With a Father. A Father cares for His children, provides for His children, disciplines His children, and guides them into the good things of life while warning them of the bad."

JJ reached out and fingered a lock of her hair, watching it curl around his finger as if clinging to him. "I've tried, you know. I prayed a couple of times. Tried to read the Bible. I don't know. He still seems like this remote God to me."

They came up to one of the benches lining the walkway, and JJ sat down. "And right now, I'd give just about anything to have the peace you always seem to have."

He glanced back up at the hospital with its endless rows of windows and concrete wings. "Even with Daria. You're concerned. You're worried. But you have a peace that God has it all under control and that in the end, it's all going to be just fine, thank you very much."

Zoe eased down next to him on the bench. "That's something that comes with knowing Him. The more time you spend with someone, the better you know his strengths and weaknesses. Well, the more time I spend with Him, the more I come to see His strength, His love, and His faithfulness."

JJ shook his head. "I don't know how to find that, Zoe. Like I said, I've tried praying."

Zoe's smile was like a burst of sunlight coming out through the dreariness. "Yeah, you've done some talking to Him, but have you done any *listening* to Him? You don't get to know someone very well if you do all the talking."

Zoe's cell phone rang, and she pulled it out of her pocket. "Hello?"

A moment later, she jumped up, closing the phone and tugging on his hand. "Daria's awake."

chapter 5

Sprawled out on the sofa, Neil Lagasse hit the remote again. And again. And again. Channel after channel until he finally settled on something that was supposed to be a comedy. It wasn't funny. Then again, he wasn't really following the plot anyway. His mind was still wrapped around finding el-Hajid and getting his reputation back at work.

The man had to be somewhere in the area. But where?

And would it be in time?

Then there was this whole assassination plot they'd heard about. Was it reliable? And if it was, who was the hit man?

So far, he and Rick had pulled the files on four known assassins operating in the United States. There wasn't much in the file on Archie Kemp, but little was known about the man except that he was good. Very, very good.

If anyone had anything on him, it would be Bevere. The man had been obsessed with Kemp for over two years. He'd studied the man under a microscope.

Somehow, Neil had to convince Bevere to let him have access to his file on Kemp. Under normal circumstances, it wouldn't be a problem. Bevere was a good guy and always willing to help out wherever he was needed, but Kemp was his pet project. He doubted Bevere would be eager to hand over all the work he'd done.

But it was worth asking. And if asking didn't work, well, he'd just have to go over Bevere's head.

He needed to know if Kemp was the assassin. If he was, Kemp could lead him to el-Hajid. Too many ifs and not enough solid information.

Frustrated, he rolled off the sofa and grabbed his coat. "Carmen! I'm going to the office for a couple of hours."

◆　◆　◆

"Hurt," Daria rasped.

"I know, baby. You banged yourself up pretty bad. What happened out there?" Zoe slipped another ice chip between Daria's chapped lips.

"Deer. Tried. . .to miss."

Relief swelled and washed over Zoe. "Well, you missed the deer. Unfortunately, the same can't be said for the tree." Zoe set the cup of ice chips down and slipped her hand around Daria's. "I'm just glad you're okay. You scared years off me."

"Shop?"

"Don't worry about the shop. Noreen is covering for you."

Daria sighed and closed her eyes. Zoe stood up. "Why don't you get some rest, kiddo? I'm going to go home and get some sleep. It's been a long twenty-four hours."

Daria murmured something. Zoe picked up her coat and slipped out quietly to wait for JJ to get back from his meeting with Chief Harris.

The chief had called and asked JJ to come in to answer some preliminary questions. Zoe felt bad that he had to go alone, but he understood and assured her that there was nothing to be accomplished by her coming along anyway. *"It's just procedure. I go in, answer some questions about the initial report, and then I'll be back. You wouldn't be allowed in with me."*

The end of the hall opened into a comfortable beige and green sitting room with seating areas scattered around a self-serve coffee station. The outside wall was floor-to-ceiling glass windows that looked out over the woods behind the hospital.

The room was empty except for one young girl in a wheelchair, sitting over at the window, staring out. She looked up at Zoe and smiled. "Hi."

"Hi." Zoe draped her coat over the back of a chair and headed for the coffee.

"You're here visiting a friend?" the girl asked.

Zoe nodded as she poured the coffee. It looked like mud. Pouring it out, she started a new pot. "My best friend was in a car accident."

Waiting for the coffee to brew, Zoe walked over and sat down near the young girl. She was probably somewhere between twelve and fifteen, wrapped in a pale blue terry cloth bathrobe with matching slippers, and wearing a cute little blue and purple fabric hat. That's when Zoe noticed the girl was bald beneath the hat.

"You escaped from upstairs."

The girl giggled. "Obvious, huh? The cancer ward is just so depressing sometimes. I like to go sit in some of the other wards to keep my head on straight." She reached a pale and fragile-looking hand toward Zoe, the fingernails tipped in iridescent pink polish. "Erin Regan."

Zoe reached out and shook the girl's hand. "Zoe Shefford."

"You have awesome hair."

For the first time in her life, Zoe was almost ashamed of her hip-length blond hair. She had so much while this girl had nothing. "Thanks."

"I had blond hair." The girl laughed, tipping her hat back a little. "When I had hair."

"I'm sorry." Zoe didn't know what else to say.

"For what? Did you do this to me?"

"Well, no, but—"

"Then don't pity me or feel sorry for me." Erin airily waved her hand. "I don't have to wash it, dry it, curl it, cut it, and I never have bad-hair days. Can you say the same?"

Zoe laughed, falling a little in love with a girl who could laugh about being bald and make it seem almost enviable. "You have a point."

"Besides, I get to wear the best hats. I design most of them myself." Erin pulled her hat off and handed it to Zoe. "I made this one."

"It's beautiful. I was admiring it when I came in." Turning it in her hands, she couldn't help notice the tiny stitches and neat workmanship. "You sewed all that design work yourself?"

"Sure."

"It's remarkable. Such tiny little stitches and they're so perfect." Zoe reluctantly handed the hat back to Erin. "Just out of curiosity, how many have you made?"

Erin flopped her hat down on her head. "I don't know. Fifty maybe. It's not like I have a whole lot to do in here, so my parents bring me all kinds of things, and I make hats."

"Would you be willing to sell some of them?"

Erin's face brightened as her eyes widened. "You want to buy one of my hats? Really?"

"Oh, I want to buy more than one, Erin. My mother owns a little boutique in town called Amy's. Maybe you've heard of it."

"Sure," Erin replied.

"I'd love to put about ten or twelve of your hats in the store and see how they sell. I bet they fly out of the store."

"Really? That would be just marvo. I'll tell my mom to bring some in for you to pick from. You really think they're good enough to sell?"

"Oh yes. I most certainly do. I know I'm going to buy a couple for myself." Zoe reached over and grabbed her purse, then began rummaging through her wallet. "Here's the store number." She handed Erin a business card. "Have your mom just take twelve hats down to the store and let my mom know how much you want to sell them for. I'll tell Mom they're coming."

Erin held the card in her hand, staring down at it. "Wow. This is so. . .thank you."

"No need to thank me. My mom and I are always on the lookout for beautiful and unique things to sell in the store."

The coffeemaker had stopped sputtering, so Zoe went over and poured herself a cup of coffee. "How long have you been here, Erin?"

"About three months."

Three months! She nearly dropped the sugar packets in her hand. "Will you be getting out soon then?"

"Hard to say," Erin replied far too easily for such a young child facing such a horrid disease. "Could be days, or weeks, or I could still be here a year from now."

"That must be hard."

"Dying is hard. Living every day in the meantime is a breeze if you keep your perspective." Erin pointed to a bucket on the counter. "Could you bring me a bottle of water?"

"Certainly." Zoe pulled a bottle of water out of the plastic bucket of ice and, picking up her coffee, walked back over to Erin and handed her the bottle. She sat back down across from the girl.

"How do you keep your perspective, Erin? You're so young. You should be at home, talking on the phone with one of your girlfriends about some cute boy at school."

Erin took several deep swallows of water and then recapped the bottle. "I can talk on the phone from here. I try to look at things from a different place. Or a different position. Like, I come down here, and this floor is all trauma patients. They've had accidents they never saw coming, and now they're fighting for their lives or dealing with the pain. I had time to understand and accept. They didn't. I have time to accept what's coming. They're trying to accept what has already happened. I like my position better, don't you?"

"You're a remarkable young woman, Erin Regan."

The girl smiled again, her pale cheeks taking on a bit of color as she blushed. "I just don't see any purpose to spending the days I have all bummed out and crying. What a waste. I see it all the time around here. Not me. I want to live every day and go out smiling, happy with the days I did have."

"There you are." JJ walked up, giving Erin a brief smile of acknowledgment before turning his attention back to Zoe. "You ready?"

"Yes." She stood up. "Erin, I would like to come and talk to you again, if I may."

Erin's face lit up again as she flashed a big grin at Zoe. "I'd like that."

"And get those hats to my mom."

"Yes, ma'am." Erin gave Zoe a saucy salute.

"I like you, Erin Regan. I'll see you soon." Zoe gave Erin's shoulder a light squeeze before turning and walking out with JJ.

"Who is the little girl with the hat?" he asked, falling into step beside her as they headed down the hall for the elevator.

"Her name is Erin. She's a cancer patient here."

JJ frowned deeply. "Cancer? And she's so young. Not that cancer is good at any age. It just seems worse when they're kids."

"I know."

"How is Daria?"

"Tired, sore, but otherwise good. She's sleeping."

"Best thing for her."

As they stepped into the empty elevator, Zoe turned and leaned into JJ's arms. "I was so afraid I was going to lose her."

JJ held her tight, stroking her hair. "Well, she's going to be fine."

"I want to go somewhere, JJ."

The elevator doors dinged open, and they stepped out. The lobby was full of activity—people coming and going, doctors and nurses rushing from one place to another, visitors with flowers and colorful balloons. The atmosphere was almost festive. "Where do you want to go? It's a little cold and raw for a walk in the park."

The restlessness nudged her harder. "I mean *somewhere. . . somewhere.*"

JJ held the lobby door open for her. "Is this a female thing?

Because I'm not sure I understand the somewhere, somewhere thing."

"Skiing for a weekend in Aspen. Snorkeling in Cancún. Maybe sightseeing in New Mexico."

They stopped at his Jeep, and she looked up at him, pleading. "I want to get away for a few days. This is the perfect time, JJ. I can get a few days off. We just pack up and go."

He opened the door for her. "I'm not opposed to it, but I don't ski, and I'm not a big fan of snorkeling."

"I'm just throwing out ideas," she replied as she climbed into the Jeep. She knew she sounded a bit sharp, so she softened her voice. "Can we talk about it at least?"

"Of course."

"How did your meeting go?" she asked as soon as he got behind the wheel.

JJ fastened his seat belt. "It went. The whole thing aggravates me. They just wanted to look at my initial report while asking me questions, trying to see if I was going to trip up somewhere and reveal that I'd lied through my teeth."

"You don't lie."

"Well, they don't know that, but by the time the questioning ended, I think they have a better understanding of what happened that night, so who knows. Maybe I'll be back to work in a matter of days."

"I hope so."

After that, silence seemed to dominate, each of them lost in their own thoughts. She stared out the window as JJ drove back to her townhouse, wishing she felt like striking up a normal conversation, but the truth was, she didn't want to talk. Not to anyone.

It surprised her to admit that she just wanted to be alone.

As the thought settled in to make itself at home, she realized it went even further. She needed time alone to pray. She needed to feel God's presence. She needed His peace and reassurance. She needed the comfort that only He could give her.

As they pulled up in her driveway, she reached over and placed her hand on JJ's, stopping him from turning the Jeep off. "I need a favor."

"What do you need?"

"I need to go be alone and pray."

One of his eyebrows lifted a little as he stared at her. How could she possibly explain the changes she could feel coming? Or the restlessness she sensed in her own spirit? Or the way her spirit sought answers to questions she couldn't even voice?

She loved this man, but lately, she felt the differences rising up between them like a wall she couldn't reach across. She loved God. He wasn't sure he wanted to serve God. She wanted to submit everything to her heavenly Father. He was still trying to figure out if God could be trusted with his soul, much less his whole life. She wanted to do things God's way. JJ still wanted to do it all his way.

Do not be yoked together with unbelievers.

Hadn't she just read that scripture last night before bed? At the time, she'd felt herself flinch from it, but she quickly read on, setting it aside in her mind. But the Word of God had a way of making itself a pest in the heart and mind.

"You want to be alone to pray? I'm not sure I understand. You want to pray, pray. I can just watch one of the games on television. And you've been asking me to put up that wallpaper trim in the kitchen. I can get started on that."

Zoe nipped her lip between her teeth, searching for a way

to explain to him without hurting him. She knew how vulnerable he was right now, but more than anything else, JJ was afraid of being alone. Afraid of his own thoughts.

She suddenly understood she was being called away to pray as much for his sake as for her own.

"I appreciate it, JJ, but I'm going to ask you to please understand. You know how I feel about you, but right now, I just need to be alone for a little while."

JJ's lips curled up in what was almost a smirk as he tilted his head. "You think I'm going to get upset. You're practically tiptoeing around my feelings. Relax, Zoe. I'm not going to get mad. Go pray. Call me when you're done."

She knew he wasn't nearly as okay with this as he was trying to pretend, but she was just going to have to trust God with him. Reaching over, she kissed him gently on the lips. "Thank you for understanding. You're going through a rough time right now, but I've been having these bad feelings about some woman who's in danger."

"Oh, right. I almost forgot about that." The reminder seemed to ease the tension from his brow, and the fine lines faded a bit. "See if you can find out who she is."

He wrapped one hand around her neck and pulled her in close, his lips soft and sweet on hers. "Call me later."

She closed her eyes as he eased the kiss a little deeper before slowly backing away. "I will."

◆　◆　◆

Justin sneezed with a sharp, quick bark as the dust flew all around him. He dropped the end of the board on the ground and wiped his sleeve under his nose. Then he knelt down and examined the board for nails. It was clean.

He picked up the end again and dragged it over to the door and propped it up against the wall. Then he went back to look through the pile of scraps in the corner of the garage for a new piece of floor for his tree fort.

He missed his grandma.

So much that he'd actually folded up the blanket in the closet and put it back on the foot of his bed, folded his pj's and put them under his pillow, straightened the bed, brushed his teeth, rinsed out his breakfast bowl and put it in the dish drainer, and wiped the table.

He didn't know how long she might be gone, but when she got home, he wanted her to see that he'd kept things neat and clean for her. That he could be a good boy. And responsible.

A few minutes later, he unearthed a piece of plywood and smiled as he pulled it out of the pile. It looked good. A little warped, but solid. It wasn't big enough to replace the entire floor of the tree fort, but it would cover the hole. Good enough.

Now he just needed some nails and his grandma's hammer. The nails he found in a jar on the shelf above the washer. The hammer would be in the kitchen in the drawer by the stove, where his grandma always kept it.

Sticking a handful of nails in his coat pocket, he went back inside the kitchen to get the hammer.

And heard rustling in the back of the house.

What should he do? His first instinct was to run outside and scream for help, but he knew that would only make things worse. Swallowing down his fear, he inched forward as quietly as he could, flinching when the floor creaked beneath his feet near the doorway to the hall.

"I know you have money hid here somewhere, old woman. Now where did you hide it?"

At the sound of his mother's muttering coming from his grandma's bedroom, he sighed in relief. It wasn't a burglar. It was just his mom, looking for money again.

When he reached the bedroom door, he was stunned to find his grandma's room in a total shambles. The bed had been stripped, the top mattress askew. The dresser drawers were all open, contents spilling onto the floor. The top of the dresser was swept clean.

"Mom! What have you done?"

His mother dumped an old purse she'd found in the closet upside down on the bed. Other than a handkerchief and a few mints, it was empty. Disgusted, she tossed it aside. "Where does she hide her stash, Justin? And don't tell me you don't know."

Kneeling down, he picked up the little music box he'd given his grandma for Christmas two years ago. It had a little red bird—a cardinal, his grandma had told him—sitting on top. When you turned the key, the bird would turn to the music. The bird was broken off. Tears filled his eyes. His grandma loved this little music box. And now it was broken.

"I asked you a question, boy! Don't you ignore me!"

A sharp slap upside his head stung, and the hovering tears welled and spilled. "I don't know, Momma. Honest, I don't. She never told me she had money hid away. It was always with her in her purse."

Swiping at the tears, he set the music box on the dresser. "Did you see Grandma? Is she okay? Is she coming home soon?"

His mother opened the nightstand drawer and began to empty it on the floor. "No, I haven't been to see her. I got things I need to do."

"But you talked to her?" Bursting with hope, he started picking up items off the floor and putting them back where they belonged.

"Of course not. I'm sure she's too sick to be taking phone calls. Don't be stupid." She fished through the pockets of clothes in the closet, ignoring that half of them were being yanked off the hangers and falling to the floor.

"Ah-ha!" With a victorious shriek, his mother turned around, quickly fishing through a small change purse. "Fifty dollars! Is that all she has stashed?"

Tucking the money in her pocket, his mother tossed the little purse onto the bed. "Well, it's better than nothing."

Justin shoved clothes back into a drawer and closed it. "Are you going to stay here with me until Grandma comes home?"

His mother, on her way out the room, looked over her shoulder at him. "You're no baby. No reason I need to be here. I gotta go to work."

"Where are you working now?" He closed another drawer.

"Never you mind. You just clean up this mess and behave yourself. I gotta run."

"But Momma! Grandma said that if they found out I was here alone, they'd take me away."

"Don't be stupid, boy. Who's going to tell them?"

He followed her down the hall, half hoping she'd change her mind and stay. It's not that he really wanted her around, but he didn't want to be alone. "But, Mom—"

"Shut up, Justin! I don't have time for all this whining!" Flinging the front door open, she glanced back only briefly. "And if you get in trouble, I'm going to come back here and beat you senseless, you hear me? I don't want no cops tracking me down because you went and got picked up for something!"

"Yes, Momma."

And then she was gone, and the house was silent again.

◆   ◆   ◆

Archie eased off the Washington Beltway onto 270 North and merged into traffic. As always, the highway north was busy, but since it was Sunday, it wasn't bumper to bumper the way it was Monday through Friday at this hour.

Once upon a time, 270 had merely been a two-lane road between Washington, D.C., and the wilds of Frederick County, which basically consisted of farms, farms, and more farms.

Then, in the late '70s and early '80s, the young married couples started moving a little farther out to buy bigger homes and more yard for less money. By the mid-'90s, Frederick County had turned into just another suburb of D.C., with disappearing farmland and mile after mile of housing developments with spectacular views of Catoctin Mountain.

"Camp David is right up there," they would boast to family and friends who came to visit.

Now, during rush hour, 270 was a four-lane parking lot.

Archie turned up the radio and rolled his shoulders to ease back into a more comfortable position as violins and horns coaxed him to relax and enjoy the ride. Forget the contracts. Forget the money. Forget the pressure. Think about the music, swirling around him, dancing in his head, filling his car.

A red pickup suddenly swerved into the lane in front of him, nearly clipping his front bumper.

"You idiot!" Archie slapped the steering wheel with one

hand. "Would you like to make it home to your nagging wife and snotty-nosed kids alive?"

Speaking of snotty-nosed kids, he wondered if the little brat in the tree was going to show up today. He wasn't sure if he wanted the kid to be there or not.

◆　◆　◆

It took Justin nearly twenty-five minutes to haul the wood to his tree fort. He glanced over from time to time at the area where he'd seen the man the day before to reassure himself that he was alone.

He was later getting to the fort than he'd planned, but he'd cleaned up his grandma's room before coming out. Just in case she came home today, he didn't want her to find her room all messed up. The bed wasn't made as neatly as Grandma made it, but it was okay. And he'd taken some of his school glue and glued the little red bird back on the music box. It tilted a little, but maybe it would be okay.

His grandma would find out what his momma had done, of course, but she'd appreciate that he'd tried to fix things afterwards. He didn't understand completely why his momma was the way she was—his grandma said it was the drugs that had a hold on her mind, making her do crazy things—but he wished she could be a regular kind of mom.

Dragging the plywood up into the tree, he set it carefully on top of the hole and then climbed back down for the hammer. Grandma said to keep praying for his momma, and he did, but so far, God hadn't done anything about her. He wasn't sure if he should keep praying or not, but Grandma would probably be real disappointed in him if he stopped.

Perched on the edge of the platform, he began to hammer in one nail after another. He loved his grandma—he really, really did—but sometimes, he couldn't help wishing someone would take him away and give him a regular kind of life.

But that wasn't going to happen. Grandma said you couldn't wish things to happen—you had to make things happen. If he went to school and got good grades and got a good job, he could have a real nice life far from the slum he lived in now.

But he'd be in school for years and years. He wanted things better now.

◆　　◆　　◆

Archie eased over into the right lane as the exit for Route 70 came into view. The mountains were shrouded in a pale gray mist, obscuring the top. Driving up and over them would be interesting. At best, he'd have to watch for deer and stupid drivers. At worst, the mist was accompanied by freezing rain and sleet, making the roads at the top like sheets of ice.

Sure enough, as he crested the mountain at Braddock Heights, he saw nothing but flashing lights and a bumper-to-bumper parking lot in front of him. It looked like an 18-wheeler had slid sideways, blocking the road and wrecking several passenger cars in the process.

Frustrated, Archie started looking for a way to cut across the median and make an illegal U-turn. He wasn't going to get there today.

chapter 6

Monday, February 13

Archie hurried across the parking lot and climbed into his car. His boss and coworkers thought he had a doctor's appointment. Smiling, he started his car and pulled out of the lot.

There was an almost childlike thrill at the idea of pulling one over on the people he worked with. The two lives of Archer Kemp. Mild-mannered man in a suit around the office by day. Ruthless killer on the hunt by night.

Amused, he drove three miles from his office and then pulled into the Home Depot parking lot. Where do you hide a nondescript white van with no noticeable markings? Among all the other contractor's vans and trucks at a Home Depot.

Parking next to the van, he left his car running and climbed into his van. Kitty was sitting in the passenger seat, feet propped up on the dashboard, listening to the radio. "Hey, lover. You're two minutes early."

Archie laughed. If there was anyone more meticulous than himself, it was his Kitty. "I hit three green lights I almost never catch."

Reaching behind the seat, he pulled out two magnetic signs for a fictitious plumbing company. He handed one to Kitty, and they both climbed out and quickly stuck them on the sides of the van. Then Kitty met him on his side of the van.

She sidled up to him, lifting her face for a kiss. He wrapped one arm around her waist and pulled her close. "You did good on this one, Kitty."

She reached up and put both arms around his neck. "Anything for you."

"Just make sure everything is ready when I get back to the house. I'm not going to have much time."

"Are you still going after the other judge tonight?"

He kissed her one more time and then gently pulled away. "I'm still planning on it."

"Okay, lover." Kitty climbed into his car and pulled out.

Archie climbed into the van. He felt for and grabbed his duffel bag, then tossed it on the passenger seat. Satisfied that he was ready, he straightened in his seat and fastened his seat belt.

While he was counting on the extensive planning to ensure that everything went smoothly, he was professional enough to understand that sometimes little things went wrong. The key was to move smoothly with the flow and not let the glitches knock you off balance. You had to be able to adjust within seconds and continue on.

What if Lisbeth Bevere didn't go to her weekly prayer meeting? What if one of the kids was sick, and she decided to stay home? What if she went to the meeting but didn't go to the usual grocery store to do her shopping? What if she had gone shopping yesterday for some reason and didn't have any reason to stop today? What if someone's car wouldn't start, and she'd called the Bevere woman for a ride?

He wouldn't know until he got to the grocery store parking lot. If she showed up and she was alone, everything would go down as planned. If she didn't show up or she wasn't alone, he'd have to call Kitty, switch vehicles, and go back to work, leaving this for another day.

Fifteen minutes later, he swung his van into the parking lot of the little strip shopping center near the Bevere home. He was banking on Lisbeth's tendency to be a creature of habit.

She drove the same routes, parked in the same area of the parking lots, shopped on the same days. If she kept to her routine, she would leave the prayer meeting between ten thirty and ten forty-five, putting her in the parking lot of the grocery store between ten forty-five and eleven.

He pulled the van into a section near where Lisbeth was always known to park and sat, idling, waiting. He glanced at his watch. Ten forty-seven.

Anticipation started to slowly build. While he preferred killing from a distance, snatching a woman in broad daylight, in the middle of a shopping center parking lot, held a certain degree of excitement he hadn't felt since back in the days when he first started killing for money. It felt good—this rush of thrill and adrenalin, the hot zing of uncertainty.

And then there she was, driving her blue minivan, slowly moving up the first lane of parking spots, looking to park near the shopping cart corral on this far side of the lot.

Archie eased the transmission into drive and took his foot off the brake, easing out, slowing moving up as she whipped into a parking spot. By the time she climbed out of her minivan, he was parked behind her. He opened the side door of the van and stepped out as she circled the rear of her vehicle.

"Lisbeth?"

Her mind must have been on her shopping list or something because it was obvious he startled her by the way she jumped a little, emitting a soft little screech. He stepped out of the van. He was so close to her he could have reached out and grabbed her.

"Yes? Do I know you?"

"I'm a friend of your husband. Donnie and I go way back. How are the kids?"

Smiling now, she turned toward him. Foolish, foolish woman. He held the hypodermic needle against his leg, his fingers tightening slowly while his thumb caressed the plunger.

"They're fine, thanks for asking. Have we ever met? I'm sorry. . .I don't remember you." She stepped forward, reaching out to shake his hand.

Something bubbled up inside of him. This was going almost too well. He reached out with his left hand to shake hers. As soon as her hand was in his, he tightened his grip and yanked her forward. With a gasp, she stumbled forward against his chest. Immediately, he brought his right hand up and jabbed the needle into her neck.

Her head tilted back, and she stared up at him, eyes wide with shock. Her mouth opened a fraction, as if she wanted to say something, but the drug was already stealing her ability to function. There was a flash of reproach in her eyes—and then fear—and then they fluttered closed.

He picked her up and swung her into the back of the van. Then he climbed in, shut the door, and stepped over her to slide into the driver's seat.

With a glance into the side mirrors, he pulled away, out of

the parking lot, and down the street, keeping his speed moderate while his heart was pounding in his chest. What a rush!

Standing behind a rifle, looking down a scope, pulling a trigger, and watching someone drop was nowhere near as exciting. Or as exhilarating.

He licked his lips, glancing into the rear and side mirrors from time to time to make sure he wasn't being followed. Man, what a feeling! It was a high unlike anything he'd felt in years. Maybe ever.

A mile down the road, he pulled into another shopping center and drove around to the back. Leaving the van idling, he jumped out and quickly removed the magnetic signs, tossing them into the store Dumpster.

Within three minutes, he was back on the road, a wide smile slashed across his face.

Zoe felt the dark heaviness descend so fast, she stumbled, grabbing the wall for support. One minute, she'd been walking back to her office after meeting with Dan about a recent case. . .and then suddenly, she felt as if someone had dropped a hot, wet wool blanket over her face.

"Zoe!" Hands suddenly grabbed her, supporting her body weight even as they guided her into her office.

"What happened?"

She recognized the male voice, husky with concern. It was Kyle Chelan, one of the other investigators at Cordette Investigations.

"I don't know."

He guided her to the nearest chair, then as soon as he

was convinced she wouldn't fall out of it, picked up her phone and connected to the receptionist. "Kelsey! Bring water and a cold compress to Zoe's office pronto!"

He slammed the phone down and knelt at Zoe's feet, rubbing her hands in his. "Your hands are like ice."

Kelsey ran in, a blur of red hair and freckles. She thrust the bottle of water at Kyle and pressed the cold compress to Zoe's forehead.

Suddenly, Dan was moving into the already crowded office. "What happened?"

"Zoe collapsed in the hall," Kyle told him, uncapping the water bottle and handing it to Zoe. "Drink some of this."

Zoe put the bottle to her lips and tipped it back. The cold water hit her throat, and she nearly purred with pleasure.

Somewhere in the distance, she heard phones ringing. Dan must have noticed because he looked at Kelsey. "Thanks, Kel, but I need you on the phones right now."

Kelsey nodded, cast a quick, concerned glance at Zoe, and hurried from the office. Dan knelt down next to her chair. "Feeling better?"

"Yeah."

"Can you tell me what happened?"

"One minute I was fine, and the next. . .I don't know. Everything just went black."

"Did you eat today?"

Zoe turned the compress over and pressed it back to her neck. "Yes. Breakfast and lunch. That wasn't it."

"Kyle, I want you to drive Zoe home and make sure she's inside before you leave. Later, you and I can take her car to her."

Zoe started to object, but Dan silenced her with a wave of

his hand. "Subject closed. You are going home. You will get in bed, and you will rest."

When Kyle went to get his coat and car keys, Dan stood up and leaned back against her desk. "You want to tell me?"

Zoe lifted her head to look up at him. It didn't bring on another wave of dizziness. A good sign. "Someone's in danger. It's been getting stronger for days, but just now, it was so strong, it stole my breath. I don't know who she is, but I've continued to pray and pray and pray. I'm not sure what I'm supposed to do now."

Dan folded his arms across his chest and studied her for a moment. "What about your friend? Rene? Have you called her?"

Zoe shook her head. "She and her husband are out of town at a pastors' conference. They won't be back until later in the week."

Dan's lips went flat as he pressed them tight. He began to drum his fingers against the desk. "Go home. Relax. Whatever is going on, you'll figure it out. You always do. Where are your car keys?"

Zoe pointed to the little tray on the corner of her desk. Dan picked them up and took the house key off the ring, handing it to her. "When Kyle gets back, he and I will bring your car to you, and I'll put your keys in your mailbox."

"Okay."

Kyle appeared in the doorway, buttoning his coat. "Let's roll."

Slowly, with Dan's hands hovering close in case she stumbled again, Zoe eased to her feet, picked up her purse, and reached for her coat hanging behind the door.

Dan held her coat for her while she slipped into it. "Call me later, if you're awake, and let me know how you're feeling."

Zoe nodded as she slowly made her way down the hall.

◆ ◆ ◆

The sky was heavy with the promise of a cold rain as Kitty watched Archie carry the sleeping Lisbeth Bevere into the spare bedroom.

"She'll be out for hours yet, but I want you to be careful. Just in case."

Kitty nodded mutely as she watched him tie Lisbeth to the metal bars on the bed.

Archie had killed before, but never had the money been so good—or the stakes so high. And for that very reason, he was being even more of a stickler for details. It was imperative that nothing went wrong.

Nothing.

Lisbeth Bevere was a wife and mother. She had parents and friends and no enemies to speak of. She was loved, respected, and had no idea that she was about to die.

And not because of anything she'd ever done. That was the only part of this that Kitty didn't care for.

Archie reached down and kissed her. "I have to get back to work. Watch her carefully. Call my cell if she starts to come around."

"Don't worry. I know what to do."

◆ ◆ ◆

Donnie Bevere sipped his coffee as he listened by phone to Neil Lagasse's spiel. In the spirit of cooperation—yada yada. For the sake of the country's security—yada yada. It might lead to nothing—yada yada.

Finally, Neil stopped long enough for Donnie to get a word in edgewise. "You want my entire file on Archie Kemp because you heard a rumor that someone may have put a contract out on a judge? You're going to jeopardize my ongoing investigation on a rumor? An *unsubstantiated* rumor?"

His partner, Jack, looked over at him, raised an eyebrow, and then shook his head as if he couldn't believe what he was overhearing.

"No, Neil. I appreciate exactly where you're coming from. Let me explain something to you. . .you know. . .in the spirit of cooperation. I've been busting my backside for over two years getting everything I could on Archie Kemp. The guy is like a ghost. What I have is pitiful considering the time I've invested. But, it's all I have; and I am not, I repeat *not*, going to just hand everything over to you so you can go follow up some rumor when you don't even know if Archie is involved."

Jack rolled his eyes as he pulled open a drawer and dug through it.

"Well, if the boss says I have to share like a good boy in third grade because the other little boys in the class haven't been doing their homework, I'll share. Until then, do your own investigation."

Donnie slammed the phone down. "Now he's threatening me. You know, ever since they formed the Homeland Security Department, those guys think they have top priority over anything and everything. All they have to do is throw out the magic words. . .*Homeland Security*. . .and everything falls into their laps."

Jack laughed as he shut the desk drawer. "Forget them. Let's go get some lunch. It's your turn to buy."

Donnie stood up and reached for his coat. "I probably could have been a little nicer about it, but I didn't get a lot of sleep last night."

Jack started grinning. "Hollywood Handsome strikes again."

"Just couldn't sleep, Jack. Tossed and turned all night. It's like you know something is about to happen and you just can't figure out what it is."

Donnie's phone rang.

"Let it go," Jack told him. "We're out to lunch."

Donnie hesitated and then turned and followed Jack out of the office. "I'm sure the problem will still be there when I get back."

"It's probably Lagasse again, looking to try another angle."

They were just at the elevator when Donnie's cell phone starting ringing. He pulled it out and looked at it. His home number.

"I have to take this." He stepped away from Jack and flipped the phone open. "What's up, babe?"

"Mr. Bevere? This is Amy. I'm not sure what to do, but Mrs. Bevere hasn't come back, and I'm going to be late for my class."

Donnie glanced at his watch. It was just after two. Lisbeth was usually back from her group meeting no later than twelve thirty. "And she hasn't called you?"

"Nah-uh. And she isn't answering her cell phone."

"Okay, let me try, and I'll call you back."

Disconnecting the call, he ignored Jack as he dialed Lisbeth's cell phone. It went right into voice mail. It was turned off. She never turned it off when she out. She worried too much that something might happen with one of the children.

Fear surged hard and fast, stealing his breath away. Something had happened to Lisbeth!

"What's up? Are we going to lunch or what?" Jack stood holding the elevator open.

Donnie stepped into the elevator. "I have something I need to go take care of. I'll call you later."

"Anything I can help with?"

If only. He shook his head. "A friend of mine has disappeared. It could be nothing, but I'm going to go check it out. Nothing for you to concern yourself with."

As soon as they were outside, Donnie dialed home. "I'm on my way!"

◆　◆　◆

The ringing was soon accompanied by pounding. And then more ringing.

Slowly, Zoe pulled herself out of the confusing fog that separated that state of dreamy sleep from wakefulness. Sitting up, she ran a hand through her hair.

The pounding continued. It was the front door, and someone was going to tear it down if she didn't open it soon.

She wasn't sure how long she'd slept, but the living room was dark. Flipping on the light, she made her way to the front door, covering her ears as the doorbell started ringing again.

"Okay, okay. I'm coming, I'm coming."

She flipped the dead bolt and opened the door. Immediately, JJ came rushing in as if wild dogs were chasing him. "Where have you been? I've been calling for over an hour. I've been ringing the bell and pounding on the door for nearly ten minutes."

"I was asleep." She shut the front door and stumbled past him into the living room. "I came home early from work. Wasn't feeling well."

"Oh." JJ shrugged off his coat and tossed it over the back of a chair. "I'm sorry. I didn't know. How do you feel now?"

"Better. Just groggy." She did a U-turn at the sofa and headed for the kitchen. "I think I need some coffee."

"You know that premonition you've been having? About a woman in danger?"

"Yeah?" Zoe pulled the coffee canister down from the cabinet and opened the lid. She held it under her nose and inhaled.

"Works better if you drink it." JJ took a filter, put it in the machine, and took the canister away from her. "Sit. I'll do this."

"Okay."

"Anyway, we know who the woman is now." JJ measured the coffee and started the machine. "Lisbeth Bevere."

Zoe was easing down into a kitchen chair, but the name had her dropping heavily into it. "Bevere? Donnie's sister?"

"Wife."

Her mind tried to wrap itself around facts that weren't making sense yet. "Wife? But Donnie's single."

"Actually, he's not."

She narrowed her eyes at him. "You knew he was married, and you didn't tell me?"

"He didn't want anyone to know. I found out by accident a few months ago. He made me swear to keep his secret."

He looked so chagrined, she didn't have the heart to nag him about it. Silence built for a second while she absorbed that piece of news. "Okay. Tell me what happened."

"Donnie called me a little bit ago. He's absolutely out of

his mind. Indications are that she's been kidnapped."

"Oh no!"

"I told Donnie we'd come, Zoe."

Her hands dropped to the table. "Absolutely." She glanced up at the clock. It was almost seven. "First thing in the morning, or did you want to try and drive down tonight?"

JJ shook his head. "Not tonight. It's icing up out there, and it's a three-hour drive in the best conditions."

"Poor Donnie."

The room fell silent for a moment except for the sound of the coffeemaker sputtering the last of the coffee. Then JJ turned and started pouring two cups.

He wasn't saying anything, but she knew what he was thinking. And it was probably killing him not to ask if she knew whether Lisbeth was still alive or not.

"I don't know, JJ."

He turned and set a mug down in front of her. "I didn't know how to ask."

"I know." And then she did. Just as she reached for her cup, she knew. "She's alive."

JJ's sigh was loud enough to make her look up at him and smile. "But he plans to kill her."

He leaned back against the counter, both hands wrapped around his mug. "Why would someone do this to Donnie?"

"All I'm getting is something about a cover-up. Someone with a lot to lose. He's really worried and willing to kill to make sure he isn't exposed." She closed her eyes, trying to pull as much information as she could. "It's like there's a puzzle and all these pieces that have to fit together just right." She opened her eyes. "Well, that makes a whole lot of sense, doesn't it?"

The look on JJ's face said he wasn't going to buy anything just yet.

"The Lord has someone else involved. I can't tell who it is, but this person will be instrumental in helping us somehow."

"Then we'll get her back alive?"

She hated to step on the hope she heard in his voice, but there were no assurances in what she felt, so she could offer none. "No guarantees, JJ. We can only try to get to her in time."

"You never met her. She's a special lady. And they have two kids, Zoe. Two little kids. Donnie will lose his mind if anything happens to her. He'll never be able to live with himself."

"He has to learn to trust God."

"Trust God!" JJ slammed his mug down on the counter. Coffee splashed out on the counter. "Is that what this is about? God is doing this so Donnie will trust Him?"

"No, JJ. God doesn't work that way. He isn't the one doing this. But He is in it with them. Donnie has to learn to trust God with his family's life. I can't give you specifics because I don't have any."

"I know exactly what you're talking about. Donnie lets everyone think he's single because he's always been terrified someone would find out he was married and use his family to get back at him."

Zoe sipped her coffee, staring down at the table without really seeing it. " 'What I feared has come upon me.' "

"What?"

"A scripture. Never mind. Donnie is going to need us, and we'll be there for him; but he's also going to have to trust God through this whole thing, regardless of how it turns out."

JJ picked up his mug, saw the spill, and grabbed a paper

towel to clean it up. "Well, that sure sounds reassuring. *Regardless of how it turns out?* What's the point of trusting God if He's not going to make sure things turn out right?"

"Things will always turn out right with God, JJ. They just don't always turn out the way we want them to."

◆　◆　◆

"Time to go, Erin."

Erin turned from the window to look at the nurse. She'd waited nearly all day here for Zoe, but she never came. Disappointed, she turned her wheelchair and rolled herself toward the nurse. "I'm coming."

The nurse stepped up behind the wheelchair and began to push Erin toward the elevator. "You need to stop hiding out on the other floors, young lady. We don't always have time to go hunt you down."

Another nurse came around the corner, spotted Erin, and smiled. "There you are. You are Erin, aren't you?"

"Yes."

The nurse handed Erin a piece of paper. "Zoe Shefford just called in. She's home sick and couldn't make it today, but she wanted to know if you would do her a favor and look in on her friend, Daria." The nurse pointed. "She's right there in room 522."

Erin looked over her shoulder at the nurse pushing her. "Can we stop in for just a minute?"

"Just a few minutes and then you have to get back to your room. Visiting hours are almost up. Are you going to make me come back and find you?"

"No. I'll be right up, I promise."

Zoe's friend, Daria, seemed a little surprised when Erin entered the room, but she offered Erin a weak smile. "Hi."

"Hi. I'm Erin. I'm a friend of Zoe's, too. She's sick today, but she wanted me to come visit you."

"I'm Daria." Daria eased herself up into a sitting position and switched off the television. "You're a friend of Zoe's, huh? Come on in. I could use the company. Cute hat, by the way. Where did you buy that?"

Erin's grin widened as she wheeled herself closer to the bed. "I made it. Zoe likes my hats, too. She's going to have her mom sell them in her store."

"They're going to be a hit, I'm sure."

She shrugged, trying to smother the urge to swell with pride. "It's something I like to do."

Daria reached for a cup of ice water. "Just how young are you?"

"Eleven."

"I thought you were about fourteen or fifteen." Daria took a couple of sips and then set the water aside.

"Most people think that. Mom says I'm an old soul." Erin looked at the bandages around Daria's head. "You were in an accident?"

"Sort of," Daria said quietly.

"How could it be *sort of* an accident?"

Erin studied Zoe's friend closely, noting the pain in her eyes and the way her eyes drifted everywhere but back to meet Erin's eyes. "Oh, I see. You have no job, no family, no friends, and decided life wasn't worth living."

Daria's eyes sliced back at Erin then, sharp and angry. "I own my own business, I have a wonderful family, and I have friends."

"Then you're just selfish. I'm really surprised that someone as nice as Zoe would be friends with someone like you."

Daria stiffened, narrowing her eyes at Erin. "You're a child. Where do you get the nerve to talk to me like this?"

"Because in case you haven't noticed, I have cancer. I'm dying. And not because I want to and not after I've had a long, wonderful life. I'll never go to my prom or graduate from high school or get married or have children. And you want me to feel sorry for you?" Erin backed her wheelchair away from the bed. "Grow up, lady. People love you, and they're going to be devastated if you die. Not that you care how other people feel."

Erin turned and wheeled out of the room. Some people held life so cheap. She'd love for them to be in her shoes for a week. Bet they'd change their attitude then!

Lisbeth's first thought was that she had the headache of all headaches. She wanted to reach out and nudge Donnie to get her some Excedrin, but when she went to move her hand, it felt as though it weighed a ton.

Her tongue felt twice its normal size. *What in heaven's name is wrong?* She tried to think back to what she'd eaten for dinner, but her thoughts wouldn't hold together, jumping like popcorn on a hot flame.

Licking her lips was a major ordeal and accomplished very little.

Then her thoughts started to slow down, and she could capture a few at a time.

Someone had slapped her. "That's not what I told you to say. Try again. Or I'll kill your little girl next."

She could see the tape recorder in someone's hand. A man. With fathomlessly evil eyes. The words written out on a piece of paper.

"Donnie. He has a coffin here. He's going to put me in the coffin and bury me alive."

Oh, God! Now she remembered. The man said he was going to kill her. That she was going to die!

Lord, Father God, please help me! Please don't let me die.

Little by little, it started to come back to her. Stopping at the grocery store the way she always did after her meeting. Getting out of the van. The man stepping out of the van. And then a needle in her neck.

Her heart slammed against her ribs, knocking the breath out of her lungs.

"I see you're awake. Did you have a nice nap, Mrs. Bevere?"

Lisbeth slowly turned her head, flinching at the pain, to look at the man in the doorway. "Why. . . ?"

It was all she could manage.

"Because your husband has something that someone wants. We're going to offer him a trade. You for the disk."

"Water." Her mouth was so dry, it hurt to swallow, and her tongue felt twice its size.

"There's no point, Mrs. Bevere. You'll be dead soon."

"No. Please. My children." The tears ran down the side of her face. Once again, she tried to lift her hands, but they wouldn't move.

He merely turned and walked out the door, shutting it firmly behind him.

chapter 7

Are you sure this is the right street?" JJ narrowed his eyes as he tried to read the street signs in the sprawling housing development.

"I'm positive." Zoe glanced down at the directions she'd written down and then back up at the narrow street lined with cookie-cutter homes, leafless oak trees, and SUVs.

"We should have been there by now."

Zoe reached over to pat his arm. "Quit complaining. If we hadn't stopped to call Matt three times, we would have been there by now."

"I just wanted to see if IAD had met yet, that's all. All hell is breaking loose back there, and I'm leaving town. You know what that looks like?"

"Like you're on leave and taking a small vacation with your girlfriend. How long has it been since you went away and relaxed for a few days somewhere?"

"I hate to point out the obvious, but this is not a vacation. Lisbeth has been missing nearly twenty-four hours without a trace. Donnie is going out of his mind with worry. We are here to help. Not exactly my idea of a vacation." He slowed down and squinted up at another street sign. "Do you know where we are?"

"Three more blocks and make a left on Poplar."

"And that's another thing!" JJ eased on the gas and sped up a little. "How many different kinds of trees can there be? This development is huge!"

"Welcome to the Washington metropolitan area, JJ. All the housing developments are big here."

The vastness made him uncomfortable, the traffic on the Beltway made him nervous, and the way all the houses were piled on top of each other made him claustrophobic. He couldn't wait to get back to the small-town comfort of Monroe where a combine crossing the road from one corn-field to another caused a traffic jam.

"This street coming up should be Poplar."

JJ's foot moved from the gas pedal to the brake as he slowed down and stared up at the street sign. POPLAR. *Finally*. He turned the wheel. "Now what?"

"One block and a right on Birch."

JJ rolled his eyes but kept his comment to himself as he slowed down again and made another turn. He was about to ask for the next direction when he realized he was in a cul-de-sac.

"Right there. The blue house."

He didn't need the last-minute instructions. Not with two police cars parked out front and an unmarked car in the driveway. He pulled his Jeep up to the curb behind a police car and parked.

"Looks like the police finally believed him."

Zoe had unbuckled her seat belt and was already jumping

out of the car. "Now the real fun begins."

JJ closed his door, then opened the back of the Jeep to haul out the suitcases. "What's that supposed to mean?"

"You know this routine, JJ. Donnie will be their first suspect, and he'll be chomping on the bit to get them off his trail and out there trying to find his wife. Makes for short tempers and long hours."

He'd almost forgotten how many cases like this she'd worked on in the past. Zoe Shefford. Famous crime psychic. Specializing in missing children. That was then. Now she was just a private investigator. But while she could denounce her psychic abilities to become a Christian, she couldn't denounce all the experience she had. It would come in handy today.

The front door opened, and Donnie stepped out. Wearing jeans, a flannel shirt, and heavy wool socks, Donnie looked a far cry from the Hollywood-handsome agent he projected when on the job. He lifted his hand, no smile on his drawn, pale face.

Zoe ran up the front walk and into Donnie's hug. "I'm so sorry, Donnie. We'll find her. You know we will."

"Thanks for coming, Zoe. I appreciate it."

JJ dropped the suitcases at their feet and reached out to take Donnie's hand. "Good to see you, Bevere. Any word?"

Donnie pulled him into a quick hug, smacking JJ's back. "Good to see you, too. Nothing yet. They're just now willing to accept that she's missing."

Donnie reached down and picked up one of the suitcases. "Come on in."

The living room wasn't all that big to start with; but adding three uniformed officers, two detectives, two kids, a woman doing her best to calm the baby down, along with Donnie,

Zoe, and himself, and you could develop claustrophobia.

Donnie made quick introductions, starting with the police and ending with the woman, a friend of Lisbeth's from church. The little brunette looked completely frazzled and overwhelmed.

Donnie took the baby from her. "I appreciate the help, Katy. We're good to go now. Tell everyone to keep the prayers going."

The woman tilted her head, looking relieved and apologetic at the same time. "Are you sure? I could stay longer if you really need me."

Donnie shook his head. "I've got help now, but thanks."

Katy disappeared into the kitchen and soon left, right behind another woman from the church who had been in the kitchen doing dishes and making coffee.

Donnie soon excused himself. "Let me take the children upstairs and put them down for their naps. I'll be right back."

JJ found that Zoe had already cut one of the detectives from the herd and had him cornered in the kitchen. "And her car was locked? No sign of forced entry?"

"None. If someone snatched her, they took her between her car and the store. Either going in or coming out."

"Have you questioned the employees?"

"Some, not all. Just the ones working this morning. So far, no one remembers her coming in."

Zoe poured coffee into a mug and handed it to the detective; then she poured one and handed it to JJ, but her attention remained on the detective. "Purse? Shoes? Keys?"

The detective shook his head as he sipped from the cup. "Nothing so far. It's like she locked the car and walked away."

Zoe leaned back against the counter. "In hopes this will save you time and trouble, I'm going to cue you in on something. I know Donnie Bevere. As does JJ here. We've worked cases with him before. He loves his wife with all his being and would never, *could never*, be involved in her disappearance. For Lisbeth's sake, forget the usual procedure of looking at Donnie as your first suspect and go find Lisbeth."

"I knew you looked familiar."

Everyone turned as the other detective stepped into the kitchen, his eyes narrowed in Zoe's direction. Hostility seemed to vibrate off him, and JJ stepped closer to Zoe.

"You're that woman. That crime psychic for missing children."

Zoe lifted her chin. "Was, Detective Harling. *Was*." She turned her attention back to the detective she was talking to. "As I was saying—"

"You *have* no say in this case, lady. End of story. We can't stop you from being here since Mr. Bevere invited you into his house, but you are not on this case. Do I make myself clear?"

JJ stepped between Zoe and Detective Harling, moving so close to Harling, the belligerent detective took a step backwards. "She's here because she's a seasoned, experienced private investigator with more years in abduction cases than you have in law enforcement of *any* kind. A smart man knows when to use all his resources, not just the ones he thinks might make him look like a hero."

Harling leaned forward, his jaw tight enough to make a muscle jump in his cheek. "Who's calling this an abduction? A woman goes to a meeting and then to the store, according to *her husband*, and doesn't come back, according to *her husband*. We have no ransom demand, no—"

Zoe stepped up next to him. "We have no ransom demand *yet*, Detective. Her *husband* is Special Agent Donnie Bevere of the Federal Bureau of Investigation. Hello! Does that ring any bells with you? His wife is missing. Ransom demand or not, someone took Lisbeth, and *your job*, should I need to remind you, is to find out who took her and bring her back safe and sound. Now, if you have trouble with that, maybe we need to call your boss and find out if he has anyone on the job who actually knows how to do the job."

Whatever Harling was about to say was lost as Donnie stormed into the room, his usual easygoing demeanor lost in a haze of outrage. "Detective Harling! I called your department in as a matter of courtesy, but if you can't act professional, please let me assure you I will be more than willing to call in my associates at the FBI to handle this and let the press know you were dismissed for lack of experience and professionalism."

Harling's face flushed red as he sputtered, "That will not be necessary."

Another voice interjected. "Excuse me, Detective?"

Both Harling and his partner turned as a uniformed officer with short brown hair and a name badge that identified him as Jassin stepped into the room with a package. "This was found on the front porch."

Harling, closest to the officer, reached out and took the package. "Who found it?"

"Willis. He went out to the car to get his cell phone and found it lying on the step. It's addressed to Mr. Bevere, here."

Donnie reached for it, but Harling turned and headed for the counter before Donnie could get his hands on it. The detective picked up a knife and carefully sliced the end, then tipped the small box. A cassette tape dropped out.

"You got a player?"

Donnie nodded and led them all into the living room. Harling slipped the tape in the player and stood there next to Donnie as the tape began to play.

"Mr. Bevere." The voice on the tape was garbled, but unmistakably male. "There's someone here who wants to talk to you. Go ahead, little lady, tell him."

Donnie gasped as Lisbeth's voice came on. "Donnie? I'm okay. I love you. Just take care of the—"

There was the sound of a slap and a soft whimper. "That's not what I told you to say. Try again. Or I'll kill your little girl next."

A sob. A sniffle. "Donnie. He has a coffin here. He's going to put me in the coffin and bury me alive."

Donnie bowed his head, clenching his fists. JJ put his hand on Donnie's shoulder. The man was wound tight enough to snap in half.

"Agent Bevere? Do you understand what's happening now? You got it? Now understand this. You get rid of the cops in your house. Pull the taps on your phone. The next time I talk to you, I don't want anyone listening in. You got that? I even smell a cop when I call next. . .I'm coming after your kids."

Special Agent Donnie Bevere could almost pinpoint the exact day he decided to join the FBI. He had just turned seven. His parents had dropped him and his younger sister, Laurie, off at their grandparents' house while they continued on to the hospital. There was a new baby coming into the family, but Donnie was more excited at the prospect of not having school for a couple of days.

He and his grandfather settled in that first night to watch a rerun of something called *The Untouchables*. Within fifteen minutes, Donnie was hooked; and by the time Eliot Ness had succeeded in foiling the gangsters once again, Donnie's young mind was filled with images of tommy guns, mobsters, and G-men.

From that day forward, his future was set. He wanted to be a G-man. He wanted to grow up and join Eliot Ness. Or be the next great Eliot Ness.

His focus never wavered. All through high school and college, he pushed himself physically and mentally, keeping his focus on the day he would apply for his dream job.

Then, during his junior year at college, his focus became divided. A soft-spoken brunette had walked up to him one day and asked for directions to the library. Rather than pointing the way, he'd closed up the book he had been reading and walked her there. By the time he left her at the library, he knew her name—Lisbeth Bushnell—and managed to convince her to go out with him on Friday night.

He married her two years later—just one month after graduating. The young couple moved into an apartment, and while Lisbeth settled into her first job as a high school counselor, Donnie left for Quantico and sixteen weeks of New Agent Training.

And for the first time since graduating, he regretted ever hearing of the FBI.

"Donnie? We'll find her, buddy. We will."

Donnie shook off his thoughts and looked over at JJ. What was the proper response? *I know we will? No problem? I'm fine?* He knew if he opened his mouth, he was going to say something closer to: *It's all my fault. Please don't try to make me feel better.*

So he just nodded, then walked over and dropped down in his recliner. Detectives were moving from one room to another, talking in monotones that scraped like claws along his nerves. Somewhere in the distance, a cell phone rang.

Then someone took his hand. He looked over. It was Zoe. She was kneeling there next to his chair.

"You know I'm not going to get into the platitudes. You and I have been up against this sort of thing many times, and we know the outcome isn't always a happy one. It wasn't for my sister, Amy. It wasn't for Lisa or Gina or DeAnne or Lori. We've buried more than our share."

He closed his eyes against her words—reminders of what he already knew. The chances of ever seeing his wife again— alive—were slim to none.

"Listen to me, Donnie Bevere. For over a week now, the Lord has had me praying for your wife. And for you. He knew this was going to happen. You have to trust Him right now like you've never trusted Him before. Regardless of the outcome, He's right here in the midst of this. Don't you dare start giving up hope yet."

She offered him a slender thread of hope, and he was so afraid to reach out for it. He squeezed her hand, still not trusting himself to speak.

"Lisbeth is counting on you to pray for her, to stay strong for her, and to care for those children. Don't you let her down. Don't you dare."

"I won't," he whispered, swallowing down emotions that threatened to take him under.

"Then let's get started finding Lisbeth."

He lifted his head and looked at her, ready to laugh in her face, but the intensity he saw there, along with something he couldn't quite understand, cut the laugh off before it could start. "What do we do first?"

"Exactly what the kidnapper is asking. Get rid of the law enforcement. Disconnect the taps."

Detective Harling thrust forward, all attitude and outrage. "Oh no, you don't. We are not going anywhere. We have an investigation underway. You do what this guy wants, and you can kiss your pretty little wife good-bye. Of course, that might be just the point, right? Set this all up, get rid of us, she dies, and you come out smelling all clean."

Before Donnie could get out of his chair, Zoe was on her feet and going nose to nose with Harling. She poked her finger in his chest, backing him up. "I've worked with some question-able people in my time, but you are coming real close to taking the award for not only the most incompetent but for the biggest fool, too. I don't care if Donnie contacts your boss or not; you can be sure that I will. I don't normally throw my weight and reputation around, but I'm willing to make an exception in your case and make sure you are known for the—"

JJ tugged on her arm. "Calm down, Zoe. This isn't helping."

Donnie placed a hand on Zoe's shoulder. "I can take it from here. Detective Harling? I want you out of my house in less than two minutes."

"You can't do that!"

Donnie reached over and picked up the phone. "I can, and I will. Watch how fast you're pulled from this investigation."

As he punched in a series of numbers, he saw Zoe flash Harling a smile that was anything but friendly. "I suggest you go quietly before your boss calls you back. And take everyone with you. This is now officially an FBI matter. And you know how the FBI is about sharing cases."

"This isn't over by a long shot," Harling growled at her. Then he turned on his heel and, motioning to his men, left the house.

Donnie hung up the phone. "The time is exactly eleven fifty-seven."

"Then we better get to work." Zoe nodded once and headed for the kitchen. "We've got a lot to do before the kidnapper calls back."

"What's first?" he asked.

"Prayer."

◆　　◆　　◆

"Any luck with Bevere's file?" Special Agent Rick Harrelson popped open his can of soda and set it down on his desk.

Neil Lagasse shook his head as he looked up from the file he was reading on a man in New York City with mob connections and known to be an assassin for hire. "He wasn't in the mood to be cooperative. I tried calling him back, but he's out of the office."

"Out on a case?" Rick reached for the phone as it started ringing, but his hand rested on top of the receiver as he waited for Neil to answer his question.

"Not that I can figure. Someone said he got a phone call yesterday at lunch and went running out of here like his house was on fire, and no one's heard from him since."

Rick lifted the phone. "Harrelson."

Neil closed the file in front of him. Bontano was sitting in Sing Sing and had been for over three months, awaiting trial for the murder of two men in Brooklyn.

Frustration hummed along Neil's nerves. He had to catch this assassin and break el-Hajid's terrorist cell wide open. Granted, he wanted to get his reputation back within the agency, but the idea of el-Hajid laughing up his sleeve hit right at Neil's ego, too.

This had become personal.

El-Hajid had escaped on *his* watch. And every time el-Hajid killed, it was because *he* had slipped up. People might not come right out and say it was *his* fault, but *he* knew it was.

And now, with those prisoners coming up from Guantánamo Bay for trial, the last thing he needed was for el-Hajid to strike.

Rick finished up his soda and hit a two-pointer in the trash can. "Okay, I got two possibles on assassins."

"Who?"

Rick was about to offer his suggestions when another agent strode over to them.

"SAIC Mann wants us in his office immediately. Task Force meeting regarding those prisoners coming in."

Neil stood up, grabbing his suit jacket off the back of the chair and swung it around, slipping his arms in the sleeves. "Something come up?"

"You mean like a full-blown press report on an operation that was supposed to be hush-hush?" The agent shook his head in disgust and headed for the conference room.

When the agent said task force, Neil hadn't expected every force known to man. He saw representatives and agents from the CIA, the U.S. Marshals Service, the NSA, the Army, the Air Force, JAG, the State Department, Maryland State Police, Virginia State Police, the D.C. chief of police, and two Marines.

He was about to make a smart comment to Rick about the White House not being there, when a man he recognized as belonging to White House Counsel strode through the door, briefcase in hand.

Neil took a spot along the wall of windows and edged a hip on the windowsill. Rick leaned against the back wall, arms folded across his chest.

Wishing he'd brought a cup of coffee with him, Neil used the time until the meeting started to check out all the men and women in the room. Attitudes rolled in waves as each agency juggled for prominence in the room, each one wanting to be seen as being at the top of the proverbial pyramid of power.

The only one who seemed oblivious to the game, or at least above playing it, was the attorney from the White House. He knew he was the only man in the room who had direct access to the president. Unless the vice pesident showed up or something, he was top dog.

The games amused Neil to some degree. In spite of all the Homeland Security marketing propaganda, the truth was, old territorial habits died hard. They could spout off all they wanted about the new "era of cooperation," but that cooperation ended with the commercials and press conferences. Then it was back to every man for himself.

Someone must have finally decided that since the Special Agent in Charge had called the meeting, he could start it, regardless of his position on the pyramid.

Towering at six-foot-four with wide shoulders and his military-style haircut, Jim Mann drew attention whether he wanted to or not.

Mann stood up, oblivious to the fact that there was a coffee stain on his tie. He ran those piercing gray eyes around the room and then slapped both hands down on the conference table, and his voice boomed, "I want to know who in tarnation opened their big mouths to the press about an operation that was supposed to be kept quiet?"

chapter 8

Tuesday, February 14

Zoe dried her hands on the towel as she hurried down the hall and opened the front door before whoever was there could ring the bell again and wake up Donnie.

The blond at the front door looked familiar, but Zoe couldn't quite place her. The woman smiled as if she could see Zoe's dilemma. "I'm Katy. We met this morning. When you first got here? All the women are taking turns making food for all of you."

Zoe opened her mouth. Shut it. Opened it. "Weren't you a brunette?"

Katy laughed, shifting a casserole dish forward. "I have a thing for wigs. You never know what color I'll be from one time to the next."

Zoe suddenly realized she was holding the door open and cold air was rushing into the house. "I'm sorry. Where are my manners? Please come in. Donnie is asleep, but I can't thank you enough for bringing food. I'm afraid none of us are really in the mood to cook."

"Well, it's just beef stew, but it'll stick to the ribs." She stepped into the house, and Zoe closed the door behind her.

"It'll be wonderful." She took the dish from Katy and led the way to the kitchen. "Donnie was up all night, and it finally got to him. He passed out on the sofa about half an hour ago, so we're letting him sleep."

Katy looked around. "It's so quiet. Where are the police?"

"We sent them away." Zoe set the casserole on the counter. "Can I offer you anything to drink?"

"You sent them away?" The woman's eyes went wide, and she broke out in a wide smile. "You found Lisbeth!"

"Oh." Zoe suddenly realized the reason for the smile. "No. I'm sorry. We haven't found her yet." She held up the coffeepot.

Smile fading, the woman shook her head, shoving her hands into her pockets. "Thanks, but I have to get home and cook for my family now. I hate to sound nosy, but why would you send the police away?"

"The kidnapper contacted Donnie and demanded that the police leave before he would negotiate further."

Katy leaned in closer, whispering. "Is that wise? I mean, I hear kidnappers do that, but then they take the money, and you don't get your family member back."

Zoe couldn't resist. She leaned toward Katy, dropping her voice down to a whisper, too. "It's okay. Donnie is FBI. I think he knows how to handle this."

"Oh. Right." She pulled her gloves out of her pocket and started pulling them on. "Well, let him know we're all praying for him and Lisbeth."

Immediately, Zoe felt chastised. She reached out and took one of Katy's hands. "I'm sorry, Katy. I didn't mean for you to take that wrong. We're all just a little stressed out around here."

"It's okay. Really. I guess I sounded a little foolish. I've just never been around a situation like this before, you know? You get married, you have kids, you go to church, PTA, the grocery store. The most exciting thing that ever happens is someone in the neighborhood getting caught having an affair, and the wife throws all his stuff out in the yard and calls the police; and the whole neighborhood goes outside to water their lawns just to watch the guy yelling because she cut up his favorite football jersey."

Zoe laughed, pulling Katy into a hug. "I'm sorry, but I wouldn't mind a bit of that for a few years."

"I want my mommy."

Zoe turned to the little voice behind her. Amanda was standing there, rubbing her eyes, a cloth doll tucked under her arm.

Her heart hurt for this little girl who didn't understand what was happening. Zoe picked her up and propped the child on her hip. "Your mommy will be home pretty soon, Mandy. Is your brother awake yet?"

Mandy nodded, her bottom lip trembling. "He's hungry."

Katy eased by. "I'll let myself out."

"Okay, thanks again. I appreciate the stew."

Katy waved and disappeared down the hall.

"Now what do you think your brother wants to eat?" Zoe said, more to herself than Mandy.

"His bottle," Mandy replied, squirming to get out of Zoe's arms.

"Bottle. Right." Zoe set Mandy on her feet and opened the refrigerator. Sure enough, there were two bottles sitting in the door. "And this has to be heated, right?"

"You take the top off and put in the micr'wabe and then shake it."

Zoe stared down at Mandy, sorting through the instructions.

"I'll do it." Donnie shuffled into the room, his blond hair sticking up at odd angles, his blue eyes dark with misery. He took the bottle from her and put it in the microwave. "Mandy, you need to go put some socks on those feet, honey. The floor is cold."

" 'Kay." Mandy skipped out of the room, content now that her dad had added a moment of normalcy to her life.

"Katy dropped off a casserole. She said the women at the church are taking turns cooking food and sending it over."

Donnie took the bottle out of the microwave and set it on the counter to cool a moment before recapping it. "We'll be bombarded with food then."

"I'll go get the baby," Zoe offered.

Donnie shook his head. "Let me. It'll keep me sane to stay busy with them."

Zoe watched him shuffle out of the room, his shoulders bent under the weight of his grief. *Father, strengthen him in this hour.*

A quick prayer on the run wasn't enough. The need was pulling too hard at her. Deciding the basement family room would be the quietest for a little while, she went downstairs and collapsed on the floor in front of the sofa.

"Father, please. For years the enemy used my gift for his purposes. I didn't know the difference until I came to know You. Whenever he used my gift, there was no eternal value. I found those children, but what did it accomplish? No one came to know You better in any of what I did. But then I turned all this over to You, and since then, I've seen what You do, Father. Karen Matthews knows You now in a way she never did before. Nora and her husband have greater faith. Dana is now one of Your children and friends with the sister she never knew she even had.

"I don't know what's going to happen to Lisbeth, but You do. Father, I'm asking You to use me to find her alive. I don't want to comfort Donnie at his wife's funeral. She's a wife and a young mother with two little children who love and need her."

She took a deep breath and lifted her face to the ceiling. "Better You should take me than let the enemy take her."

◆　◆　◆

Archie was sliding his favorite rifle—a .308-caliber thunderstick custom-built on a Remington Model 700 bolt-action receiver, holding five match-grade 168-grain boattail hollowpoint bullets in a spring-loaded magazine, topped with a Leupold 3.5 x 10 variable power scope—into the case. It was his pride and joy and the sweetest thing he'd ever fired, right down to the leather cheek pad on the stock.

Kitty walked through the door, drying her hands with a dish towel. "So the hit on the judge is on?"

"Yes." Archie didn't bother buttoning his coat after slipping it on. Picking up the gun case, he walked over to the door, then turned. "I'll only be gone for a couple of hours. If anything goes wrong, you know what to do."

Kitty sidled over to him, wrapping her arms around his neck, pressing in close. "Kill the woman, go directly to the storage unit, switch cars with the one stored in there, drive directly to Richmond, and wait there for you to contact me."

◆　◆　◆

She knew the routine by heart. Every time he went out on a

job, he would make her repeat his instructions. Routine, routine, routine. The man was a fanatic about having every detail down to the last fiber.

"Good girl. I'll see you in a bit. Stay close to the phone."

"I know." She quickly smiled when she saw something flash in his eyes. Most of the time, Archie was the easiest person in the world to be around, but when he thought she was mocking him or talking down to him, his temper would flare faster than flash paper. "I won't go to bed until you're home."

He stared at her a long moment and then, without a word, turned and walked out. As the door clicked shut behind him, she heaved a sigh of relief. Another close one. The older she got, the harder it was to pretend to still be the sweet, pliable kid she had once been. She had opinions now. And a need to be something more than just his shadow and gofer.

Tamping down her resentment, she went into the kitchen and hung up the dish towel. He was always telling her how smart she was, how bright she was, how capable she was, but did he really take her seriously? Not really. Even if he latched on to an idea she came up with, he'd eventually begin to talk as if it were his idea all along.

Picking up the tray she'd prepared, she headed downstairs. Outside the room, she paused a moment, taking a deep breath and preparing herself for the confrontation ahead.

Then she opened the door and turned on the light.

Lisbeth blinked a few times, turning her head slowly toward Kitty.

She set the tray down. "I know you must be hungry as well as thirsty, so I brought you something."

"No," Lisbeth whispered in a scratchy voice.

"No, you're not hungry? I find that hard to believe." Kitty

put a straw in the glass of water and sat down on the edge of the bed. "Drink a little at a time. I don't want you gulping it down and then throwing it all back up."

Lisbeth blinked. "I don't understand."

"What's to understand? Now, here. Drink."

Placing one hand under Lisbeth's head, she lifted Lisbeth up a little so the woman could drink. Lisbeth sipped slowly. After a couple of swallows, Kitty pulled the water away. "Easy."

"Why?" Lisbeth licked her lips as tears filled her eyes. "Why are you doing this, Katy?"

When the doorbell rang the third time and neither Zoe nor Donnie showed up to answer it, JJ got up off the sofa to take care of it. He'd been reading over Donnie's old case files for hours, hoping to spot something, or someone, that jumped out and looked like a potential lead in Lisbeth's abduction. So far, he hadn't found a thing.

He opened the door. It took him a minute to recognize the man standing there, hunched down in an overcoat. "Jack Fleming. How are you?"

Jack looked shocked to see JJ standing at Donnie's door. "Detective Johnson? A little out of your jurisdiction, aren't you?"

"Just visiting as a friend. Come on in."

Jack stepped into the house, unbuttoning his coat. "I've been trying to get in touch with Donnie, but he's not returning my calls. We've got some important things going on. Decided to come over and find out what the problem was."

JJ shut the door. "You mean Donnie didn't call you?"

A noise on the stairs captured their attention. The look

on Jack's face was so priceless, JJ wanted to laugh. Then again, his own face probably looked about the same the afternoon he walked into Donnie's hotel room and found out Donnie had a wife and kids.

Donnie was coming down the stairs, holding Mandy's hand as she two-footed the steps.

"Okay," Jack said. "Somebody talk to me."

"What are you doing here, Jack?" Donnie reached the bottom of the stairs and released Mandy's hand.

"I've been calling you for two days, partner. All hell is breaking loose around the office, and you are nowhere to be found."

"All hell is breaking loose around here, too."

Jack looked at Mandy, who was running off to the kitchen, then back to Donnie. "Whose kid?"

"Mine," Donnie said. "For the record, I'm not single. I'm married. I have two kids. I haven't told you because I didn't want anyone to know. Not that it did me any good. My wife has been abducted."

"Married?"

Donnie led the way into the living room. Jack followed on his heels like a little terrier. "Why didn't you ever tell me? We're partners."

"Never mind. I'm not in the mood to go into it right now. But I'm glad you stopped over. We could use your help." He eased wearily down in the recliner. "JJ's going over some of our bigger cases. Any ideas who would want to get back at me by taking Lisbeth?"

Jack continued to stand there and stare at Donnie. JJ eased around Jack and returned to his spot on the sofa. This was Donnie's problem. He'd let Donnie handle it.

"Let me get this straight. You're married, and you didn't tell me. No, you let me think you had a number of girlfriends. And this goes on for years. And then. . .the minute something happens, you call Johnson. Not me. Your partner. You call a detective you worked with on a couple of cases. Am I getting this right?"

JJ looked up from the file in front of him, wondering if he should step in and say something. Donnie was hurting, and this wasn't the time for Jack to be jumping all over him because he didn't know something he felt he should know.

Donnie rubbed one hand over his face. "Look, Jack. I'm sorry I never told you. I never wanted anyone to know. Not even JJ. But he stumbled on the truth. I didn't tell him. And he's kept my secret. Not that it's done me any good, because someone found out about Lisbeth, and now she's gone. Now, you can either lick your wounds somewhere else, or you can help us find my wife. Your choice."

Jack stared at Donnie for a long moment, then turned and looked over at JJ. He unbuttoned his coat. "What do we know so far?"

"The kidnapper demanded I get rid of the police who were here."

Jack pulled at his trouser legs before sitting down near JJ on the sofa. "How did they know the police were. . ." He waved his hand. "Standard procedure. Okay, what else?"

"He said that once the police were gone, he'd call with his demands. And if I didn't get rid of the police, he'd come after my daughter next."

Donnie looked down at his hands, clasped tightly in his lap. "He said he had a coffin and was going to bury Lisbeth alive."

Jack muttered something under his breath. "Okay, who do you suspect?"

Donnie raised his head. "I don't know. I feel like my mind has turned to mush. I've never felt so helpless in my life."

"I've narrowed this pile down to four possibles," JJ interjected. "All four of them threatened to retaliate."

Jack reached out and turned JJ's notepad around and read the names. "Larry Sickler is in prison. He was picked up six months ago on a weapons charge."

JJ reached over and crossed out the name. Jack held out his hand. "Give me some of those files. I can probably go through them faster than you can."

After handing Jack a stack of file folders, Jack looked through the tabs. "How did you get these, Donnie?"

"I kept my own copies here in my home office. There's nothing in those files I couldn't remember off the top of my head if I needed to."

Jack laughed. "Easy to say when you have a photographic memory like you do." He tossed the first three file folders down. "No, no, and no way. Saunders is dead."

When the phone rang a few minutes later, all three men jumped. JJ had just noticed that Zoe hadn't made an appearance and was about to go looking for her. He stopped in his tracks and looked at Donnie. Nodding in understanding, Donnie took a deep breath, picked up the phone, and hit the speaker option so everyone could hear the conversation.

"Bevere."

"I'm so glad you're a smart man, Special Agent Bevere. It makes working with you so much easier."

"I want to talk to my wife."

Immediately, JJ manned the phone tracer, trying to get a

fix on the caller's location.

"I'm so sorry. She's taking a nap right now, but I'll see what I can do for you a little later. You have a flash drive. The owner wants it back. You deliver the flash drive; I give you your wife. Deal?"

"I don't know what you're talking about!"

"Oh, I think you do. Don't play games with your wife's life, Bevere."

"Do you have any idea how many of those things we confiscate in a year's time? You have to give me something more to go on!"

"I'm going to bury your wife alive, Bevere. Now I'm going to be real considerate and install a small breathing tube into the coffin so she can get a little bit of air, but you know, anything can happen. Snow. Rain. Leaves blowing over it. If I were you, I'd find that drive and have it ready the next time I call. The longer you take, the less time she has."

Donnie came up out of the chair and started striding from one end of the room to the other. "You are sick! Let me tell you something. My wife dies, and I'll make sure you wish it had been you in that coffin, because her suffering will look like mercy compared to what I'm going to make you go through."

The man laughed, and the sound ran down JJ's back like ice water.

"Oh, I think you're smarter than that, Bevere. Get the flash drive."

JJ whipped a hand in the air, rolling it in a signal to Donnie to keep the man talking. Donnie jumped on it.

"I can't get anything tonight! Anything like that is at the office and locked up in evidence. You need to at least tell me which case and then give me time to go through all that stuff and find it."

"I'll call you tomorrow. I suggest you have that drive."

"Wait! I want—"

But the caller was gone. JJ slammed his hand down on his knee. "He knows. He knows we're tracing. He didn't stay on long enough."

Donnie reached over and disconnected his end of the call. "He's going to bury her alive."

"Trust your heavenly Father, Donnie." Zoe strode into the room like a warrior looking for the battle. "Her life is in His hands, not this madman's."

Donnie whirled around, his face mottled red and white. "Her life is in a coffin. What am I supposed to do with that?"

"Trust Him. You didn't before. You tried to protect her with lies. Now protect her with truth. God's truth. She is in His hands, and He has not forgotten her. Regardless of what happens, her life is in His hands. Trust Him with that."

Her voice had started out soft and sure, but she ended with such force that even JJ stepped back.

Donnie looked as if someone had sucker-punched him. "I didn't mean for it to be about lies. The men just assumed, and I let them. It seemed the best way to protect my family."

"I realize that, Donnie. I'm not judging you for what you did in the past. Never look back. Just see where you are, and do it the Father's way from this moment forward." She reached out and stroked the side of his face with her hand as if soothing away the bitter sting of her words. "God is faithful, Donnie."

"I don't know how to trust Him in this, Zoe. I keep thinking I'm going to have to face life without her. Raise our kids without her. Explain to them someday that the reason she died was because of my job."

JJ saw the tears gathering in his friend's eyes and turned away. He couldn't stand to see it. He understood Donnie's fear. When his fiancée had been murdered, he thought he'd go insane before he buried himself in his work. Then falling for Zoe and seeing her brush so close to death had nearly undone him.

There was a knock at the door, but it seemed that JJ was the only one who heard it. Slipping out of the room, he opened the door.

His jaw dropped.

"Lisbeth!"

◆　◆　◆

Justin huddled in his grandmother's bed, watching her little TV sitting on the tall dresser in the corner. It had lousy reception, but the room had blinds as well as curtains and faced the back of the house, so no one would see the flickering light. He was so tired of being alone, hiding from people, eating leftovers, and wondering if and when his grandma was coming home.

He hadn't been to school now for two days. How long could he be missing from classes before they sent someone by to check on him? He wondered if Mr. Fiske, the principal, had called to ask if there was a problem.

His grandma hadn't told him what to do if this went on for more than a day or two. What if he ran out of food? Now that his mother had taken his grandma's money, he couldn't even go to the little store down the street and buy some bread or cereal.

Bored with the offerings of the night, he stared at the screen and tried not to think that his grandma might not be coming back at all. Then what would he do?

◆   ◆   ◆

"Maureen?" Donnie stared at the woman in the doorway. Slowly, he climbed to his feet. "What are you doing here?"

JJ stepped back from the door. "Come on in."

Maureen shot JJ a warm smile as she passed him on her way into the living room. "Okay, Don. What's going on, and where is my sister?"

Now he remembered why he'd been having a sinking sensation all day that he was overlooking something important. "You and Lisbeth were supposed to go shopping for your wedding dress tonight. I'm sorry, Maureen. I should have called you."

"Where is she?"

Donnie looked around the room, wishing he could be anywhere but here and doing anything but this. "You have to promise me that you won't tell your parents what I'm going to tell you. At least, not yet. Your dad's health hasn't been all that good since—"

"Cut to the chase, Donnie. I've had the worst feeling all day that something horrible was happening, and the look on your face has me ready to have a heart attack. Spill it."

"Lisbeth has been abducted."

Maureen staggered backwards, and Zoe, closest to her, reached out and grabbed her. She guided Maureen over to a chair. "Sit. I'll get you some water."

Maureen didn't respond, just stared down at the floor, her

face drained of color. By the time Zoe returned with a glass of water, she was trembling.

"What are you doing to get my sister back?"

"Everything," Zoe told her before Donnie could respond. She knelt down next to Maureen. "My name is Zoe Shefford... that man over there is Detective Josiah Johnson, and the gentleman on the sofa is Special Agent Jack Fleming. Together, we're going to do everything possible to get your sister back safe and sound."

Maureen stared at Zoe for a long moment, then lifted her face to Donnie. "When did this happen?"

"Yesterday."

"Yesterday!" Maureen screeched. "She's been gone two days? And you didn't think to call her family? What are you thinking, Donnie? We have a right to know!"

Donnie looked completely lost and so miserable, Zoe wanted to rush over to him and hold him close. Somehow, she didn't think the sister-in-law would appreciate it.

"I'm sorry, Maureen. I probably should have called, but I was hoping she'd be back by now. I didn't want your dad to find out. That's the last thing he needs right now."

Maureen set her water down with a solid *thunk*. "What he needs is to know that his daughter is in danger so he can be praying for her. Lisbeth deserves to have everyone praying, Donnie. Not just Special Agent Bevere, superhero."

Donnie groaned. "Don't go there, Maureen. I'm at the edge of my sanity as it is."

"Well, what do you want from me, Don? Sympathy? Once again, you're only thinking of yourself!"

Zoe looked at JJ, hoping to find some indication as to whether one of them should step in and help out. JJ had his hands in his pockets and was staring at the floor, obviously as uncomfortable as she was. She glanced over at Jack. He had his nose buried in a file folder, making every effort to stay out of the family dispute.

Maureen jerked to her feet. "I'm calling Mom and Dad. They have a right to know. When I get off the phone, I want to know exactly what we're dealing with. Is there a ransom demand? I don't have a lot of money and neither does Pete, but we'll—"

"There's no ransom demand," Donnie interjected.

His sister-in-law stared at him for a moment, then turned and marched into the kitchen to make her phone call. Donnie sank down in his recliner. "I'm sorry, folks. That must have been a little awkward."

"A little," JJ admitted. "What flash drive, Donnie?"

Donnie heaved a heavy sigh. "About three months ago, Jack and I busted a gang in Boston. Along with everything else we found, there was a flash drive with encrypted files. I've been working on cracking the encryption."

Jack closed the file he had in his hand. "I still think we need to call in the cavalry. We can't keep this a secret forever."

"Where's the flash drive?" Zoe asked.

"Downstairs in my office."

Jack groaned. "Are you crazy? I thought you'd given it to the guys over in systems to work on."

"They have a copy. They haven't had a bit of luck. They've got a ton of work over there, and this drive isn't getting their full attention. I know there's something important on there."

"Duh. They just took your wife in order to get it back." Jack flopped back in his seat.

Zoe raised her hand. "Hello, guys. Could we get back on

track here?" She turned to Donnie. "If you have the drive here, why didn't you just make the deal?"

"Because the minute I hand him that drive, I'm dead, and so is Lisbeth. Our only shot is to find out what is on that drive so we can find out who is behind this."

"I was afraid you were going to say that." Zoe pursed her lips, thinking.

"Look, I'm close, okay? Real close. I have to do this."

JJ tilted his head. "What aren't you telling us, Donnie?"

Donnie looked at Jack and then back to JJ, shoving his hands in his pockets. "We found a cache of weapons when we made the bust."

"And?" JJ prompted.

"And they were American-made military issue."

The ramifications hit Zoe like a fist to the gut. "An American soldier is selling our enemies our own weapons to use against us?"

Donnie nodded soberly. "And we think this goes high up. That's why I know they'll kill to keep this from getting out."

"How high up?" JJ asked softly.

"I don't know, but I don't think this is just some supply officer passing things off the back of a transport. A captain. Maybe a general."

JJ nodded. "Maybe as high as the Pentagon. Great. What about FBI resources? We could use all the help we can get."

Zoe stepped in. "We need this to go to the media. Someone in that shopping center may have seen something, JJ. I can understand why you're reluctant, Donnie, but we need a possible witness. We need to be chasing this guy from every angle, just in case you don't get the information we need off that drive."

Maureen stepped into the living room, hand in hand with Mandy. "I'm taking Mandy upstairs. Dad's on the phone and wants to talk to you, Donnie."

With a long glare, she marched past Donnie and headed upstairs.

◆ ◆ ◆

Donnie sat at the kitchen table, head bent, one hand on the phone, the other covering his eyes as he listened to his father-in-law plead in the midst of weeping. "I'm not going to argue with what you did. I understand what you were thinking, but you were wrong. Just find my daughter, Don. Find Lisbeth."

"I'm going to do all I can, I swear. I won't leave a single stone unturned." He pinched at the bridge of his nose, trying to press back the tears that fought to break free. If they did, he'd never be able to stop. His heart was absolutely shattered, and with each passing moment, he fell deeper into a pain he never thought he'd feel.

Lisbeth was his life. His best friend. His soul mate. How could he live without her?

Why are You doing this to me, God?

"Momma and I are going to come down, Donnie. Maureen said she would take care of the children until we get there. We can't do much, but Momma can cook and clean, and we'll watch the children and at least take that worry off your mind. You just concentrate on finding our Lisbeth."

It was on the tip of Donnie's tongue to tell them not to come, but he realized that Lisbeth was more than just his wife—she was a mother and a daughter and a sister. These people were worrying as much as he was. They needed to be here. To feel they were doing something, anything, to help.

"I'll see you when you get here." Donnie slowly hung up the phone.

He sat there, head bent for a couple of minutes, trying to rein in his emotions and get a handle on his fear. This was not the time to be falling apart. His friends and his partner were out there flailing around, trying to find clues while he was sitting around feeling sorry for himself.

It was time to pull it together. If anyone knew his enemies, he did.

Wiping his hand over his face, he stood up. Maureen was standing there, looking at him as if trying to decide whether to hug him or hit him. "I'm sorry, Maureen. I was just trying to keep everyone else from worrying."

"I know that, Donnie. Mom told me that she and Dad were coming down. They won't get here until tomorrow afternoon at the earliest. I'm going to take the babies to my house for the night. Get them out of all this tension. I'll bring them back when Mom and Dad get here."

He wanted to argue with that, too. First his wife, now his kids. His world was being stripped clean. At the same time, he knew his children were picking up on the tension.

"I'll help you get their stuff together."

As he turned to leave the kitchen, Maureen touched his arm. It hurt to look at her, so much like her older sister—the same eyes, the same sweet smile.

"For what it's worth, Donnie, I don't blame you for trying to protect all of us, but this isn't the time for it. We need to gather together and hold each other up, not retreat to our own little islands of pain. We're a family. You're part of this family. We take care of our own, no matter what."

He couldn't stop the tears now. She pulled them out of him as deftly as a surgeon with a delicate hand and a sharp scalpel. When she stepped up and opened her arms, he collapsed against her, the sobs racking through him as she rubbed one hand across his back.

"We'll find her, Donnie. We'll get her back. God is faithful."

"He's faithful, Maureen. But He doesn't always stop evil from having its way."

◆　◆　◆

Archie leaned against the Dumpster as he checked his watch. After calling Bevere from the pay phone, he'd made his way across town, parked in a mall parking garage, and then walked the two blocks to set up his position behind the apartment complex. Up on the third floor, Judge Kessler was visiting his mistress while his wife waited at home, thinking her devoted husband was going over to the gym for a late workout.

Yeah. Some workout.

But the judge should be coming out any minute, and when he did, it would be the end of all his little secrets. By morning, everyone would know that the honorable judge hadn't been so honorable after all, keeping a mistress and cheating on his wife.

As if on cue, Judge Kessler stepped out of the back door of the apartment complex and, buttoning his coat, strolled cheerily toward his car.

Archie lifted his rifle and brought the scope's crosshairs center on Kessler's head. Patiently, he waited, following Kessler as he crossed the lot. A few feet from Kessler's car, he would step into the light and when he did, Archie would be ready.

His finger slowly caressed the trigger. . .waiting.

Then Kessler was there, illuminated under the parking lot light.

Archie pulled the trigger and held his stance just long enough to see Kessler jerk violently before crumpling to the ground.

In spite of the silencer, Archie glanced around to make sure no one had heard the little pop, but no additional lights came on, no faces appeared at windows.

Turning, Archie disappeared into the night.

chapter 9

D onnie leaned against the kitchen counter, nursing his coffee as JJ and Zoe sat at the table, going over the game plan. Showers, clean clothes, and coffee hid the fact that they had been up all night. Jack had finally crashed on the sofa until six. Then he'd gotten up and gone home to shower and change. He planned on returning before the press conference at nine.

Taking another sip of coffee, Donnie glanced up at the clock. Eight twenty. A few miles away, the media vans would be filling up the parking lot of his church, jockeying for position, and setting up their cameras and microphones.

How Zoe pulled it all together in the middle of the night, he'd never know, but she had.

Donnie had finally called his boss and filled him in. To say his boss was upset was an understatement. His ears were still ringing from the dressing-down, but in the end, Jim Mann had come through, offering resources and help.

His stomach clenched as he swallowed more coffee, burning in revolt. He hadn't eaten any of the stew the night before, nor had he touched the breakfast Zoe prepared. In fact, all he'd had was coffee and water since Monday morning. No wonder his stomach was giving him fits.

He looked over at his breakfast plate, sitting on the stove. Picking up a slice of toast, he took a bite. It felt like cold sawdust in his mouth. He swallowed and tossed the rest back to his plate.

Lisbeth would be fussing around him if she were here, giving him the what for as she tempted him with something to eat.

He swallowed down the tears. How could he have made it this far in life without her? How could he ever get through the rest of his life without her? It had been her support and love that had given him the strength to make it through training at the academy.

Closing his eyes, he let the memory overtake him.

Donnie hadn't been sure what to expect when he arrived at the FBI Academy, but he wasn't disappointed. In addition to the FBI Academy, the DEA was running their own exercises on the 385-acre complex, and the Marines were conducting basic training just down the road.

The sprawling complex of beige brick buildings reminded him of college, as did his room in the Madison dormitory. Two people to a room, two rooms sharing a bath, and little to no privacy. The rooms were small and were all furnished exactly alike with two single beds, two small desks, and one bookshelf.

But the similarity to college life ended the morning training began. Like all the other trainees, he was dressed in his new uniform—tan cargo pants, navy blue polo shirt with the FBI Academy logo on the left breast, ID badge, fake handcuffs, and a red plastic gun the same size and weight as a Glock. New agents were required to wear the fake gun and handcuffs to help them grow accustomed to the weight and feel. Or so the theory went. Donnie was pretty sure that the supervisors just valued their lives too much to hand over loaded guns to a group of adrenaline junkies before they had those junkies under control.

And then suddenly, Donnie was thrown headfirst into training hell. Classes in white-collar crime, civil rights, profiling, counterintelligence, drug cases, and organized crime. Lessons in interrogation, arrest tactics, driving maneuvers, undercover work, and computers. Lectures on criminology, legal rights, forensics, ethics, and FBI history. And when he wasn't sitting in a classroom, he was doing push-ups and sit-ups, running the track, climbing the rope, tackling the towering Marine training wall, dancing through tire obstacle courses, and suffering through body-fat testing. Then it was off to firearm training. Stand and shoot at a paper target, sit and shoot, shoot with your right hand, now with your left. Reload. Run, drop, shoot, and then run some more. Belly crawl, shoot, reload, and shoot again. Running drills, night-firing drills, and Hogan's Alley. Shooting with a Glock .40, an M16 rifle, a Remington Model 870 shotgun, and a Heckler & Koch MP5/10 submachine gun.

There were nights Donnie could hear the shots and smell the powder in his sleep.

Academically, Donnie had an edge—a nearly photographic memory that kept him at the top of his classes. But between the classroom, the physical endurance, the firearms, and the hours, he was losing weight, losing sleep, and by week ten, losing faith in his ability to finish the training.

He called Lisbeth one Sunday evening, discouraged, exhausted, and desperately missing her. "I can't do this, Lisbeth," he'd told her wearily. "I thought I could handle it, but I was wrong."

She had been so quiet on the phone, he thought he'd lost the connection. "Lisbeth?"

"Some people are called by God from a young age to do special things for Him, Donnie. Even our pastor told you that he felt called when he was just ten years old. You've always known this is what you were called to do. What He called you to do, He has equipped you to do. Stop trying to do this in your own strength, and rely on Him to get you through."

Donnie had felt her words pierce him like a hot blade. She had been right. From the moment he'd stepped foot on the complex, he'd barely prayed at all. His arrogance had brought him to this, not his lack of ability.

I just remembered once again why the Lord brought you into my life, Lisbeth. I love you, and I miss you like crazy.

He couldn't remember the rest of the conversation; it had been like so many others, discussing, sharing, reaching out, and staying close through the phone, but it had ended with them praying together on the phone—the first of many times they would do so.

Now, once again, his arrogance had brought him to this, not his lack of ability. Zoe had been right. He'd tried to keep his family safe in his own ability, not trusting God with their lives and their safety. He'd left God out of the equation.

And now he needed God to step in and make things right. If it wasn't too late.

But there was no time to pray. His boss, Special Agent in Charge Jim Mann, was striding into the room, commanding everyone's attention with little more than a glance around the room.

JJ stood up first, reaching out to shake Mann's hand. "Lieutenant Josiah Johnson, detective with Monroe County Sheriff's Department. Just call me JJ."

Mann nodded, shaking JJ's hand.

Then Zoe stood up, but Mann waved her off. "Zoe Shefford. We worked together in Chicago a few years back on an abduction from a private school. Nice to see you again."

"Agent Mann. Pleasure to see you again, as well."

"Any sense of where this is going?" Mann directed his question at Zoe.

"On the surface, it looks like a typical hit for hire. This guy is strictly the middleman. Grab the woman, get the data, and kill her and Donnie. Collect his money and be gone. Giving this guy the drive will accomplish nothing. Honestly, I have my doubts he'll walk away alive either, but he may have already figured that out and is making provision for it."

◆ ◆ ◆

"And the man we're dealing with?"

Zoe took a mug out of the cabinet and poured Mann a cup of coffee. "He's meticulous. He not only found out that Donnie was married, but he also had her schedule down pat. This guy isn't going to mess up easily. He definitely intends to kill Lisbeth. He says he's going to give her air in the coffin, and he might, but it won't be for long. If anything, he'll do it for a day or two just to play with her for his own sick gratification; but then he'll seal it up, and that will be that. He can't afford to have her found alive. There's something else I've picked up on. I think this guy and Donnie have crossed paths before. He has a grudge against Donnie and is going to enjoy killing him when he gets the chance. He's looking forward to it."

JJ picked up where Zoe left off. "He's very arrogant, which is nothing new in this type of abduction. He took her in broad daylight with little or no fear of being caught. Toying with Donnie merely increases his arrogance. He truly believes he's at least a couple steps ahead of us and will remain there all the way. The key is going to be maintaining that illusion with him. The moment he thinks we're getting close, he'll end the game quickly."

Mann reached for the sugar. "How did he know you called off the police?"

Zoe tucked a strand of hair behind her ear. "We're not entirely sure. It's possible he was watching and saw them leave in a huff."

"Or he has the house bugged." Mann finally turned and looked at Donnie. "Has it been swept yet?"

Donnie shook his head. "No."

"Get it done. Now. The man could be listening in to everything we say. What about the phones?"

"The police said they're clear."

Mann nodded. "He's soon going to know that the FBI is involved. What do you think his next move will be?"

Donnie set his mug down in the sink, trying to keep his hands from shaking. "I don't know. It could make things worse. Or he may just call and insist I back you off."

Mann turned to Zoe. "Impressions?"

"He'll be expecting this. Donnie is one of your own, so keeping you out would be unrealistic. He's made allowances for that, and it's bought him extra time so far. I don't think it's going to throw him off stride at all."

With a nod, Mann glanced up at the clock. "Since we have a few minutes, I want to let you know. A federal judge was murdered last night. Assassinated outside an apartment complex in Arlington."

Zoe closed her eyes. "It's the same man. The man who has Lisbeth."

Suddenly the pieces of the puzzle started to fall into place for Donnie. "Archie Kemp!"

"Who?" JJ asked.

"Archie Kemp." Hope surged, and Donnie could feel the smile forming on his lips. "He's an assassin I've been chasing for two years. This week, a couple of fellow agents asked me to give them all I had on him because there was a rumor that a hit was going down on a federal judge."

Mann narrowed his eyes. "Did you give them your files?"

Donnie shook his head. "It was only moments before I got word on Lisbeth. I completely forgot about it, but no, I didn't give them my files."

"I want that file," Mann informed him, jabbing in his direction with his finger. "In the meantime, no one so much as whispers the name Archie Kemp. We need to make sure before we go considering him our top suspect. Who were the agents looking at Kemp?"

"Lagasse and Harrelson."

"They're working security for the prisoners coming in from Gitmo for trial." Mann groaned. "Kessler was one of the judges to preside over the trial. We got a serious problem, people. This is far more than an abduction."

"So Kemp, if it is Kemp, is working for terrorists?" JJ looked over at Donnie. "Would Kemp do that?"

"For enough money, Kemp would do anything. He has no

loyalties." For the first time since hearing Lisbeth was missing, Donnie had hope. It wasn't much—just a glimmer—but it was enough.

JJ shook his head. "Since when does al-Qaeda use hired assassins to do their dirty work? If this Archie Kemp has got Lisbeth, it's not because of al-Qaeda."

Mann set his coffee mug down on the counter. "You're saying an American is killing these judges? That doesn't make sense."

"All I'm saying is that I've never heard of al-Qaeda using hired assassins. They have plenty of their own. A guy straps a bomb to his chest, walks up to a judge, and boom. Judge is history. Why pay money for someone like Kemp when they can use that money for more weapons?"

Mann glanced at the clock again. "We can call this off."

It was a question, an offer, a last-minute check now that they had a possible suspect. But it was only a possibility, not a definite.

Donnie picked up his cell phone and clipped it to his belt. "We can't afford to go chasing after Kemp only to find out it wasn't him. Lagasse said they had several assassins they were looking at. It could be any of them. We need to put this out there and see if we get any leads."

His boss nodded. "Then let's do this, people. Let's get this woman home safe and sound."

Lisbeth woke to find the room too dark to see anything, but she was pretty sure she was alone. It boggled her mind that someone she knew, someone she attended church with, prayed with, laughed with—was involved in her abduction and was planning to kill her.

How in heaven's name could this have happened? Lorraine's warnings didn't seem so off base now. The woman had been far wiser than Lisbeth had been willing to give her credit for. It was easy to look back now and see how determined Katy had been to infiltrate Lisbeth's inner circle and befriend her. Now, what had once looked like new-believer enthusiasm had far darker implications.

As if summoned by her thoughts, the door opened, and Kitty strolled in, flipping on the lights. Lisbeth stared at her, realizing that for the first time she was seeing the real Katy. If that was even her real name. No wig this morning—just red hair curling lightly around her shoulders.

"Why, Katy?"

"It's Kitty. Not Katy. Might as well call me by my right name. And this isn't about me, Lisbeth. Archie was hired to do a job, so here you are. My job was simply to get close to you and learn your schedule. Now, as far as Archie is concerned, you could lie here and starve to death, so don't get too nasty with me. At least I'm giving you food and water. Which Archie wouldn't be too happy about if he knew."

"Where is he? This Archie?"

"Gone to work."

"Let me go, Kitty. My husband won't give up until he finds Archie and kills him."

Kitty laughed. "I can't do that. Archie would put a bullet in me so quick, I'd never see it coming. Thanks, but no thanks. I like you, but I'm not willing to die for you."

Kneeling down, Kitty began to loosen Lisbeth's bonds. "You can go to bathroom, wash up, and eat. Then back you go. Give me one bit of trouble, and I have a needle handy. You'll be in la-la land before you can get two feet."

Lisbeth merely blinked, trying to figure out if she could, indeed, overpower Kitty and escape.

Kitty's smile was laced with steel. "And need I remind you that the drugs Archie has in those needles aren't all that healthy for your baby."

Lisbeth felt her heart lurch. "How did you know I was pregnant?" She hadn't even told Donnie yet.

"A woman knows these things. So try to escape and harm your baby. Your choice."

Kitty pulled off the ropes and pulled Lisbeth to a sitting position. Lisbeth rubbed at her wrists, flexing her fingers and wrists, trying to get the circulation back.

"Katy. . .Kitty, please don't do this. I have children at home. You know Mandy and Cody. You've played with them. How can you hurt them like this?"

Kitty stood, hands on her hips, staring down at Lisbeth without a trace of emotion showing anywhere. "You have cute kids. They'll get over this. Now, do you want to use the bathroom and eat, or not?"

Lisbeth struggled to her feet. For a second—just a split second—she wanted to slam into Kitty, knock her to the ground, and make a run for it. But she felt the weakness in her legs and knew she'd never make it.

Resigning herself to cooperating—at least for now—Lisbeth let Kitty lead her out of the room.

◆　◆　◆

Zoe let her gaze move over the crowd as Donnie explained to the reporters about Lisbeth's abduction. They all wore badges, identifications from the different agencies they represented. The *Washington Post*, *USA Today*, Fox News, CNN, CBS, ABC, NBC, MSNBC, Reuters, and the Associated Press, among many others. Everyone had their attention focused completely on Donnie. No one seemed to be watching her or JJ.

If the killer were there, he was well hidden.

"So we're asking anyone who was in that parking lot on Monday morning between eleven thirty and noon to call us at this one-eight-hundred number." Mann stopped for a second and, intentional or not, his long pause drew their attention even closer. "There's a young wife and mother missing from her home today for one reason, and one reason only—her husband has been pursuing a killer working for terrorists and putting this country at risk. He should take note—every law enforcement agency in the country is coming after him."

The reporters loved that little sound bite, and immediately hands went up, pressing forward with a barrage of questions.

Mann took the first question and then another. Then a reporter Zoe recognized from Fox caught her eye as he stepped forward. "Miss Shefford is well-known for her work with abducted children. Was one of Mrs. Bevere's children taken with her? Is that why Miss Shefford is here?"

Mann shook his head. "No. There was a threat issued against the children, but we moved them to a secure location, and they are with other family members. Miss Shefford is here because she is a friend of the family and is here as much for emotional support as she is for her expertise in abductions."

She felt JJ's breath against her ear as he leaned in close. "I'll be inside the church."

"Why?" she whispered.

"Because Chief Harris is watching this and must have seen

me. He's calling me on my cell. I need to go talk to him."

Zoe saw one reporter watching JJ as he melted in behind some of the law enforcement officers standing around her and Donnie, but the reporter didn't jump in and bring anyone's attention to JJ. As soon as she felt she could ease back, she joined JJ inside the church.

He was pacing inside the sanctuary, cell phone to his ear. "Yes, sir."

JJ saw her and rolled his eyes. "Yes, sir, but—"

Zoe smothered the urge to laugh and took a seat in one of the pews while JJ listened.

"Yes, sir."

JJ walked over to her and touched her shoulder. She reached up and squeezed his hand in support. She could just imagine the dressing-down he was getting.

"Sir, I am here because Agent Bevere is a friend of mine. He called and wanted my help. Now, if I recall correctly, I am on leave, so what I do with my own time is my own business. I've called in and talked to Matt and Lieutenant Summers in IAD. They both know where I am if I'm needed for any further questioning. I am *not* jeopardizing anything."

Uh-oh. Harris was going to try and jerk JJ back to Monroe County and sit on him. And no way would JJ let him. She'd bet anything that JJ would suddenly be needed back for questioning within the next few days.

"And pigs fly with pink wings. Sir, no disrespect intended, but you're off base here, and I'm not leaving Donnie until this is resolved. If Summers needs me, he'll call me, and I'll be there within a matter of hours; until then, I'm on my own time. . .*sir.*"

That last *sir* was about as sarcastic as Zoe had ever heard coming from JJ. He snapped the phone closed and then turned it off. "Oh my, the battery must have died."

Zoe laughed as she stood up. "He's watching his political backside; you know that. If locals see you here, they're going to assume you're here working a case and not on administrative leave at all. You're supposed to be home, whipped and properly chastised, not off working a big case with the FBI."

"Well, the day I roll over and play dead to make those politicians happy, you can close the coffin and bury me, because I *will* be dead."

Patting his arm in a quiet show of support, she said, "And I'm sure Harris knows better than to think for one minute that you're going to pack up and come running home just because he told you to. He's known you far too long to even entertain the idea. He's just covering his bases, JJ. This way, anyone comes to him about you, he can honestly say that he ordered you home and you are thumbing your nose at them all."

"I need to quit the force. Be done with all that garbage once and for all. Why don't we just start up our own investigators agency? Go into business for ourselves. Partners."

Zoe stared at him, trying to figure out just how serious he was. It was hard to tell. Finally, she sighed. "There isn't enough business for two agencies in Monroe, and I don't think it would be fair of us to take business away from Dan."

"Then we specialize. Work abduction cases nationwide. Then we won't be taking anything from him."

"JJ—"

"I know, but it feels good to think we might."

She laughed up at him. "Well, you never know what the future holds, but for now, let's concentrate on getting Lisbeth home, shall we?"

There was something in the intensity of his gaze that stole her breath. She swallowed hard, trying to understand why it felt as if the earth were shifting under her feet. "What is it, JJ?"

He reached up, cupping her cheek with his palm, his thumb caressing softly. It sent a shiver down her spine. "I've been trying to tell you for days, but it seems that every time I go to tell you, something interrupts us."

"Tell me what?"

"That—"

The door suddenly burst open, and Donnie, Mann, and several other agents spilled in, everyone talking at once.

JJ blew out a frustrated breath and dropped his hand. She heard him mutter something under his breath but couldn't make out what he said.

chapter 10

N eil opened another piece of nicotine gum and shoved it in his mouth, grimacing as he did. If ever he needed a cigarette, it was now. All hell was breaking loose over the assassination of a federal judge. Law enforcement was falling over themselves trying to find evidence. Any lead would be coveted.

So far, they hadn't found a thing.

Naturally, the press was having a field day with Kessler's life, as well as death. His mistress had been exposed, her picture plastered on the front page of all the newspapers. His wife was hiding in her home, sending out her attorney to merely say, "No comment."

Which only enflamed the press more.

And, of course, the press was going crazy speculating about the connection between the upcoming terrorist trials and the murder of one of the judges. He figured by the end of the day, other judges would be screaming for protection.

And on top of everything else, it seemed Hollywood-handsome Donnie Bevere had been hiding a wife and kids in the suburbs, and now the wife was missing. Once again, there was speculation that it was somehow tied to the murder of the judge.

A whole lot of speculation and not one solid lead to be had.

He needed a cigarette. And a stiff drink.

Glancing at his watch, he stood up. "Time to go meet Jamal, partner."

Rick Harrelson nodded as he finished jotting notes down, then stood up and grabbed his coat. "You drive?"

"Sure."

Jamal had called not long after the press conference that morning regarding Bevere's wife. He said that he had information about el-Hajid but wasn't going to talk over the phone. He told Neil to meet him at a small bar in D.C. around three. It was now two thirty.

"How's your tooth?" Neil asked his partner as they headed out of the building. Rick had come in in the morning with an abscessed tooth and had gone to the dentist during lunch, returning with a swollen jaw and a mouthful of cotton.

"The painkillers are just barely taking the edge off," Rick mumbled.

"You sure you feel up to this? I can go alone."

Rick shook his head as he climbed into the car. "I'll be fine."

Due to the usual gridlock that was known as D.C. traffic, it took them nearly forty minutes to get to the club. Inside, the place was dark and fairly quiet. The bartender, wiping down glasses, nodded in their direction.

Jamal was nowhere to be seen.

Neil checked his watch. It was just a quarter after. No way Jamal would have given up on them and left already.

"Let's grab a table and wait. He must be running late, too."

Rick nodded. "Get me an OJ and tell him to hold the ice.

Oh, and get me a straw."

After getting Rick's orange juice and a coffee for himself, they settled down to wait for Jamal. By four, it was fairly obvious he wasn't going to show up. Neil had tried calling him but only got Jamal's voice mail.

"He's not going to show. Probably found some blow and is holed up somewhere, oblivious to the world."

Rick merely nodded. "Let's head back to the office, and then I'm going home. Maybe I'll feel better tomorrow."

On the way out the door, they passed two young men coming in. One of them looked familiar to Neil. He intercepted the men. "You seen Jamal? He was supposed to meet my friend and me, and he hasn't shown up."

The one whom Neil was addressing looked up at him with a bored expression that was tugging his mouth down into a frown. "You ain't heard the word? Jamal got hisself whacked this morning."

"Whacked? He's dead?"

"Thass what I said, man. You deaf as well as ugly?"

The other young man laughed and slid away, heading for the bar. The one Neil was talking to started to follow his friend. Neil grabbed his arm.

"What happened to Jamal?"

"I tole ya; he got whacked. Someone put a bullet in his head down at his crib." The man let his gaze drift from Neil to Rick, and then back again. "Guess he talked to you pigs one too many times, ya know?"

◆　◆　◆

Mack and Jane Bushnell arrived in a flurry of hugs, tears, and questions about their daughter's abduction. Mack Bushnell, in spite of minor heart problems six months earlier, was a robust-looking man with a thick head of gray hair, mustache and beard, broad shoulders, and a thick neck. Retired, his hands still showed the scars of years working for the railroad. Now, most of his days were spent in his workshop, building and restoring fine pieces of furniture. Quick to smile and slow to anger, Mack was an even-tempered man with a deep, abiding faith that never failed to impress Donnie.

His wife, Jane, was a tall, trim woman with auburn hair that never showed a trace of gray, big brown eyes, and the cameo looks she had passed on to her daughters. She was a woman who liked keeping busy and, even when sitting still, gave the impression of movement.

Mack settled into Donnie's recliner; Jane perched herself on the edge of the sofa, twisting a handkerchief with her fingers; and for over an hour, Donnie sat with them, reassuring them that everything that could be done was being done.

"The Lord is faithful," Mack said. "We have to trust Him in all of this. I know it didn't take Him by surprise."

"No, it didn't," Donnie admitted. "Zoe said the Lord started calling her to pray for Lisbeth weeks ago, so He saw it coming."

Jane raised an eyebrow. "This woman says the Lord told her to pray for Lisbeth weeks ago?"

"Not quite that specific, Mom. Zoe felt she was to pray for a woman who was facing danger, but she didn't know who it was until this happened."

Finally, Mack said Donnie needed to get back to work, and Jane busied herself making beds, doing laundry, and sweeping floors.

Donnie joined JJ and Zoe in the family room where JJ was going over the tapes of the caller again, trying to pick up any background sounds they might have missed. He pulled the headphones off when Donnie joined them.

"Anything?"

JJ shook his head. "I'm pretty sure he was calling from a pay phone each time, but I'm not picking up anything to help us."

Zoe let out a heavy sigh and releasing her hair from the barrette, shook it out, running her fingers through it and massaging her scalp. "So Archie Kemp is an alias. Did you find anything at all about what his real name might be?"

"Not a thing," Donnie told her. "The guy is good. Real good. Not so much as a fingerprint or a spent shell at any of the crime scenes. The only reason we even have the name Archie Kemp is from what we've picked up from the streets during the investigations."

"He almost always kills by rifle, different calibers, which means different weapons. Almost always from a distance. Almost always high-profile targets. And has never missed that I can see." Zoe tossed back her head and gathered her hair together to replace the barrette. "Lisbeth is an anomaly. Why?"

Donnie's brows drew tight over his nose. "What do you mean?"

Zoe leaned back in her chair. "If Archie works by his usual MO, he kidnaps Lisbeth, records her voice for your benefit, and then puts a bullet in her head and tosses her."

Donnie closed his eyes, going pale. "Thank you for that visual."

"Sorry." Zoe grimaced. "But what I'm saying is, why all the stuff with the coffin and giving her enough air to last a few days?"

"To make me give up the drive immediately."

Zoe tilted her head, giving him a pointed look. "Come on, Bevere. You're smarter than that."

Donnie took a moment, trying to pull back emotionally from the scene and look at it all objectively. It wasn't easy. "He wants to torment me."

"Bingo. Now why?"

"I have no idea."

Zoe huffed, looking frustrated. "Because you've gotten too close. You've made him nervous."

Donnie snorted softly as he stretched his legs out in front of him. "I'm not close at all."

JJ leaned forward. "Or. . .he thinks you may get too close."

"Meaning?"

"Meaning he somehow found out that you were targeting him. That you have been compiling a personal file on him, and he doesn't like being on your radar."

Zoe picked up her pen and mindlessly began tapping it on the table. "So you're thinking he may be someone Donnie either knows, or someone who has heard about it, maybe someone who knows someone Donnie works with."

Donnie shook his head. "No way it's someone I know. I don't talk about my work outside the office. Not even to Lisbeth. She's never heard the name Archie Kemp."

"What about at work?"

Again, Donnie shook his head. "Wrong angle. This is something I work on from time to time. A pet project. It's not something that would become a subject of conversation for anyone. Almost every agent has someone who is the bane of their existence, who they'd like to take down. It's not that big a deal that someone would mention it around their dinner table some night."

"Okay, forget that angle then. What else do we have?" JJ twisted the top off a bottle of water and took a long drink.

"We know that some of the terrorists are being brought in for trial and that one of the judges scheduled to preside over the trial has been assassinated. It's all connected somehow."

"I still want to know how he found out about Lisbeth." Donnie folded his arms across his chest.

Zoe gave his shoulder a quick pat. "He followed you home and watched. Saw a woman and kids here. Got close enough to Lisbeth to see the wedding ring. Not that hard to figure out, Donnie."

"But I'm careful about that. I don't use the same route home every day. I've never seen a vehicle tailing me." He sounded almost petulant and hoped his friends would understand he was just trying to chew on one bone to keep from choking on another. He was terrified for Lisbeth. And for himself.

Zoe was going to go further with the subject matter, but her cell phone rang. She flipped it open. "Hello?"

It was Noreen, Daria's sister. "Zoe? Where are you?"

"Outside D.C. on a case. Why? Is something wrong with Daria? I thought she was out of the woods."

"She is medically, but she's gone back to not talking to anyone. Completely withdrawn from all of us. In fact, she seems almost angry or hostile. I just thought maybe you knew what was going on."

Zoe closed her eyes, frustration at her friend nudging her. "I have no idea. She seemed fine when I saw her. I even told this young girl I met at the hospital to visit Daria. If what you say is true, I'm worried now about Erin. She's barely a teen-ager and has cancer."

"What's her name?" Noreen asked. "I'll check and make sure Daria didn't devastate the poor kid."

Zoe shifted gears, trying to think back a few days. "Erin. Erin. . .Regan. That's it. Erin Regan. Like I said, young, maybe twelve or fourteen. Designs the most adorable hats. My mom is carrying them in her store now."

"I'll check on her. When are you going to be home?"

"I have no idea, Noreen."

"Is this about that FBI agent's wife who's missing?"

"Yes." And that was as far as Zoe was willing to go in talk-ing about the case. Noreen must have caught on quick because she changed the subject back to Daria.

"Okay, well, let me know when you're back, and check in on Daria if you have time."

"I will. Thanks, Noreen."

"Daria?" JJ asked as Zoe closed her phone.

"Yeah, she's acting all withdrawn and sullen again. I guess it was too much to ask that she was starting to get through all this."

Donnie jerked to his feet and started pacing. "I thought this guy was going to be calling."

"Be glad he hasn't. Mann has three people working on that drive, and no one has cracked it yet."

"Daddy!" Mandy's voice bounded down the stairs just ahead of the sound of her feet double-footing them.

Donnie walked over to the staircase, and Mandy jumped into his arms from near the bottom. "Guess what? We went to Aunt Maureen's, and we had pizza and ice cream; and then we watched movies, and look!" Mandy put her hands in her daddy's face. "We painted my nails!"

"Wow! They're so pretty. Sounds like you had a great time."

"Yep." Mandy nodded firmly and then began to squirm in Donnie's arms. "Where's Mommy? I want to show her."

"Mommy isn't home yet, Mandy Bear."

"Why not?"

"I explained this to you already, Mandy. Remember how I said that sometimes Daddy goes away for a few days and then he comes home?"

Mandy nodded, curls bouncing. "Yes."

"And I told you that this time it was your mom's turn to go away for a few days."

"But I want her home!"

"Well, your grandma and grandpa are here to visit you, and you're going to go stay with them for a few days. Did you say hello to them?"

Mandy nodded again. "Papa gave me a quarter."

"He did? Why?"

" 'Cause he said I'm so 'dorable."

Donnie laughed. "They spoil you, kiddo."

"They do? Is that good?"

"It's fine, Mandy Bear. It's what grandparents do. Why don't you go up and make sure Cody is behaving himself. I'll be up soon."

"Okay." She turned and started running back up the stairs. "But he don't listen to me."

Zoe laughed. "She really is precious, Donnie. What a personality that little girl has."

"That's what scares me. She has no control over her tongue at all. Says anything that comes to mind."

JJ snorted in a good-natured way. "Oh, then she's a female."

Zoe reached over and slapped JJ's arm. "Hey!"

"I better go upstairs and help Mom pack for the kids." Donnie started up the stairs. "I wish they could stay here with me."

"Donnie, you know you won't be here every minute to protect them. Having them tucked away in a safe place is the best way to go for everyone. Especially you." Zoe tried to give him an encouraging smile. "Let Mandy think of it as an adventure."

◆　◆　◆

Jack picked up the stack of mail on Donnie's desk and breezed through it real quick. When he came across a plain white envelope with a loopy handwriting, he slammed his fist on Donnie's desk. How could he have been so stupid? Grabbing Donnie's phone, he quickly dialed his partner's cell phone. As soon as Donnie answered, Jack began talking fast.

"I forgot! I'm sorry, I forgot! Before your wife was taken, a letter came here to the office warning that she was going to be killed. I thought it was for me at first; and then when I saw it was addressed to you, I thought it was a joke, and I trashed it. I'm sorry, partner."

"Well, it's of no consequence now. If you threw it away, it's long gone."

Jack held up the phone cord to circle the desk and sit down. "Another one just came in."

"Another one?" Donnie nearly barked the words. "What does it say?"

"Hold on. Let me open it." Balancing the phone between shoulder and chin, he grabbed Donnie's letter opener and slit the envelope. Then he shook out the letter and used the letter opener and a pen to unfold it.

"It says. . . He's going to bury her Wednesday night, but—"

"That's tonight! He's going to kill her tonight!"

"Hold on, Donnie. There's more. It also says, 'I don't know where yet. I'll stay in touch. Don't tell anyone I've contacted you.' That's it, partner. Not much to go on."

"Who is going to stay in touch? Who wrote that letter? What does he know? That maniac's playing with me again!"

"We'll find her, partner."

"He's going to bury her tonight, Jack. That doesn't give us much time, does it?"

◆　◆　◆

Donnie hung up the phone and returned to the living room where his in-laws were preparing to leave with his children. The FBI agent who would be guarding them at the hotel was standing at the door, checking his watch and looking a little annoyed.

Mandy had her bottom lip puffed out while her grandfather was trying to explain once again about the swimming pool and room service. It didn't look to be flying with her.

"I want to stay here and wait for Mommy."

Donnie's heart clenched. He'd been so busy focusing on his pain, he'd forgotten that his children were hurting, too. Okay, Mandy was hurting. Fortunately, Cody was too young to do more than sense that something wasn't quite right. Still, Lisbeth had never been away from them before, and Mandy couldn't even talk to her on the phone to help with her fears.

He knelt down and took his daughter's hands in his. "Mandy, I need you to talk to you."

"What?" she pouted, glaring at him.

Wrestling with what to say and how to say it drove him to pick her up and carry her over to the sofa. He sat her down in his lap. "I wasn't going to tell you this because I thought maybe you were too young, but you're a big girl, aren't you?"

" 'Course," Mandy replied, lifting her chin a little. "Mommy says so."

Wrapping one of her curls around his finger, he swallowed the urge to cry. "Mandy, the truth is, Mommy is lost, and I have to go find her. Do you understand?"

"Mommy's lost? Like when Andy Bear was lost at Disney World?" Andy Bear was a stuffed bear someone had given her when she was born and was always in her crib. From the time she was old enough to hold onto it, it became her constant companion.

"Just like Andy Bear. And we found your bear, didn't we?"

Mandy nodded, but he saw the tears welling up in her eyes. "Will you find Mommy in lost and found, too?"

"I wish it were that easy, Mandy, but no. There is no lost and found for mommies. I have to go find her. And if I'm going to go find her and bring her home, I can't be here to take care of you and your little brother. Do you understand?"

"So if we go with Gamma and Papa, you can go find Mommy?"

"Yes."

"Okay." Mandy threw her arms around his neck and kissed him on the cheek, then wiggled out of his lap and ran to her papa and took his hand. "Let's go, Papa. Hurry up."

As soon as the door closed behind them, Donnie dropped his head, buried his face in his hands, and let the tears stream down his cheeks. They were going to kill his wife in a matter of hours, and he had no idea where to begin looking for her.

They had been through so much together. Life hadn't always been easy, but it had been worth it with her at his side.

After graduating from the academy at the top of his class, he had been assigned to the Washington, D.C., office. Settled into their dream jobs, he and Lisbeth laid out their plan. Work for three years and save. Buy a house. Wait two more years to get the house the way they wanted it and then start a family. Everything went like clockwork, until it came time to start a family. Three years went by, and Lisbeth never got pregnant.

They had just started discussing the possibility of fertility tests, artificial insemination, or even adoption when Lisbeth finally shut down. For weeks, she refused to talk about children at all.

Finally, she came to Donnie one night and curled up in his lap. With tears in her eyes, she told him that she had started to feel as though she were struggling against the will of God and, after much prayer, had come to terms with never having children. "I've been praying and praying about this. I think maybe the Lord wanted me to accept the fact that we may never have children; and it wasn't easy, but I am willing to accept that."

The empty nursery eventually became an office for Donnie, and life went on. Eighteen months later, Donnie had come home from investigating the murder of a child in Seattle, thankful that he and Lisbeth had never had children. Seeing that small, sweet child—broken, tortured, and tossed in a ditch—was almost more than Donnie could handle.

He'd stumbled home, numb and hurting, looking forward to just spending some quiet time with Lisbeth. But Lisbeth, oblivious to his pain, had a whirlwind evening planned that included dinner out at a nice restaurant and then a play.

It was only the look in her eyes that made him go along, pretending to be as excited about the evening as she was. And then, in the middle of dinner, she gave him the news that changed his life forever.

She was expecting their first child.

At the time, he smiled, laughed, and let her think he was thrilled about it, but inside, he was questioning God's wisdom.

Then the day came when Amanda was born, and from the moment Mandy had been placed in his arms, he understood that God had more than one way of healing the pain in a person's life.

But what could God ever use to heal the pain of losing his wife?

◆ ◆ ◆

"Don't do this. Please, don't do this." Lisbeth let her body go limp as Archie pulled her off the cot she'd been tied to. "This won't stop my husband, don't you understand? He'll hunt you down like a dog."

He jerked her up, sending sharp jabs of knifelike pain through her shoulders and arms. "Lady, I can kill you now and end this, but I thought you'd at least like to give your husband a chance to save you."

"You're not going to let him find me. Who are you kidding?"

He shoved her forward. She stumbled toward the door, catching sight of Kitty standing just outside the door. "Katy! Don't let him do this! You'll be an accessory to murder. Can you live with that?"

"You'd be surprised at what I've learned to live with." Kitty looked up at Archie, her face holding no expression whatsoever, and Lisbeth's hopes that Kitty would help her faded quickly. "Hey, baby, what do you want me to do?"

"Get me the duct tape. I'm not going to listen to this broad's whining the whole way."

By the time Archie had Lisbeth in her coat and in the garage, Kitty was cutting off a piece of duct tape and handing it to Archie. "You want me to go with you?"

Archie shook his head as he slapped the tape across Lisbeth's mouth, picked her up, and dumped her in the back of the van. "I've already got the coffin in the ground. All I have to do is dump her in and cover her up. No need for you to go."

"I could just go along for the ride."

Archie tied the knot in the ropes around Lisbeth's feet and stood back. "I said I didn't need you to go!"

The sharpness of his tone had Kitty backing up. "Fine!" She turned and ran back into the house.

Archie swore under his breath, slammed the van door closed, and went into the house after her. Lisbeth immediately began wiggling around, trying to see if she could get loose. No such luck. Archie tied a mean knot.

Rolling to her side, she rocked herself to her knees and looked out the van windows. The garage door was closed, but there was a side door that led to the yard.

Slowly, she sidled her way to the van's side door. Turning her back to the door, she struggled to get her hands on the handle. The strain on her shoulders was painful, but she just gritted her teeth hard and bent her body even more.

Her fingers touched the handle. Then they wrapped around it. She paused, took a deep breath, and then yanked the handle up. Pain shot through her arms and shoulders, nearly making her scream.

Panting from the effort and the racking twinges in her joints, she paused for a second. Took a deep breath. Clamped her teeth together. Then she jerked upwards.

The door clicked open. Her heart thundered in her chest as she glanced back over at the door. So far, no Archie. *Keep him in there a little longer, Kitty. Just a few more minutes.*

Grabbing the door, she shoved sideways. The door slid open a little further. She swung her feet out first, easing herself into a standing position. Here came the hard part. She had to hop across the empty bay of the garage, open the door, hop outside, and somehow manage to get someone's attention.

She could do this. She could. *She had to.*

The first hop nearly sent her to her knees, but she used the momentum to hop again; and this time, she managed to keep her balance a little better. Four hops. Five. Two more and she was nearly there.

She glanced over her shoulder. The door to the house remained closed. She hopped again. And then once more.

She was at the door. Quickly, she turned her back to the door and fumbled for the knob. Please open. Please.

The knob turned.

She pushed backwards, falling though the door as it swung open.

"Ahhh!" She had no control over the soft exclamation of pain as the shock of landing with her arms trapped behind her, vibrated with burning agony.

No time to think about the pain. She rolled to her knees and struggled to her feet. Quickly, she glanced around, trying to get her bearings. To her right, the backyard yawned into the seemingly endless dark. Definitely not going that way. To her left, the front yard stretched in an easy slope down to a dark road. Not a street lamp in sight. In front of her, she could just make out a neighboring house.

She started hopping again, one bone-jarring jump after another in the direction of the house. If she could just get to their door. If she could just get their attention.

In the middle of a hop, she suddenly went sprawling face-first to the ground. At first, she thought she'd lost her balance. And then there was this hot breath sweeping across her ear.

"Going somewhere, Mrs. Bevere?"

◆　◆　◆

Zoe ran down the stairs and through the family room to Donnie's home office. The door was shut. She knocked. "Donnie!"

When he didn't answer within a reasonable amount of time, she knocked again. . .louder. "Donnie. Special Agent Mann is here. He needs to talk to you right away. Donnie?"

The door swung open. Donnie stood there, shirttails only half tucked in, slacks wrinkled, eyes red rimmed and heavy with dark circles.

Zoe reached out and took his hand, dragging him back into his office. She pushed him down in his chair. Once he was seated, she put her hands on her hips. "So tell me, would you like me to call the paper and have Lisbeth's obit run tomorrow?"

Donnie's eyes grew wide, and his jaw dropped; then there was this little twitch in his left eye. "That's not funny."

"It wasn't meant to be. You've all but got her dead and buried, so I just thought I'd help you out here."

Donnie went to stand. Zoe shoved him back down. "Don't you even think of moving. Now I want to ask you a question,

Donnie, and you best think long and hard before you answer. Is Jesus just your Savior, or is He your Lord, as well?"

Donnie stared up at her, the look telling her he couldn't decide if she'd lost her marbles, or was just short a few watts. "Is He what?"

"Well, some people look at Jesus as their ticket to heaven, and that's about all there is to their relationship with Him. If He's your Lord, it means that you turn everything over to His will and guidance. He's in charge, not you. You trust Him to keep you on course. So which is it, Bevere?"

"He's Lord and Savior, Zoe. What a stupid question."

"I don't think it's so stupid. For two days you've wandered around this house like a ghost—here but not here. You act like Lisbeth is gone and never coming back. I'm truly surprised you haven't planned the funeral. In all of that, I haven't seen a trace of trust in your Lord. If He's in charge and He's God, what are you doing?"

Donnie's lips thinned as he narrowed his eyes. "There's no guarantee that we'll find her alive, Zoe. You know that. We've seen too much, you and I. . .too many lives ended before their time, too many grieving family members left behind."

"No, there's no guarantee for anything. But you're not even trying. You walk around, barely functioning. If we're going to get her back alive, we need your help, Donnie. We need you to trust that God had me praying for Lisbeth for a reason. That He worked it so JJ was off work during the very time you needed him to be here. He's working on your behalf, and you're doing nothing."

This time, Donnie made it to his feet, jerking upwards so fast, Zoe stepped back, caught off guard. "My wife is in the hands of a sick killer. Do you know how that makes me feel?"

"Frankly, at this moment, Donnie, I don't care. What I do care about is getting Lisbeth home as quickly as possible, and that means we need you to get your head on straight, get upstairs, and help us figure out our next move."

When he clenched his fists, Zoe had a fleeting thought that he might actually swing at her, but the thought was gone as quickly as it appeared. "Donnie, I know you're hurting, and we're hurting for you. But if we truly believe that God is in charge and working on our behalf, we have to step out in faith and follow Him. That means doing everything we can to find Lisbeth!"

"I can't think straight, Zoe! Do you understand that? I can't stop thinking about her, about what he might be doing to her. What she might be suffering through. What life could be like without her."

Zoe folded her arms across her chest and glared at him. "Let me ask you something else. Have you prayed?"

Donnie's eyes fell away from her, and she had her answer before he opened his mouth and said, "I've tried. I really have tried."

Zoe reached out and took his hands. "All you had to do was ask for help, my friend." She closed her eyes. "Father, we thank You and we praise You that even before evil struck, You were preparing the way. We thank You that even when we are paralyzed in fear, You are faithful. Father, I ask that You give my brother peace, the peace that surpasses all understanding. Give him a clear mind that can focus on what You have called him to do in this hour. Give him the faith to stand in this hour and lean on You, trust in You, and hear Your voice. Father, we give thanks that You are with Lisbeth in this hour. Hold her close, infuse her with faith, and keep her safe. And now,

Father, we ask that You help us find her. Give us guidance in this hour to see through the fog of deception and stand on Your truth. In Jesus' most precious name, amen and amen."

Donnie took a deep breath as Zoe released his hands. He squared his shoulders. "Thanks, Zoe."

"You're welcome. Now, your boss is here. We need you upstairs."

Donnie ran his fingers through his hair and then tucked his shirt in. "Zoe, in case I haven't said it so far, I'm saying it now. Thanks for being here."

"Let's just go find your wife."

❖   ❖   ❖

By the time they reached the living room, Donnie could actually feel his mind clearing a little, like fog slowly burning away by the sun. The fear, that overriding, mind-choking fear, was still there, but held at bay like a thick chain around the neck of a snarling, hungry junkyard dog.

His supervisor, Jim Mann, was leaning over JJ's shoulder, shaking his head. "We've looked at all that and come up empty. He must have had those magnetic signs on the side of the van, and they were totally bogus. There is no Jasper and Sons Plumbing Company."

"Did you run the partial plate you got off the store's security camera?"

"To the tune of over four thousand white vans of that year and make and model registered to a male resident in the state." Mann looked up, saw Donnie, and slowly straightened to his full height. "Donnie."

"Sir."

One of Mann's eyebrows shot up and a look of amusement sparkled in his eyes. "Sir?"

Rather than try to explain the sudden return of the professional courtesy so lacking in him over the past few days, he shrugged.

Donnie looked around the room as he headed for his recliner. Jack was perched on the edge of the sofa chair, hands clasped between his knees. Another agent was strolling from living room to kitchen, chattering away on a cell phone. "Where do we stand?"

Jim Mann hiked up his slacks at the thighs and sat down next to JJ. "They broke the code. The drive contains shipment dates, items, and quantities."

"That's it?"

Mann stared at the floor. "I'm sorry, Donnie."

Donnie jerked to his feet, all hope for getting Lisbeth back alive going up like flash paper. "That can't be all! They wouldn't go to these lengths for a record of shipments they already have!"

His boss looked up him, expression shuttered tight. "There were no names, no places, nothing that would help us figure out who is behind this. I'm sorry, Donnie. It's a dead end."

◆   ◆   ◆

Lisbeth tried to scream through the duct tape, but Archie merely smiled as he dropped her to the cold, hard ground. "Go ahead and scream. There's no one out here to hear you."

She watched him brush off a sheet of plywood and lift it. Her grave. Fear rose up to choke off her breathing as her heart skipped painfully. She tried to crawl backwards, but there was nowhere to go that he wouldn't just drag her back.

She was going to die. Buried alive in a grave. A cold, dark grave. *Oh, God, my Father, be with me, please. If this is Your will that I die now, be merciful and let me die quickly. Father, please help me endure this.*

Thoughts flooded her being—Mandy laughing, running to her with open arms for a hug and kiss; Cody cooing, staring up at her as he lay in her arms; Donnie pulling her down on the sofa, wrapping his arms around her, whispering words of love and devotion; a baby whom she would never hold, who would never see life.

I don't want to die, Lord. I'm sorry I'm not being stronger, but I just don't want to die. I want to go home to my family. I want to hold my children and my husband and see my parents and my sister. I'm not ready to leave them.

But time had run out. Archie turned, grinning at the little bit of progress she'd made to crawl away from him. Shaking his head, he walked over and hauled her to her feet.

"Any last words, Mrs. Bevere?"

"May God forgive you."

Laughing, Archie wrapped his arms around her waist and hauled her back to the grave. "Original. But I doubt God is even paying attention."

"Oh, He's paying attention; trust me."

"Well, if He is, it doesn't matter much to Him, now does it?"

"That's just your misguided opinion of the matter."

They reached the edge. Her whole body went stiff as she saw the coffin sitting open, waiting for her. "Don't do this. Please don't do this."

Her words had no effect at all. Stepping down into the

shallow hole, he set her into the coffin. She wanted to be strong, to glare at him, to spit in his face as he laid her down inside, but she could only cry.

He pulled out a knife, and she stiffened. This was it. *Father God, wrap me in Your arms and hold me.*

"Good-bye, Mrs. Bevere."

chapter 11

Wednesday, February 15

The room sat in stunned silence as Mann left, his agents in tow, leaving Donnie, JJ, Jack, and Zoe to digest this latest blow.

Zoe dropped her head, folding her hands into her hair. She couldn't believe that it was going to end like this. There had to be another road they could take. *Think, Zoe.* The disk didn't contain anything worth killing for, so why did they want it so badly? Why were they willing to risk so much just to get their hands on it?

"I don't believe it."

Zoe lifted her head to look over at Donnie. "What?"

"It doesn't fly. How could there be nothing incriminating on that drive?" His jaw clenched; a combative light flushed his cheeks and hardened his voice. "I want to try that drive again for myself."

"I thought Mann had it." JJ sounded tired, frustrated.

"I never told him about the copy I had here. Only the one I handed over." He stood up, looking around at each of them. "I'm having enough trouble trusting God with Lisbeth's life, much less trusting a government agency with it."

Jack choked out a laugh. "Trust Donnie to always have something hidden up his sleeve." He slapped his thighs. "Okay, we need a game plan."

"We need a computer nerd with a penchant for hacking." JJ stood up and headed for the kitchen. "I think it's going to be a long night. I'm making coffee."

"He's right. We need someone who can help us with this drive." Donnie shot to his feet, started pacing.

"Wait a minute!" Jack stared up at Donnie. "You really think Mann is holding out on us?"

"He has to be."

Zoe couldn't help but agree. "It's the only thing that makes sense. They found something on that drive that's way bigger than they thought. They're going to play this by their rules, and Lisbeth is just a casualty."

"Oh, come on, people. This is our boss. We work for these people. I've never known them to do something like this! Mann isn't like that."

Donnie glanced over at his partner. "How do you know? How do you really know what goes on behind our backs? They send us out there to catch the bad guys, but do you really think they tell us everything?"

"It doesn't matter," Zoe interjected softly into Donnie's anger. "They aren't the ones who matter. This guy is going to call you in a matter of hours and want the drive. You're going to agree to anything he asks."

JJ stepped into the room. "Are you crazy? You know that flash drive is the only chance for Lisbeth. For Donnie, too."

"I never said we were going to give him what he wanted. I just said you were going to agree to give him what he asks for."

◆   ◆   ◆

Archie pressed the knife to Lisbeth's throat. She went still, holding her breath. "Now listen to me very carefully. I'm going to close the lid of this coffin. There's a PVC tube here that will keep you from running out of air. It's going to be cold, and it's going to be dark, but don't waste what little air you have trying to lift the lid and escape. You're going to be buried under a couple feet of dirt. It will be a waste of time and energy."

She swallowed hard, never blinking.

"As soon as I leave here, I'm going to give your husband a call and see if he's willing to pay to get you back. If he is, you may see daylight again. If he tries to double-cross me, or if he doesn't bring me that flash drive, then I'm the last face you'll ever see."

Smiling, he eased the knife from her throat and cut the rope on her hands. "Never let it be said that Archie Kemp couldn't give a girl a fighting chance."

He stood up. Put his hand on the lid. Winked at her. And then the lid slammed shut.

Lisbeth jerked, stunned, immediately enveloped in a smothering darkness. She heard the first shovelful of dirt hit the top of the casket.

"No!" She reached up and tried to press against the lid. It didn't budge. She beat on it. "Don't do this! No! God, help me. Please help me."

I will never leave you nor forsake you.

◆   ◆   ◆

The voices woke Justin. He blinked. Grandma was home? He

started to move. Felt the wood beneath his hand. And then he remembered.

He had been in the tree fort, dreading going back to the empty house. He must have fallen asleep.

Then what voice was he hearing?

He crept over to the edge and peered through the tarp. The man was back!

His breath caught in this throat as he watched the man throwing dirt into the hole. He was burying something.

The man's flashlight threw eerie shadows all around him as he tossed one shovelful of dirt after another. But in between, Justin could hear something else. A faint sound coming from the hole.

The sound of a woman screaming.

Heart pounding, Justin could only watch in horror as the man finished, picked up his flashlight, and walked away.

Justin sat there, wondering if he should go down and get a closer look. Wondering if the woman was dead now. Wondering if the man was coming back.

Wondering what he was supposed to do now.

Call the police and tell them?

He couldn't. If he did, they would find out about Grandma and the hospital and take him away to a foster home.

He heard the sound of a car start up in the distance. Then it moved away, and all was silent again. He looked back down at the grave.

Go home?

Or go look?

With shaking hands, he eased away from the tarp, pressing himself against the trunk of the tree. But what if she weren't dead? What if she were alive and as scared as he was?

Peeking through the tarp, he looked around. Nothing

moved in the shadows. Backing off the platform, he quickly climbed down.

But he couldn't make himself run over to where the woman was buried. Every step was worse than the last, as his mind screamed at him to run.

Finally, he was close enough to hear her crying. Praying. He eased up closer. He saw the white pipe sticking up out of the ground. Kneeling down next to it, he realized he could hear her even better.

"Hello?" he whispered softly.

The crying stopped, and there was only silence. He leaned down closer to the pipe. "Are you there?"

"Hello? Is someone there? Help me, please!"

"I don't know what to do."

"Call the police. Please. Tell them I'm here. My name is Lisbeth Bevere. My husband works for the FBI. Can you remember that? Lisbeth Bevere."

He rocked back on his heels. *Her husband is an FBI agent? That's worse than cops, even.* He scrambled to his feet and backed away.

He couldn't call the police. He couldn't.

"Hello," she called out to him. "Can you hear me? Are you there?"

He didn't answer her as he stared down at the ground. If he helped her, they would take him away from his grandma and put him in some foster home.

Turning on his heel, he ran for home.

◆   ◆   ◆

Donnie stared at the computer screen. Typed another command.

Stared again. Shaking his head, he flopped back in his chair. "I'm not getting anywhere."

Zoe looked up, her hands clasped between her knees. "You've been at this for three hours. Take a break. Clear your mind."

"All I can think about is Lisbeth, buried alive. She could already be dead, Zoe."

"You know in your heart she's not. I know in mine. We keep going. We'll find something."

Donnie reached back and began rubbing his neck. "Why hasn't he called? I expected him to have called by now."

As if summoned by Donnie's fear, the phone rang. Donnie grabbed it on the first ring as JJ raced to start the trace. "Hello?"

"Do you have it?"

"Yes. Where is Lisbeth? I want to talk to my wife."

"I told you, she'll be waiting for you in the ground. Now, pay attention, because I'm only going to say this once. Take the Beltway around to 270 North. When you get into Frederick, take I-70 West."

Donnie wrote the directions down as fast as he could, glancing over at JJ. Time. He needed to buy JJ time.

"You got all that?"

Donnie looked down at the directions to a property out in the middle of nowhere. "Let me read this back and make sure—"

"If you don't have it right, your wife dies." The man laughed. "Oh, and Bevere? Come alone. I see any of your FBI agent friends, and I'll kill her right then and there."

The man hung up before Donnie could say anything else.

JJ shook his head. "He knows."

Donnie hung up the phone. "That's it then. I take him the drive."

"We," JJ said. "We take him the drive. We've been over this. Stick to the plan. Jack and I will be backing you up."

"You heard him, JJ. He even thinks you or Jack are there, and he'll kill Lisbeth."

JJ grabbed Donnie by the upper arms. "He's going to kill her anyway. And he's going to kill you. There is no bargaining with this. We do this according to plan. Got that?"

Donnie stared up at JJ, then slowly nodded. "Okay. We do this according to the plan."

JJ took the directions and went to the map spread out on the credenza.

Jack came in the office with a platter of sandwiches. "You know, my son has a friend who might be able to help us. He's supposed to be a real whiz with computers. I can't remember his name, but I can call my son and see if the kid can help us."

Zoe looked over at Donnie. "Copy the files to your hard drive. Make two copies on your hard drive. Let the boy work on one copy. It can't hurt. He can be working on it while we're gone."

Donnie looked at his watch. "It's after midnight."

Jack laughed as he set the sandwiches down on the desk. "Oh, to have babies again. For my son and his friends, the night is just getting started."

Pulling out his cell phone, Jack dialed. "Patrick?" Jack put a finger in his ear. "Can you hear me?"

Shaking his head, Jack waited. "He's at a party. Going to step outside so he can hear—yeah, Patrick. You know that friend of yours, the one always working on everyone's computers? Warthog? Okay, Warthog. We have a problem with some encrypted files. Any chance Warthog could help us out?"

Donnie thought about Mandy as a teenager. No. Don't. She was more than a handful now. He might not survive Mandy as a teenager.

Jack closed his phone. "He's going to call this Warthog and call me back."

"Warthog?"

"Don't ask. All these kids have these gaming handles they go by even when they're not online. I think Patrick is known as the Red Falcon. What can I say?"

"I'm definitely putting Mandy in a convent somewhere until she's thirty-five."

Zoe laughed as she reached for a sandwich. "You're not Catholic."

"I'll convert if that's what it takes to get Mandy through the teen years with my sanity intact."

"Just get a big gun, and let all the boys see it." Jack's phone rang. He flipped it open. "Patrick? Great. Yeah, this might take all night and most of tomorrow. Tell him we'll make it worth his while. Sure, you can come with him if you like. Let me give you the address."

Donnie tuned Jack out as he sat down and began copying the files from the flash drive to his hard drive, then making another copy under a different name.

"Okay, the boys will be here in about twenty. All they ask is pizza and soda."

Donnie pulled the flash drive and stuck it in his pocket. "By the phone in the kitchen. Order them whatever they want. It's on me. Order sodas, too. I doubt Lisbeth has enough for teenage boys."

Jack nodded and headed upstairs. JJ waved Donnie and

Zoe over to the map. "The area he's taking you to looks like just farmland. He's bringing you in from the south. It looks like residential housing here to the east and north, and a highway over here to the west. Jack can come in here from the east. Zoe and I will come in from the north."

Donnie looked at the map. Somewhere on that property, his wife was slowly dying. No. Don't think of that right now. God is in control. God is in control. "Okay. As soon as the boys get here, I'm gone."

JJ nodded to Zoe. "Then we're leaving now so we can circle around and get behind him." He reached out and placed a hand on Donnie's shoulder. "We've all done this before. We know what we're up against. We'll get her back alive. I promise. Keep your cell phone on."

Zoe held out her hands. "Let's pray."

◆　◆　◆

Zoe climbed into JJ's Jeep and buckled her seat belt. If it weren't for the adrenalin, she wasn't sure she'd still be on her feet. Fatigue pulled at her, making her crave a soft bed and a warm blanket. The little catnaps she'd been taking over the past two days weren't much help at all.

"We should have brought a gallon of coffee with us. We may need it." JJ checked the heat and turned the blower on low as he waited for the vehicle to warm up.

"I think I've already gone through a gallon. Just in the last hour. Have we thought of everything, JJ?"

"I certainly hope so." He turned in his seat, rubbing a thumb across the dark circles under her eyes. "You look as bad as I feel."

"You sweet talker, you."

He smiled, straightened in his seat, and put the Jeep into reverse. "Do you really think Mann is holding out on Donnie?"

"I don't doubt it for a second. No one would go to this much trouble for some sales figures. There's more in those files."

"Makes you think, doesn't it? The almighty FBI and they're turning their back on one of their own."

Traffic was light as they headed around the Beltway into Maryland. At one spot, they could see the top of the Washington Monument. "We'll have to come back and see the sights, one of these days," JJ remarked.

"You've never done D.C.?"

He shook his head. "Never had the pleasure. I've done New York City. Does that count?"

"No." Zoe laughed. "This is the nation's capital. Home of the Lincoln Memorial, the Smithsonian, the White House, Congress."

"And that is better than New York how?"

Zoe tipped her head, glaring at him. "Not better. Different. If you'd seen D.C., I'd be telling you now about Times Square, Wall Street, the Statue of Liberty, Ellis Island, and the Empire State Building."

"I was fortunate enough to be one of those who saw it before 9/11," he replied soberly. "I saw the towers. Had lunch there."

"Me, too."

"Do you think it'll happen again?"

Zoe stared out at the lights of the capital as they circled it. "I don't know. Sometimes I think the government is on top of it, and other times, I don't think they know what they're doing. They confiscate your fingernail clippers after making you wait two hours in line at the airport and then let illegals walk across the border without so much as a by-your-leave. They want the right to delve into private computers and listen in on cell phones and then don't even bother checking shipping containers coming in at our ports."

JJ saw the merge for 270 and changed lanes. "I guess, to use one of your favorite expressions, we just have to trust God."

◆　◆　◆

Donnie looked up from the computer screen as Jack walked in with two teenage boys. It was easy enough to pick out which one was Patrick. He was taller than his father, but had the same facial structure and eyes.

Which meant Warthog was a thin young man with shoulder-length hair, an earring in his eyebrow, and a quick, easy smile. "Mr. Bevere." He held out his hand, and Donnie shook it.

"You must be Warthog."

The boy shrugged. "You can call me Bobby. No big."

"Well, I appreciate you coming over and giving this a try." Donnie pulled out the chair at the desk. "Have a seat, and I'll leave you to see what you can do."

"I don't try." Warthog sat down and stared at the computer screen for a moment. "I do."

"Well, this is a very complicated encryption."

"And I'm a very complicated expert." He flashed a quick reassuring smile. "It may not be fast, but it'll be done."

Jack's son, Patrick, pulled over a chair and dropped down next to his friend, already enthralled with what was on the screen.

"Then I'll leave you boys to it. The pizzas are here. Sodas

are in the fridge. You have the cell phone number to call if you have any questions."

Already engrossed in the work, Warthog merely gave a nod of his head as his fingers raced across the keyboard.

Upstairs, Jack was waiting at the front door with Donnie's coat. "I started your car for you. Heat should be up shortly."

"Thanks."

Outside, Donnie stopped on the sidewalk and turned to Jack. "I appreciate everything."

"Partner." Jack gave a little salute and headed for his car.

Donnie pulled out of his driveway, his cell phone on the seat beside him, the radio turned off, with only his thoughts for company. He didn't want to think about Lisbeth lying in that coffin, cold and terrified and wondering if he'd reach her in time. He didn't want to think about raising two children without their mother. And he didn't want to think about what he was going to do to Mann if Warthog was able to break the code and that file contained what Donnie thought it contained.

So he tried to keep his thoughts centered on his faith, instead. He knew he had failed some important test with the Lord, but he couldn't worry with beating himself over it just yet. In spite of all his years of thinking he'd been trusting God, the truth was, he had only been trusting Him on a superficial level.

I'm sorry, Lord. I don't know how this is going to turn out, and that scares me. I admit it. I've been wrestling with You for three days, trying to get You to assure me that Lisbeth is coming home. You've seemed so far away, but I know You're not. You're right here. You always are. I guess this comes down to Your will or mine. I want my wife home, and if it's not Your will for her to come home, I'm going to be mad at You. I have to work through that.

He glanced up in his rearview mirror and didn't see Jack's

car. Knowing Jack, he didn't trust that Lisbeth's abductor wasn't watching to see if anyone came with Donnie and peeled off in a different direction somewhere during the drive.

But he was back there somewhere.

And God was up ahead somewhere. Comforting Lisbeth. Preparing the way for Donnie.

I'm sorry, Father. Forgive me. I'm trying to get to that point of just trusting in You regardless of the outcome. I really am. Help me get there. This is another one of those things I can't do in my own strength.

◆ ◆ ◆

Lisbeth's voice was raspy as she yelled again for someone to help her. Her mouth was so dry, her lips were cracking, and her throat was hurting. She was so cold and so miserable.

Had the person gone for help? Surely help would have arrived by now if he had. Despair persisted, and she pressed it down again.

She wasn't going to give up. Donnie would come for her. He would. He'd move heaven and earth if he had to, but he'd come for her.

And he'd get there in time. He had to.

In spite of the pipe, the air was heavy and hard to breathe. She arched up, trying to get her mouth near the pipe, trying to pull in fresh air.

Please. Someone help me.

◆ ◆ ◆

Justin sat in the closet, his knees under his chin, his arms wrapped around his legs. He rocked, keening softly as he tried to drive out the image of that woman in the ground.

Hours had passed. Maybe she was dead now. And if she was dead, he had killed her because he hadn't helped her.

He could be a murderer!

He whimpered a little louder. Rocked a little harder. No one had ever told him what to do in a situation like this. He didn't want anyone to die. But he didn't want to go away to some foster home. He didn't want to be taken away from his grandma, never to see her again. He didn't want to go away and never see his friend Ty again.

What to do, what to do, what to do.

Why wasn't his grandma here to help him? If she were home, she'd call the police and tell them about that lady in the hole, and they'd get her out—and everything would be just fine.

But Grandma wasn't home, and that lady was going to die, and it would be all his fault.

Dropping his head to his knees, he sobbed.

chapter 12

C heck the map again."
Zoe flipped on the little penlight and ran it over the map spread out in her lap. "Left on Kiln. Should be about three blocks up."

JJ slowed down at each little intersection to check the street signs. There were no streetlights to help him out.

Sure enough, the third intersection was Kiln. He made a left. "Now we look for some place to park."

Zoe continued to look at the map. "It looks like there might be a park or something up ahead on the right. No, never mind. If the police see a car unattended in the park, they'll want to check it out."

JJ eyed what appeared to be an old apartment building as he passed by it. Most likely built some forty years earlier, it was a sad-looking place with cardboard over some of the windows and graffiti on the brick exterior. Most of the cars in the lot were old, rusty, and well-used. His Jeep would more than likely stick out like a sore thumb. Then again, it would more than likely stick out anywhere in the area.

Finally, they were back in a residential area. He pulled up to the curb, parking between a pickup truck and an old El Camino. "This will do."

Zoe folded the map and tucked it back in the console. Then she pulled out her gloves. It was going to be a long hike through the woods, so both of them had dressed in jeans, heavy sweatshirts, and sturdy boots.

After setting the alarm on the Jeep, they cut through a backyard without a fence and entered the woods. JJ turned on a flashlight, keeping it pointed at the ground.

"From the map, it looks like we're going to have to hike about a mile. When we get close, we'll have to go on without the light. Just stay right behind me, and you should be okay."

Zoe nodded. "I'm good."

JJ gave her a quick glance and then went back to leading them through the brush, ducking under a low branch. "Do I have to warn you to be careful and not take any unnecessary chances?"

"I'll be fine. This time, I'm carrying a gun."

He wasn't sure that made her any safer. "I'd still feel better if you decided to become an accountant or something."

"I've been doing this kind of work too long to stop now. JJ?"

"What?"

"He's here."

"Who?"

"I can feel him. We don't need to go as far as we thought. Turn off the flashlight."

JJ switched it off, stopping. "How far?" he whispered.

"I'm not sure. But if we keep going straight ahead, we're going to trip right over him in about five minutes."

That made him smile. He reached back and squeezed her

hand. Then he tucked the flashlight away and pulled out the gun Donnie had loaned him. From here on, they'd go slow and quiet.

"Hey, Zoe?" he whispered softly.

"What?" she said softly in his ear, tickling it.

"I hope you're praying."

"I've never stopped."

Suddenly, a bright light flashed in their eyes. "Stop right there, you two."

JJ put his hand up, shielding his eyes. It was a woman's voice, but was she a police officer? Park ranger?

"Who are you?" Zoe asked, and something in her voice put him on alert.

The flashlight lowered a little, and JJ could make out the woman in the down coat. "Wait. You're Lisbeth's friend. Katy."

"She's in on it, JJ."

Katy stepped forward, raising a 9mm pistol. "I can't let you stop this. I'm sorry."

"Can't let. . .do you have any idea what is about to happen? He's going to kill Donnie and Lisbeth."

"I know. But he has to get that information back. It's too important."

JJ felt Zoe's hand at the small of his back, rubbing softly. *Easy. Stay calm.*

"Important enough that a good man and his wife have to die? Their children have to be orphaned?" JJ slid his thumb across the safety on his pistol and eased it off.

"I tried to warn Donnie to watch out for her."

"You were the one who sent the warning letters," Zoe replied.

"Yes. Look, I don't want Donnie or Lisbeth to die. But if Archie doesn't retrieve that flash drive, a whole lot of people are going to die. I know it's hard for you to understand, but you're going to have to trust me on this."

JJ snorted as disgust rose up in him. "Trust you. You stand there ready to kill me, kill Zoe, and let your boyfriend kill Donnie and Lisbeth, and it's all for some glorious cause—is that it?"

"Something like that, yes. If I could change it, I would, but this is the way it has to be."

A shadow of movement behind Kitty caught JJ's attention. He had a split second to make a decision, but before he could even sort through the facts and weigh the pros and cons, training kicked in.

He took half a step forward. "You're with Archie Kemp, right?"

"That's one of his names, yes."

Another half step. "He's a trained killer, Katy. He kills without thought or regret. How could you possibly want to defend him, much less help him?"

"I'm not defending him. I know he'd kill me just as fast as he would anyone else."

He eased up a little more. "Then why don't you want to be free of him?"

"I do want to be free of him, don't you see? I'm not going—"

Jack brought the gun down across the back of Kitty's neck, cutting her off midsentence. She dropped like a stone.

"I don't know what you're doing here, Jack, but I'm glad you are." JJ knelt down and pressed two fingers against Kitty's neck. "She's fine. Just out cold."

"That was the point," Jack retorted. "I don't kill unless I have to. Especially women."

Zoe stripped off her belt. "Tie her up. We have to get going, or Donnie's going to be handling this all by himself."

"We need to gag her, or she'll just scream and give us away."

◆　　◆　　◆

Donnie found the driveway and turned in, slowing down as he hit one rut after another. Trees and overgrown brush closed in around him, sometimes scraping against the side of the car.

A few minutes later, he came upon the old farmhouse. At one time, it had been a home, full of laughter and meals and love. But those days were long gone. Abandoned, ignored, forsaken, and from the way the roof sagged, the front porch leaned, and the slightly tilted foundation, it looked not only abandoned, but condemned.

He drove around to the side, as he had been instructed, and parked. He sat there for a second, staring out into the woods behind the house. The headlights could only penetrate a few feet beyond the trees, and then darkness reigned once more.

Somewhere out there, Lisbeth was waiting. *Please, God. Orchestrate this down to the last second. Keep Lisbeth safe until we find her.*

Cutting the engine, he slowly climbed out of the car. Walk of faith. Faith that God was in control. Faith that Lisbeth was still alive. Faith that JJ and Zoe and Jack were out there somewhere, ready to swoop in and capture this man. Faith that he would tell them where Lisbeth was.

He made his way across the small patch of backyard to the edge of the woods, stepping over old tires, discarded lumber, and trash. There was a white ribbon dangling from a tree limb, just as he had been told there would be. He entered the woods at the marker and walked forward a few hundred feet. He came to the creek and stopped.

Donnie looked around, but it was too dark to see anything or anyone.

"You have the flash drive?"

Donnie turned to his left, in the direction of the voice. "Yes. Where is Lisbeth?"

The man stepped out of the shadows and turned on his flashlight. "Hand it over."

Donnie reached into his pocket and extracted it. Holding it out, he stepped closer.

And stopped as realization ran through his blood like a bitter nor'easter. "You're Archie Kemp?"

"The one and only." He held out his hand. "Give it to me."

Donnie just stood there, shocked into place. "No wonder I could never get a handle on you. Why you always seemed to be one step ahead of me."

Archie laughed, clearly delighted at having the upper hand. "Never expected me to be hiding in plain sight, did you?"

"Rick Harrelson, right? Homeland Security?"

"Right you are. Batting a thousand this morning, Bevere. Hey, if it's any consolation, you were a formidable opponent. I almost hate to kill you."

"Just tell me something, Harrelson. Is Lisbeth still alive?" *Where are you, JJ? Jack? Zoe?*

"Oh, I'm sure she is. After I kill you, I'll go close up that air pipe. Now hand over the flash drive."

"Aren't you curious as to whether or not there's another copy?"

Rick laughed, once more delighted in having the upper hand. "Oh, you mean the one you gave Special Agent in Charge Jim Mann? How stupid do you think I am, Bevere? You seem to overlook the fact that while you were studying Archie Kemp, I was studying you. Of course, I had the advantage of knowing whom I was studying and getting to work around him from time to time. You, on the other hand, were studying someone who didn't even exist."

"Why, Rick? Do you have any idea the damage this could do?"

"Money, Bevere. Lots and lots of money."

Donnie wrestled for conversation. He had to keep Rick talking, or he was dead. *Come on, Jack. JJ. Somebody!*

"Is Mann in on this with you?"

"First of all, this isn't *my* deal, okay. I'm just the guy they hired to get it from you. As for Mann, nah. . .I played him just as easily as I played you." He narrowed his eyes at Donnie. "Just give me the drive, Bevere. There isn't that much time."

"Why not? What's your rush, Rick?"

"Criminy, Bevere. Are you really that stupid? The flight coming in from Gitmo day after tomorrow." He held out his hand. "Give me the drive."

"Drop it, Harrelson." Jack stepped out from behind a tree, his weapon palmed in both hands, aimed straight at Rick.

Rick only laughed again as he maneuvered himself, backing away but keeping Donnie and Jack in front of him. "Hey, Jack. Figured you wouldn't miss the party."

"Just drop your weapon, Rick. It doesn't have to go any further." Jack stepped over a fallen log, keeping his weapon trained on Rick.

"No can do, pal. Doesn't work that way. Think I'm stupid

enough to come out here without backup of my own?"

"If you're talking about your girlfriend, I'm afraid I've already taken her out of the equation."

For the first time, Rick didn't seem quite so confident. His gun wavered, revealing the slight tremble in his hands. His eyes darted left to right. He backed up a step.

Then he raised his gun at Jack and fired.

Jack, anticipating the move, jumped sideways, hit the ground, and rolled.

Donnie dropped to the ground and dug under his coat for his own gun. Then Rick turned the gun on Donnie.

Another shot rang out as Donnie rolled, hoping to avoid the shot.

When he raised his head, JJ was stepping out of the woods and kneeling down to check on Rick who was sprawled on the ground.

Donnie sprang to his feet. "Tell me you didn't kill him!"

"I didn't even shoot him," JJ replied as he stood up slowly. "Jack fired to keep you from getting killed."

"Is he dead?" Donnie stood over Rick, fear screaming in his heart. He couldn't be dead. *Don't let him be dead.* But Donnie knew the answer before JJ spoke.

"Yes."

Donnie dropped to his knees. "He never told us where he buried Lisbeth."

◆　◆　◆

Dawn crept over the horizon in a struggle to break through a heavy gray sky. Light was muted as investigators diligently worked on wrapping up the crime scene.

Donnie sat on the hood of his car, hunched down in his coat while Mann finished up his interview with Katy. Kitty. Whatever her name was.

Donnie still wasn't sure he trusted Mann, but JJ was hovering close enough that if Kitty said anything about Lisbeth's whereabouts, JJ would hear it.

So far, she was still swearing that she didn't know, that Archie, as she called him, had refused to take her along when he buried Lisbeth. He called her later and told her where to meet him. She had no idea if Lisbeth was alive or not. A unit had been called to search their residence.

The state police had brought in the dogs, and they were, at that very moment, searching the woods for Lisbeth.

Zoe was leaning against JJ's Jeep, now parked right behind Donnie's car, and talking on her cell phone to someone.

It had gone south so quick.

What was on that flash drive? There was no doubt in his mind that Mann knew. And that made Donnie want to grab his boss's lapels and shake him until his teeth rattled. Or fell out.

Donnie wanted to be out there in those woods, but he'd been given strict orders to sit tight. Mann was not happy with him. Well, he wasn't too happy with Mann, either.

At the sound of footsteps, he turned and watched Zoe approach him, two cups of steaming coffee in hand. She handed him one. "One of the officers went for coffee."

Donnie wrapped both hands around the cup. "Thanks."

Zoe blew lightly across the top of her cup and then sipped cautiously. "How are you holding up?"

"Barely," he replied. "We have to find her, Zoe."

"We will."

He nodded his head over in Kitty's direction. "I never

saw that coming. She was in our home, befriended my wife, attended our church. And it was all so she could get close enough to attack."

"And what hurts most is that you thought she was okay because she attended your church. She slipped in under your radar because you thought she was a Christian."

Donnie digested that for a moment, then nodded. "Yeah. I think that pretty much sums it up. You don't expect it to come at you from inside the church."

"The times we live in dictate that we not judge people by what they say or how they dress, or even what church they attend, but as the Bible teaches, to judge them by the Spirit." She patted his arm. "Don't beat yourself up about it."

He continued to stare over at Kitty, who was still answering questions. "One of Lisbeth's friends tried to tell Lisbeth that something wasn't right about Katy. Kitty. Whatever her name is. We all just blew it off."

"She hit me wrong, too, but I chalked it up as stress over Lisbeth rather than taking a good, long look." She looked over at him, her gaze steady. Solid.

He took comfort in that steadiness and pulled deep down inside for more strength. This wasn't over yet.

Lisbeth was out there, and time was running out.

chapter 13

Justin screwed the cap on the bottle of water and stuck it down in his backpack. He rubbed his eyes and reached for the straws and fruit snacks, then tucked them down in the pack with the water.

He still wasn't sure what he was supposed to do, but he knew he had to do something. Maybe if he took her food and water, he could help her stay alive until she was found. Or until Grandma came home and could call the police.

Looking around, trying to think if there was anything else he should take, he zipped his pack closed. He had some dry cereal, a handful of peanuts, a carrot he'd broken down into small pieces, the fruit snacks that were supposed to be for his lunch box, and water. There weren't many kinds of foods small enough to drop down a tube to someone.

Dressing warmly—jeans, shirt, sweatshirt, sweater, coat, his grandmother's gloves, and his cap—he picked up the pack and slipped out the back door, making sure he had his key tucked down deep in his pocket.

Trudging through the woods, he kept looking up at the

sky. It was that pale gray color it got just before it snowed.

When he got close, he slowed down. What if she were already dead? Swallowing hard, he approached cautiously. "Hello? Lady?"

Silence. He felt a sting behind his eyes. Kneeling down beside the pipe, he leaned closer. "Lady? Are you. . . awake?"

"Hello?"

The sound of her voice, weak and raspy, sent a shiver of pleasure up his back. He settled himself on the ground and pulled his pack into his lap. Unzipped it. "I brought you some food and water. It's not much, but it's all I have."

"Police. Call the police. Please."

He set the bottle of water down. "I can't. I'm sorry. They'll take me away."

There was a moment of silence that echoed in his heart like one of his grandma's looks of disappointment. "Do you want some water?"

"Yes."

She sounded as if she were merely accepting second prize at the carnival—a cheap plastic toy instead of the big teddy bear. He understood. His whole life was like that.

"What's your name?" she asked in that soft, sweet voice that tore at his heart.

"Justin. I live on the other side of the woods with my grandma. She's in the hospital. That's why I can't call the police for you." He stared down at the bottle of water in his hands. "I want to, lady. I do. I don't want you to die. That's why I brought you stuff."

"I appreciate the thought, Justin. How old are you?"

"Seven. But I'll be eight in July." He stared down at the

pipe. "If I pour this water down the pipe, are you going to be able to drink it?"

There was a rustling sound and then a hiss of frustration. "I don't think so."

He ripped open the fruit snacks and dropped a couple down the pipe. "Can you get those?"

A moment later, she replied. "Yes. Thanks."

While dropping fruit snacks, he thought about the water, trying to work out the problem. When all the fruit snacks were gone, he started dropping cereal. "I don't know what to do about the water, lady."

"Lisbeth. My name is Lisbeth."

"Lisbeth," he repeated, his tongue twisting around the name. "You need water, right?"

"Yes. I'm thinking. Justin? Why can't you call the police for me?"

"If I call them, they'll take me away and put me in a foster home. My grandma told me not to let anyone know I'm alone. Just till she gets home."

"When will she be home?"

"I don't know. They took her to the hospital a few days ago. I don't know." He looked up as the first flakes of snow began to fall. "It's starting to snow."

"Justin, I need to get home to my family. Do you understand? I have two little children. A little girl and a little boy. My son is just a baby. They need me, sweetheart. They need me to come home to them."

He thought she might be crying, but he couldn't say for sure. Bowing his head, he twisted and untwisted the top on the bottle of water. "I'm afraid, Lisbeth. They'll take me away from my grandma. I don't want to go to a foster home. I want to stay with my grandma."

"I understand, Justin. I do. At the same time, you're too young to be alone like this. Do you have food? And money to buy food? And are you going to school?"

"Grandma left me money, but my momma found it and took it. I have some food left. There's stuff in the freezer— hamburger and stuff—but I promised Grandma I wouldn't use the stove. Just the microwave."

"Justin, listen to me, honey. My husband works for the FBI. Do you know what that is?"

"Yeah."

"Even if they take you and put you in a foster home, my husband can make sure that you come back home to your grandmother as soon as she gets out of the hospital."

It all sounded good and right, but he knew that grownups lied to get what they wanted. And Lisbeth wanted him to call the police.

He climbed to his feet and picked up his backpack. "I have to go. I'll try to figure out how to get you some water. Then I'll be back."

"Wait! Justin!"

Ignoring the plea in her voice and the way it made him feel, he turned and ran for home.

◆　◆　◆

Lisbeth kicked out her foot in frustration when Justin left. She wanted to scream, but her throat hurt too much. And why waste the energy? She might need it later. Hungry, thirsty, cold, tired, and despondent, she allowed herself a few tears.

She was going to die here. She was resigned to that now.

Or at least, she was at that moment. Her emotions had been all over the board for the past eight hours, bouncing from sky-high hope that Donnie or the police were going to show up at any moment, to heart-wrenching acceptance of impending death.

There had been tears, and plenty of them. There had been deep reflection, and plenty of it. And most of all, there had been nearly endless prayer.

And memories. Bittersweet memories of meeting Donnie on campus, falling in love with his sweet smile, his endless enthusiasm, his dreams of making a difference in the world. Of Mandy and the first time she'd held her daughter in her arms, her first birthday, her first Christmas, her boundless energy and delightful laugh. Cody, his toothless smile and the way his eyes would light up when she came into the room. Her parents and their love. Her sister and her loyalty.

Groping with her hand, she reached out and fingered the little pile of cereal next to her head. Slowly, her heart stopped hurting, and her spirits lifted just a little. Justin was just a child, caught up in something far bigger than he could handle, but he'd brought her fruit snacks and cereal.

Neil Lagasse stared at the empty desk across from his, trying to comprehend the rumors invading every corner of the agency. His partner, Rick Harrelson, had been assassinating people under the name Archie Kemp for years, using his position with the agency to gather inside information and hinder investigations. His partner, Rick Harrelson aka Archie Kemp, had kidnapped Bevere's wife, buried her alive, and then tried to kill Bevere.

His partner was dead, killed by Special Agent Jack Fleming.

His fellow agents passed by, some giving him the look that said they figured him stupid for not knowing his partner was a hired killer, the others looking at him with wary glances that said they wondered if he were dangerous, too.

First el-Hajid. Now this. He could see his career going up in flames. He'd be lucky if all they did was assign him to the South Dakota office after this.

His phone buzzed. He picked it up. "Lagasse."

His supervisor, Jim Mann, was on the line. "I need to see you in my office immediately."

Neil swallowed hard. "I'll be right there."

He hung up the phone, stood up, and slipped into his suit coat, buttoning it as he made his way to Mann's office. *Here it comes: We have an opening in South Dakota; you start there on Monday. Be on the next plane out of town, and don't call us. We'll call you.*

Taking a deep breath, he knocked on Mann's door and then opened it. "You wanted to see me, sir?"

Jim Mann looked up from the computer screen in front of him and waved toward a chair. "Have a seat."

With his lungs jammed into his throat, Neil sat stiffly, folding his hands in his lap. Then folded them across his chest. Then dropped them to his thighs and took a deep breath.

Mann swiveled his chair around, placing both hands on the desk blotter. "You worked with Harrelson for what, four years, right?"

Neil swallowed hard, trying to get air into his lungs. "Yes, sir."

"I want you to take the man's life apart. Find anything and everything you can about him. Friends, acquaintances. Talk to his old school buddies. I want him under a microscope."

Relief toyed with him. "Yes, sir."

Mann leaned back in his chair, fingering the ends of his tie. "Harrelson was a sociopath. I don't want you beating yourself up because you didn't see him for what he was. He was very good at deceiving people. Including me. Get over to his house and oversee the evidence gathering over there."

"Yes, sir." Air filled his lungs, making him giddy and light-headed.

"Get on it. I want this like yesterday."

Neil jumped to his feet. "I'm on it."

"Oh, and Lagasse."

Neil stopped and slowly turned around. "Sir?"

"This does not mean el-Hajid is off your radar. I want him found."

"Sir," he replied smartly and hurried out of the office.

◆　◆　◆

JJ dug into his eggs with enthusiasm, easily ignoring all the noise in the crowded diner buzzing around him. He dabbed a corner of his toast into the egg yoke and nearly moaned in pleasure when he took a bite.

"You are enjoying that entirely too much." Zoe wrinkled her nose as he dunked his toast again.

"I'm starving. This is good. What's not to enjoy?" He noticed that she'd barely touched her waffle. "Why aren't you hungry?"

"I don't know. Too much on my mind." She shoved her plate aside and wrapped her hands around her orange juice glass. "They went over almost every inch of those woods and not a trace of Lisbeth. He buried her somewhere else. But where? I called Dan, and he's looking to see if Rick owned any properties anywhere else. The problem is, what if he owns the property under another alias? I really wish Jack had winged him instead of killed him."

JJ picked up a slice of bacon, waving it as he talked. "Even if Jack had winged him, we have no guarantee he would have told us anything." He took a bite and tossed the rest back to his plate.

Zoe kept eyeing his bacon like a hungry wolf eyes a young moose. "And Kitty didn't say anything at all that could help us?"

JJ shook his head, picked up a strip of bacon, and handed it to her. "You're drooling. No, she insists that Rick wouldn't tell her where he buried Lisbeth. I gotta tell you, my instincts are screaming around her. Something still doesn't fit. She warns Donnie that Lisbeth is going to be taken. Then she pulls a gun on us to keep us from stopping Rick from killing Donnie. It makes no sense to me. The woman has an agenda, and I'd like to know what it is."

Zoe lifted an eyebrow. "Maybe she planned on stealing the drive from Rick and making a little side deal of her own, selling it to the highest bidder or something."

"Well, Mann took her into custody, so we may never find out the real story there. If I read him right, he's going to keep her well hidden."

"Probably." She chomped down on more bacon.

"What we need is for the Lord to give you some clear direction. Even a vision would be welcome at this point."

Zoe choked midswallow, sending her into coughing spasms. JJ leaned over and gave her a few pats on the back. "Chew slowly and swallow. Didn't your mother ever teach you how to eat properly? I swear, I can't take you anywhere."

She stared at him, a few tears trickling down her face as a result of her choking. "What did you just say?"

"I said we need God to give you—"

"I heard what you said. I just don't believe my ears. Josiah Johnson. Are you telling me that you finally believe God speaks to people?"

He frowned, wishing she wasn't going to make such an issue out of this. "I've known you almost a year, Shefford. I've seen what God does with you. How He uses you. Even a hardnose like me can only deny the truth for just so long."

Zoe leaned back in her seat. Reached for her juice. Took a drink. Never took her eyes off him. He smiled at her. "Wow, Shefford. Are you telling me you didn't have enough faith to believe that I'd eventually come to accept it?"

"You just took me by surprise, is all."

He leaned forward. "How about I surprise you again? I'm in love with you, Zoe Shefford."

Donnie dragged himself into the house and pushed the front door closed behind him. He wanted to crawl into a bed, pull the covers over his head, and not wake up for a year.

Instead, he toed off his shoes, tossed his coat over the stair rail, and made his way into the kitchen. He flipped on the little countertop television and then headed for the coffee.

A murmur of voices and a sudden excited whoop sent every sense on high alert. He nearly reached for his gun when he remembered Warthog and Patrick.

He nearly ran down the stairs and across the family room to his office. Pausing in the doorway, he took in the scene. Pizza boxes and soda cans were littering his desk. A couple of napkins, balled up and tossed like basketballs to the trash can, lay on the floor. *No points, fellas.*

Patrick was standing up behind Warthog, eyes narrowed, lips moving silently as he read whatever was on the screen. Warthog was arched over the keyboard, hands still, reading as well.

Neither boy seemed to notice he was there.

"Please tell me you have something for me."

Both boys jumped as if spooked by a ghost. Patrick even threw one hand over his chest.

"Mr. Bevere." Warthog blinked. "Sir."

Donnie strolled over to the boys, hands in his pockets. "How's it going?"

"I just broke through one set of files. It's mostly numbers. Dates, quantities, stuff like that. But here's the kicker. This guy is smart. You see these codes here?"

Donnie stared at the screen. They were just numbers to him. A random string of numbers. "Yeah?"

"There's another file within this one, and that's what I need to break open next."

Donnie stared at the screen again. "A file within a file?"

"It's slick, no doubt. But I've seen it before. We send files like this over the Web sometimes. You know. Hiding things from our parents." He blushed, quickly turning his attention back to the screen.

Donnie placed a hand on Warthog's shoulder. Squeezed gently. "You've done an amazing job, son. I'm impressed."

Warthog lit up like Times Square. "Thanks, sir."

"You boys hungry? I can make us some breakfast. Did you get any sleep at all?"

"We power napped around four, so I'm cool for a while. But yeah, I could do with some eats." Warthog turned his attention back to the computer, sitting up a little straighter.

Donnie looked over at Patrick. "Food?"

Patrick shrugged. "I could eat."

The last thing Donnie felt like doing was cooking, but it was the least he could do for the boys. So when his in-laws walked in the door five minutes later, he nearly fell at Jane Bushnell's feet in gratitude.

"I am so glad to see you." He picked Mandy up when she leaped into his arms. "Hi, Mandy Bear. I missed you."

"I miss you, too. Did you find Mommy?"

"Not yet, sweetie. But we're getting close."

When she wiggled in his arms, he set her down. She was off and running, heading upstairs to her toys.

Jane eyed the carton of eggs and pancake mix on the counter. "Let me put Cody down in his crib, and I'll make you some breakfast."

"I have two teenage boys downstairs who need to be fed."

"I can handle it," she said as she disappeared down the hall.

Donnie sat down at the table with Mack. "I'm surprised to see you back here, but I guess they pulled the agent now that there's no danger to the kids."

Mack folded his hands on the table. "Are you really closer? The agent wouldn't tell us squat, only that there was no more danger and that Lisbeth hadn't been found."

Donnie rolled his head, trying to work out the fatigue that had settled between his shoulder blades. "We found the man who took her, but he was killed before he could tell us where he buried her. We're tearing his life apart right now, trying to figure out where he might have taken her."

Mack paled, dropping his eyes. "He could have buried her anywhere, son."

"I know. I'm just trying to trust God, here."

"I hear ya. All I can pray for these days is the strength to accept whatever happens."

Jane swept back into the room, pushing the sleeves of her sweater to her elbows. "And that's all of that kind of talk we're going to have in this house. When my daughter gets home, I'm not going to like having to tell her that her father and her husband were walking around here with their chins resting on their kneecaps. I believe my daughter is coming home. End of discussion."

Mack's lips twitched. "I think I'll start some coffee."

❖　❖　❖

Kitty paced the small interrogation room, ignoring the mirror on the wall and the prying eyes of the men on the other side of that mirror watching every move she made. She knew they were frustrated that she wasn't giving them what they wanted, but too bad for them.

She didn't trust any of them.

Except Donnie Bevere. And for sure, they weren't going to let her talk to him.

She'd already tried asking to speak to him, and they'd just brushed her off with some excuse about him not being available. If he knew she wanted to talk to him, he'd be available, and she knew it. They weren't telling him.

Another reason she didn't trust them.

Archie was dead. She wasn't sure how she felt about that. Part of her was grieving. She'd been with him for so many years it was hard not to miss him. But another part of her didn't care at all. She felt free. Free of him and his expectations.

Her headache was still throbbing in spite of the aspirin she'd taken. Maybe it was a good thing Archie was dead. If he'd found out she'd let someone sneak up behind her and conk her on the head, he'd have killed her.

She stopped, turned, and leaned back against the concrete wall, staring at the pale green tile floor. She had to get out of here. Easier said than done, but she had to escape.

Pressing her fingertips to her temples, she rubbed lightly. *Think, girl. How do you get away? How do you give these jerks the slip? You have to finish what you started.*

Pushing off the wall, she started pacing again. How much did they know? Archie had been so good at sleight of hand and illusion. Now she had to see how much she'd learned from him over the years.

Walking over to the table, she dropped down in the chair, burying her head in her hands. She let her shoulders shake a little and drummed up a few tears by thinking back about the day her mother had died. How alone she'd felt. How scared she'd been.

Sure enough, two men strolled into the room a few minutes later, shoulders squared with confidence that they'd finally broken her.

The one who had been playing "bad cop" leaned against the wall, arms folded across his chest, glaring at her. The "good cop" sat down across the table from her. "Kathryn, would you like something to drink? Water? Soda?"

She sniffled loudly. "Soda. Please."

The bad cop, acting quite put out, left the room. As soon as the door closed, the good cop leaned forward, hands clasped on the table in front of him. "Honey, I know you're just caught up in something not of your doing. Harrelson took advantage of your youth and your innocence. He's gone now. He can't hurt you or control you anymore. You can be free of all this. We just need to know who hired him."

She sniffled again. He reached into his pocket and pulled out a handkerchief. Handed it to her. She took it and wiped her eyes. "I don't know his name. Archie never told me stuff like that. He kept all that stuff in that little notebook of his."

She could almost feel the man jumping in his seat. "What notebook, Kathryn?"

"That little black one that he kept. If it wasn't on him, then he must have put it back in the deposit box. I have a key at the house."

"You can get into the deposit box?"

Wiping her eyes, she gave him the most pitiful look she could muster up and looked pointedly around the room. "Well, not anymore, but you can probably get the bank to let you into it."

She nearly held her breath, waiting for the idiot to take the bait. She knew as well as he did that it would take a court order, which would take a day or more and that was time they didn't have. They wouldn't like it, but they would take her to the house to get the key and to the bank to get the book.

Sure enough, he smiled indulgently. "Let me see what happened to that soda you wanted. What about some food? Are you hungry?"

She lifted her shoulders in a little shrug. "I guess."

chapter 14

Kitty sat quietly in the backseat of the sedan, her hands cuffed and in her lap. She hadn't counted on the handcuffs, but it was just another obstacle for her to overcome.

It had taken the better part of two hours, but the good cop had obviously convinced the powers that be that she was a good little girl, conned by a bad man into doing bad things, and that she was now completely broken and putty in his hands.

Fools.

So now she was on her way to the house she'd shared with Archie, the bad cop in the front seat with the driver and the good cop in the backseat with her.

Staring out the window, she ran through her plan again and again. If Archie had taught her nothing else, he taught her that good planning was critical to success.

And she had to be successful if she wanted to escape.

Had to escape.

"I know you must be terrified, Kathryn, but we're going to see that the judge understands how Archie forced you to cooperate with him and that you feared for your life. You've never been arrested, and that will show the judge that none of this is your fault. You were just a young girl, not even eighteen, and Archie used that."

Kitty was so deep in thought, she nearly missed hearing what the good cop was saying to her. She dropped her head, twisting her fingers together. *Don't blow it now, girl. Pay attention.*

"What about your parents? Do they know where you are?"

Kitty shook her head. "My mom died when I was fourteen. My stepfather didn't want me around after that, so I've been on my own ever since."

She thought about playing the old "my stepfather abused me" card, but it had been played so many times, it didn't even evoke much sympathy from people anymore.

"You poor thing. Tossed out of your home and still practically a baby. No wonder Archie found you an easy mark."

Kitty kept her head down. It wouldn't do to have the man see her rolling her eyes.

Her story wasn't all that far from the truth anyway. Her mother had died when she was fourteen, and her stepfather hadn't wanted her around, but he hadn't kicked her out. He just ignored her, and she left on her own.

He had probably been as glad to see her go as she was to leave. Not that he was a bad guy, really. Just a little too straight and uptight. Everything in its place, meals at designated times, rules and more rules and expectations of rules. It all got so boring. And confining.

Kitty steeled herself to act almost reluctant when they arrived at the house. Good cop held open the car door, and she just sat there for a minute, staring at the house.

"It'll be okay, Kathryn. He's not here anymore. You'll be fine."

Slowly, she scooted out and followed him to the front door. She let him lead the way into the house. And then into the living room.

They had ripped the house apart. Books on the floor, pillows tossed off the sofa, chairs overturned, papers strewn everywhere, drawers opened and dumped.

Bad cop stayed at the front door while good cop urged her to get the key. She led him down the hallway and into the bedroom. Once again, the room had been turned inside out. She stepped over clothes, linens, and shoes to the dresser. All the drawers had been pulled out and dumped on the floor. She eased the dresser away from the wall and slid her hand behind it, ripping off the key that was taped to the back.

She held the key out to good cop. "I really need to use the bathroom real quick. Is that okay?"

Good cop took the key, nodding to her. "Make it quick, okay?"

She held out her hands. For a moment, he stared at her, then he ducked his head in the bathroom, looked around, and not seeing a window, nodded. He tucked the key she'd given him in his shirt pocket and then unlocked the handcuffs.

Stepping into the bathroom, she shut the door and locked it quietly. Then she pushed back the shower curtain and gently lifted down the plastic shelving that Archie had installed to hold soaps and shampoos. She quietly set it aside and slid open the frosted glass window hidden behind it. She turned and closed the shower curtain. Why make it easy for them?

A little bounce on her toes and she jumped up, then swung her legs through and dropped to the ground below. She crouched there on the ground for a few seconds, making sure there was no one around. Then she bolted toward the house next door, disappearing around the hedges.

◆　◆　◆

JJ stared at his notes, tapping his pen idly on the page. It was frustrating beyond words. The FBI had jumped in and shut them out of everything. They had no access to Kitty, the house she and Harrelson shared, or any evidence they may have found there.

He looked across the room at Zoe, who was tucked in a sofa chair, feet beneath her, going over the printouts that Warthog had given her.

"Has Dan called?"

Zoe looked over at him, blinking as she shifted mental gears. "No. Not yet."

He watched her drop her attention back to the printouts.

"Finding anything interesting?"

"If I'm reading this right, there are four sources for the shipments. Another column has the dates the shipments went out and then the quantity. What I haven't figured out yet are these little number/letter combinations. I'm going to guess and say it's the initials of the person responsible for shipping and his cut of the profits." She sighed, shifting in her chair. "Maybe when Warthog decodes that other file, it will explain the rest of this."

They both looked up as Donnie came walking into the room, carrying a stack of papers. "Kitty escaped."

JJ gaped at Donnie, thoughts warring with each other. He couldn't help it. Some small part of him was glad she had.

"How did she escape?"

"Seems she and Rick had covered the bathroom window with some shelf, and no one noticed it. When they took her back to the house to retrieve a key, she said she had to use the bathroom, and, abracadabra. . .out the window she went." Donnie sat down on the coffee table, setting the papers beside him. "They're searching high and low for her, but I don't think they're going to find her."

JJ set his notebook down. "Not unless she wants to be found. Mann must be pulling his hair out."

Donnie didn't look the least bit concerned. "I feel so bad for him."

Zoe pointed at the stack of papers with her pencil. "What's all that?"

"These," Donnie replied, setting his hand on top of them, "are leads called in to the hotline. Seems all these people have seen Lisbeth. Mann thought we could help out by going through them all and weeding them down to legitimate leads."

Zoe tossed her printout to the end table beside her chair and held out her hands. "Give me some. I'll start going through them."

Donnie lifted a third of them and handed them to her. Then he gave some to JJ. "I'll take the rest."

Zoe laughed as she read the first one. "Get this. A lady in Richmond says she saw Lisbeth shopping at Wal-Mart yesterday evening around seven. She was buying groceries."

"Hey," JJ piped up. "She's bound to get hungry buried there underground." Suddenly, he closed his eyes and groaned. "I'm sorry, Donnie. That was thoughtless of me."

Donnie waved it off. "I understand. I'm a little punchy myself right now. This one says that Lisbeth was seen driving a white sports car in Annapolis this morning."

One by one, they worked on the stack, laughing at some, dismissing others, setting some aside as possibilities.

Suddenly, Zoe sat up straighter, making a little sound somewhere between a gasp and a screech. "Someone called in. Wouldn't leave a name. Said he saw a man burying a woman in the woods. She's alive and needs help."

Donnie jumped up and reached for the report. "Where?"

"They wouldn't leave an address. Just that it was the woods on Garrett Road near the old shoe factory."

Donnie's hands were shaking. "But where?"

"It's a three-oh-one area code. Braddock Heights. Right near where we met Rick."

JJ set his stack aside and took the report from Donnie. He read it over. "It's a long shot, but it fits. I'd be more inclined to check this out before checking out the mall in Richmond."

Donnie grabbed the phone and called Mann. After explaining about the lead, he requested the search dogs and was turned down.

Donnie slammed the phone onto the receiver. "He won't authorize to have the search teams brought out on a wild goose chase. He says at least an inch of snow has fallen up there, and the dogs would be worthless."

"Then we go ourselves." Zoe looked down at her sweats. "I just need to change into something warmer, and then we're out of here."

JJ watched Zoe run up the stairs. It sounded like a good lead. Maybe too good. Too good to be true. "When did they see this man bury this woman alive? We know he buried Lisbeth last night. If this person saw it happen last night, why are they waiting until"—he glanced down at the time of the incoming call on the sheet—"one thirteen this afternoon?"

"Maybe he didn't want to get involved. Maybe he had an attack of conscience and finally called it in." Donnie threw his hands up. "I don't know, but you have to admit, it's the closest thing we have to a real lead."

JJ could understand Donnie wanting to jump at every credible lead. Heaven knew he was all for checking it out himself, but he still had questions.

Zoe came bouncing down the stairs, boots in hand. "Donnie, I probably don't have to say this, but don't let yourself get too caught up in this lead. I'm not so sure it's what it appears to be."

JJ felt something skip inside him, a little piece of awareness that he didn't totally understand, but it made him feel. . . *right.*

"I know. I know. Don't get my hopes up." Donnie shrugged into his coat. "But you have to admit, it sounds legit."

Zoe tied her boots. "I know it sounds legit, and it may be; but you're too close. I don't want you to get too upset if it turns out to be a crank, that's all."

"I won't, I promise." Donnie strode for the front door.

"And pigs fly with blue wings," JJ whispered softly.

Zoe must have heard him though. She punched his arm lightly as he passed her.

JJ was about to defend himself when Warthog came running into the room, waving some papers. "I did it! I did it!"

Donnie had already disappeared through the door. JJ took the papers and started looking them over. "Amazing." He turned and grinned at the teen. "Great job. Now go get some rest. We'll be back in a couple of hours."

Warthog nodded, still grinning ear to ear. "I really did it."

"Yes, son. You really did."

Zoe was waiting for him on the front porch. "Are you driving?"

"Sure."

She held out her hand. "Good, let me read those while you drive."

"You don't miss a trick, do you?"

"Nope."

He handed her the printout and went for his keys. Her cell phone rang. "Shefford. Sure, hold on a sec." She handed him her phone. "It's Matt."

"Yeah, partner. What's going down?" He followed Zoe to his Jeep as he listened to Matt.

"The press is all over this, JJ. They're accusing you of running away in one breath, and with the next breath, scream that you're ignoring your suspension by being involved in a high profile case. Harris is pulling his hair out. He wants you back here, tail tucked between your legs."

He climbed into the Jeep, ignoring Donnie's impatient look from the backseat. "No way, partner. Can't happen right now. Let me call you back later, okay?"

He closed the phone and handed it back to Zoe. "Now, anything interesting in that file?"

"Oh yeah," Zoe replied without taking her eyes from it. "We're talking explosive."

◆　◆　◆

Justin knelt down beside the pipe. It was full of snow. Quickly, he brushed a patch of snow away from the pipe and sat down. Digging a spoon out of his pack, he dug as much snow out of the pipe as he could. Then he blew in it, trying to clear the pipe of snow. "Miss Lisbeth?"

He knocked on the pipe and stared down into it. It was too dark to see if snow still blocked it or if it was clear. "Hello?"

"Justin?"

She sounded so tired. Maybe he'd woken her up.

He stared down the pipe. "Are you okay, Lisbeth?"

"I'm just very cold, Justin. Very cold and very sleepy. Please call the police for me, honey. I really need you to do that. It's getting hard to breathe down here."

Wrapping his arms around his waist, he started rocking. "I'm sorry. I don't know what to do."

"I know, Justin. This is hard for you. But. . .I just don't know how much longer—"

She didn't finish. She didn't have to. He understood. She was dying. And it was all his fault.

"I taped a whole bunch of straws together, and I think I can get you some water now."

"Okay."

"And I brought you some more fruit snacks."

She didn't respond. Swallowing hard, he rocked harder. What was he supposed to do? He couldn't let her just die. What would his grandma say if she knew what was happening? Would she tell him to just let the lady die? Or would she tell him to go call the police?

God, please tell me what to do.

"Please, call the police, Justin. You don't have to tell them your name. Just tell them where I am."

Justin jumped to his feet. "Okay, Lisbeth. I'll go call."

Then he turned and ran for home.

◆　　◆　　◆

Donnie stared at the information on the paper Zoe handed him in disbelief, his fists crushing the paper. "They're stealing weapons from four of our military bases and selling it to terrorists. They have some operation here. This makes me sick to my stomach."

JJ gave him a quick glance in the rearview mirror. "Does it say who the ringleaders are?"

"All the names are here. Including the main man himself. Roger Rupert."

"Sounds like that name means something to you."

"Oh yes. I'm quite familiar with Rupert. General Roger Rupert. He's a friend of Jim Mann's."

Zoe's head whipped around. "But Rick said Mann wasn't in on this."

Donnie smoothed out the paper and looked it over again. "Rick may not have known. Or he could have been lying."

"Or," JJ offered, "Mann doesn't know what his pal is up to."

"Well, if I wasn't sure whether to trust him or not, I definitely don't trust him now." Donnie slid back in his seat, dropping his head to the headrest. "No wonder they were willing to go to such lengths to get this information back. This could blow D.C. wide open. Rupert has some powerful friends in Congress, as well as in the military."

Zoe turned in her seat. "But what does any of this have to do with that plane coming in tomorrow? Rick specifically said the timing was critical because of that plane."

Donnie pulled out his cell phone and dialed. "I don't know, but let's see if we can find out. Jack. It's me. Do me a favor. I'm going to give you five names. Run them for me. Find out what you can and call me back." He rattled off the names, all Middle Eastern-sounding, and disconnected the call. "If I'm right, one or more of the men on that flight is knee-deep in this and could bring Rupert down if he ever took the stand."

JJ whistled. "I never thought of that angle. But it would explain a few things. Let's hope Jack finds something solid for us. In the meantime, whom do we turn to? We can't go to Mann for fear he'll bury this. And maybe us. Know anyone else who will take this and do something with it?"

"I'm thinking."

"Well, you may have to think about it later. We're here." JJ pulled up to the curb and parked.

Donnie climbed out and looked around. It was, for the most part, a poor, racially mixed neighborhood with an air of desperation and need. The woods, encompassing about twenty acres, sat in the middle of the area as if holding off the encroachment of civilization while being swallowed up in it.

"She's not here," Zoe said as she looked around.

"Please don't tell me that," Donnie replied, flinching.

"I'm sorry. I'm just telling you what I sense. She's not here."

"Well, let's just take a quick walk-through, just to make sure." JJ slipped on his sunglasses. "We've come all this way."

Zoe nodded. "I'm willing."

The snow wasn't deep at all, but covering brush, vines, and holes, it made for slow and cautious going. They fanned out, staying within sight of each other, but trying to cover as much ground as they could. They took turns calling out her name and then stopping to listen in hopes of hearing her reply.

Talk about long shots, Donnie thought. They were looking for a needle in a haystack.

They came upon a small clearing and stopped. A woman sat there on a fallen log. "About time you got here. I was starting to think you wouldn't show up."

"Katy." Donnie clenched his fists. "What are you doing here?"

"*Kitty*. I need to talk to you, and I didn't know any other way of drawing you out." She stood up, stamping her feet against the cold. "First of all, I don't know where Lisbeth is. I wish I did. And if I did, I would tell you. Or go after her myself. I tried to get Archie to take me along, but he refused."

She looked at each one of them in turn before finally settling her gaze back on Donnie. "Have you found out what's on that drive yet?"

"What if I have?"

"Because they plan on blowing that plane up, and while everyone is going crazy thinking it's a terrorist attack, they're going to be moving weapons on the other side of the airport. There's a shipment of surface-to-air missiles headed for South America. Purchased by members of al-Qaeda."

Donnie stiffened in an attempt not to stagger backwards at the enormity of what she was saying. *If* what she was saying were true.

"And I should believe you? Why?"

She hunched down in her coat, kicking at the snow. "I tried to warn you before all this started. I had to be careful Archie didn't catch on, or I'd be dead right now. I'm not your enemy, Donnie. I know you don't have a reason in the world to trust me, but I'm telling you the truth. I just want this madman who hired Archie stopped before they get an opportunity to pull off another attack somewhere."

"I believe her," Zoe interjected. "Just in case it matters."

Donnie didn't reply as he studied Kitty for himself. "Why couldn't you just tell me this one morning at church? Archie wasn't there. He wouldn't have known."

Kitty smiled a little. "And you would have called in the Feds, and I would have been taken into custody, and Archie would have known."

"Why was he hired to kill the judges? What did they have to do with anything?"

"One of the judges has been suspicious of this guy. The one pulling all the strings. Archie said he had been talking to the other judges. Word got out. This man is one very bad character, Donnie. He doesn't care who he kills. You get in his way, and you're dead."

Donnie rubbed his face, mulling it all over and trying to sort it out. "What are you looking to accomplish?"

"I'm going to stop this guy. You know, I may not be the most upright, moral person in the world, but this is my country, too. I don't like people messing with it." She took one step toward him. "Archie taught me well. I have one of his sniper rifles. I'm going to take this guy out."

Donnie shook his head. "No. You can't do that, Kitty. It's murder."

"What he's going to do is mass murder!"

"Then we arrest him. He goes to trial. He goes to jail."

"Arrest him!" She threw her hands in the air. "Who? You? With what backup? You really think anyone is going to help you? You tell anyone about this, and you're dead, too."

"Kitty, I appreciate what you're saying, but you can't just go shoot a guy because he's breaking the law. Leave this to law enforcement."

"Donnie, I know you're one of the good guys, but you're

not hearing me." She turned to JJ, eyeing him critically. "You. You know how the world works. Tell him. Tell him he can't trust the Feds."

JJ returned her gaze, and for a long moment, it almost looked like a battle of wills to see who would back down first. But then JJ turned to Donnie and jerked his head in Katy's direction. "She's right. We already have our suspicions about Mann. So whom do we go to?"

"We do it ourselves," Zoe offered. "FBI. State police detective. You are law enforcement. Bring him down. Arrest him. Let the press know you've arrested him so no one can make it disappear. Or us."

Donnie folded his arms across his chest. "In case you have all forgotten, my wife is out here somewhere, buried alive and fighting for her life. We can't be looking for her and taking down the general at the same time. We have to find Lisbeth."

"And that plane is coming in tomorrow at Andrews. At quarter after twelve, that plane is going to land, and by the time the wheels stop rolling, it's going sky-high. Everyone on that plane is going to die." Kitty's desperation was written all over her face, digging dark circles under her eyes and bracketing her mouth as she frowned. "You save one life. . .or you save many."

JJ lifted a hand, stepping in to take control of the conversation. "Kitty, do you have any idea at all where Rick might have taken Lisbeth? Did he own any property out here somewhere that we wouldn't know about?"

"I don't know. He didn't like sharing too much with anyone. Including me. When I found out about this thing with selling our weapons to our enemy, I started digging, but I didn't find much. I know he grew up in this area, but that's all I know."

"What are you thinking, JJ?" Zoe asked.

"I'm thinking you and Kitty find Lisbeth. Donnie and I go after General Rupert."

Kitty shook her head. "It's not that I'm not willing to go find Lisbeth. I want her found alive as much as you do, but I can't just go parading around town with Zoe. In case it slipped your notice, I escaped from the Feds. They're looking for me."

"Well, you can't just hide out here in the woods. Come on back with us. The last place the Feds would think to look for you is at my place." Donnie dug into his eyes with the heels of his hands. "At least you can have a hot shower, a warm bed, and some food. We can figure out what we're going to do. We're just wasting time standing here freezing in the woods."

"You're a Fed." Kitty's voice softened. "Doesn't it go against your oath or something to harbor a fugitive?"

"Have you committed a crime? Did you shoot someone? Murder someone? Were you the one who abducted Lisbeth?"

Kitty shook her head, then reached up and pulled her cap down tighter over her hair. "No. I observed, took notes, gave them to Archie, but I've never done anything you could call illegal."

"Then you're not a fugitive, and I'm not harboring you. I'm protecting you from people who want to use you. Or worse."

◆　◆　◆

Justin's hands were shaking as he dialed nine-one-one. He had to do this. He had to do this.

"Emergency. How can I help you?"

"That woman who is missing? Lisbeth Bevere. A man buried her out here in the woods. She said to call you and tell you to tell her husband she's alive and for you to come dig her up."

"Can I have your name please?"

"She said I didn't have to give it to you. You're just supposed to tell her husband that she's in the woods near Hamilton Avenue Park. The one near the old shoe factory. There's a tree fort right near where she's buried. And tell him—"

"Can I have your address, please?"

"No," he insisted and then rushed breathlessly through his message again, trying not to trip over his words as he rushed to get them all out. "Just tell him to come help her. She's cold, and she says it's getting hard to breathe. You have to hurry and help her, or she's gonna die."

He slammed the phone down and stared at it. He'd done it. It was too late to take it back, and truthfully, he didn't want to. It felt good to know that help was coming for Lisbeth.

He zipped up his coat and darted back out the door.

chapter 15

Neil Lagasse felt sick to his stomach. The further he dug into his ex-partner's life and activities, the worse he felt. All the pieces were starting to fall into place. Rick had been on stakeout with him when el-Hajid had escaped. It had been Rick who helped el-Hajid escape, letting Neil take the fall for it.

The morning Jamal had called to say he had discovered where el-Hajid was hiding, Rick had claimed to have a dentist's appointment. There had been no dentist. Rick had slipped away and murdered Jamal before he could talk.

The day Lisbeth Bevere had been abducted, Rick had taken a long lunch break to go to the doctor. There had been no doctor's appointment. He'd walked out of the office, abducted Lisbeth Bevere, and returned to work as cool as a cucumber.

And he had been one cool customer.

The whole time he'd been asking for Bevere's file on Archie Kemp, he'd merely been checking to see how much Bevere had on him.

What better way to foil an investigation than to be looking

over the shoulders of the ones investigating you.

Neil combed his fingers through his hair, blowing out a heavy breath. The search of Rick's house had uncovered three handguns, one with a scope; two hunting rifles; and three sniper rifles, all mounted with high-powered scopes; money; passports and identification in four different names; and bank account records from the Caymans.

From the amount of money in the account, Rick had been at this a long time.

So far, he hadn't been able to locate any property in Rick's name. Obviously, Rick didn't plan on staying in the country or didn't want to be tied to property if he had to leave quickly. The house he and Kitty shared was rented. The cars were leased. The old van was paid for but was in Kitty's name.

Ah, Kitty. What a little surprise she'd turned out to be. The two agents responsible for babysitting her were probably still feeling the sting of Mann's wrath when she gave them the slip. Neil had to laugh. The key she'd given them had been to a locker at the airport. All they'd found in it had been clothes, wigs, and more fake identification.

The one thing they hadn't found was the rifle used to kill the judge.

Somewhere out there, Rick had another hiding place. And who knew what all they'd find when they uncovered it.

◆　　◆　　◆

Lisbeth clenched and unclenched her fists, fighting the urge to fall asleep. Breathing was more and more labored as she fought for air. If she could only lift her mouth high enough to suck air through the pipe, but she'd already wasted too much time trying that and failing.

Stay awake. Stay alive.

Do You remember when I wanted to grow up and be a singer? How You must have laughed at me, prancing around the house with the vacuum cleaner cord, pretending it was a microphone, singing bad enough to make the dog hide. Sometimes, I miss those days, Lord. Mom making dinner in the kitchen, and the smells filling the little house on Livingston Street. Dad out in the garage, puttering around with something until dinner was ready.

Life was so simple back then. I just thought it was complicated. Acne before a big date. A boy I liked who never asked me out. A lousy grade after I studied so hard. Not making cheerleader tryouts. Having to be home by ten or I'd be grounded.

Lisbeth choked out a little sob. *I want to go home, Father. I want to go home and call my mother and tell her that I really do appreciate all the love and discipline she gave me over the years. I want to tell my dad that his jokes really were funny, but it was considered uncool to laugh at your old man. And I want to tell Maureen that I really thought she should have been homecoming queen. She was always so much prettier than Janette Marlow.*

She blinked at the tears. *I want to go home and hold my son in my arms, watch him sleep, wrap his little fingers around mine, savor that sweet baby smell of his. I love the way his little mouth is still puckering long after the bottle is finished and taken away and he's fast asleep.*

I want to take a walk with Mandy and listen to her explain to me how the world works through her eyes, watch her skip with enthusiasm at the sight of a puppy, and watch in fascination as a bird soars through the sky.

And Father, I want to tell my husband one more time that he is the most remarkable man I've ever met and how I always felt blessed to be loved by him.

Her eyes drifted closed, too heavy to hold open. *Lord, I wanted to bring this child I'm carrying into the world and show him or her how wonderful You are.*

"Lisbeth!"

"Mmm?"

"Lisbeth! Wake up! The police are coming!"

She could hear the voice calling her, but she just wanted to pull the covers over her head and go back to sleep.

The pinging noise annoyed her. "Go 'way," she mumbled.

"Lisbeth, you have to wake up! The police are coming. Do you hear me? I called the police."

Justin's words finally penetrated her dreams, pulling her reluctantly back.

"Lisbeth!"

He sounded terrified, screaming down the pipe at her.

"Yeah. Yeah, I'm here." She tried to shift, hoping to find a more comfortable position. Another waste of time. Everything ached, and she felt weak, dizzy.

"Did you hear me? The police are coming, okay? I called them."

Thank You, God. "I hear you, Justin. Thank you!"

They were coming.

She just had to hold on a little longer. The police were coming, and she was going to get out of this alive.

❖   ❖   ❖

Dispatcher Irene Dowells handed the call report to her supervisor. "Another call about the missing Bevere woman. This one sounded like a kid."

Sergeant Pallitto glanced over the report and handed it back to her. "Go ahead and fax it over to the FBI office. It's probably another crank call, but we have orders to fax everything in."

"You want me to dispatch a unit to the scene?"

Pallitto shook his head. "Not for an obvious crank call. Let the Feds follow up on it."

◆　◆　◆

Zoe rocked her foot as she talked to Daria on the phone. "She's just a kid, Daria. And a sweet one at that. I can't even imagine having the strength she has if I were in her shoes."

She flashed JJ a smile—*thank you*—as he set a glass of soda down in front of her. Wrapping her hand around it, she watched Lisbeth's mother chop vegetables for a soup or stew as she listened to Daria complain about Erin.

"I'm sorry she hurt your feelings. So, you're getting out of the hospital tomorrow?"

Mandy ran through the kitchen, clutching a bear and giggling as her grandfather chased her, always staying within inches of catching her.

A buzzer went off, and Jane picked up a pot holder and opened the oven door. The tantalizing smell of chocolate chip cookies exploded into the room.

"No, we haven't found her yet, but we're getting close. The police just dropped off another stack of leads from the one-eight-hundred number, so JJ and I are going through those as we speak."

JJ looked up at her from across the table and smiled as he

placed another lead sheet in the discard pile.

"Okay, sweetie. I'll talk to you tomorrow or the day after."

Zoe closed the cell phone, set it on the table, and headed over to the counter where Jane was lifting cookies from the pan and transferring them to a cooling rack.

"Go ahead and take one," she said. "I made them to be eaten."

"I want one, too," JJ piped up as he read another lead, rubbing his eyes. "How's Daria?"

Zoe snagged a couple cookies, dropped one off in front of JJ, and picked up a stack of leads to work on. "She and Erin met, and Erin came down hard on her for feeling sorry for herself; so now Daria doesn't want the child anywhere near her, and Erin is refusing to visit Daria anymore."

"She'll get over it."

"Which one?" Zoe laughed.

"Gotta go for the hard questions, don't you?"

Zoe kissed the top of his head. "How's Donnie doing?"

"He's got Warthog tracking the general's finances. He wants to talk to a judge about a warrant, but Kitty is still adamant that if he tries to go that route, the general will be tipped off and escape. Or kill us." He glanced at another sheet and discounted it as a case of mistaken identity.

"As much as I hate to admit it, she's probably right."

"You know Donnie. By the book all the way."

Zoe eased down into her chair. "But he could take the general into custody and then go for the warrant."

"Arrested in the act?" JJ looked skeptical. "And what are we going to catch him doing? Neglecting to recycle?"

"Let's follow him going somewhere, do a little road rage tailgating, and when he speeds up, we get him for reckless driving and speeding." Zoe took a bite out of her cookie.

"You are dangerous, woman."

Donnie stepped into the room with a wide smile. "We got him."

Zoe set her cookie down and brushed the crumbs from her fingers. "How?"

"We found his bank account in the islands. We found cell phone records to and from Rick Harrelson. And we found cell phone records to a mosque in Detroit that just happens to be under investigation for harboring terrorists." He pulled out a chair and sat down. "All that, along with Kitty's testimony of the general's call to Rick, hiring him to kill the judges. . .and we got him."

"But I thought Kitty wasn't aware of the name of the man who called Rick?" JJ picked up his glass.

Donnie lifted his shoulders in a slight shrug, rolling his eyes up to stare at the ceiling. "She just told me that it was General Rupert."

JJ laughed. "So much for by-the-book, straight-arrow Bevere. So Kitty is going along with the idea of going to a judge for a warrant?"

Zoe reached for another cookie. "Where is Kitty?"

"She's helping Warthog." Donnie reached over, broke off a piece of Zoe's cookie, and popped it in his mouth. "I reminded her that the general put a contract out on Judge Ronald Williamson. How can we not trust him?"

"Good point," Zoe responded.

JJ folded his arms on the table and leaned forward. "So, what's the plan?"

"I'm going to see Judge Williamson about a warrant. You guys can stay on the leads. Warthog is going to keep working on finding whatever he can on the general. The more we find, the more nails we put into his coffin. When I get back, we regroup and take it from there." Donnie stood up. "Jack called. He's been trying to join us, but Mann has him running in circles at the office, obviously trying to cut down on our access to information and keep us out of the loop."

Zoe squared the reports in front of her. "We'll make do without Mann's help, but heaven help him if I find out he was in on this with the general."

◆ ◆ ◆

Donnie was barely five minutes from his house when he knew he had a tail. The question was, who put them there? Mann? The general? Someone else?

Well, if they wanted to play, he'd play. But he was going to change the rules a bit. He pulled out his cell phone and called JJ. "I got a tail. I need you to help me shake them. Ask Mack if you can borrow his car. Meet me at the Wal-Mart on Dale Highway. I'll be inside the store in the men's department. Keep an eye out for a tail on you, too."

He moved into the left lane, pulled a U-turn, and zipped into the Wal-Mart parking lot. Parking the car as close to the front door as he could, he took his time, sauntering into the store as if he had nothing more on his mind than shopping.

As soon as he was in the store, he ducked into the café and slipped into a booth, keeping his head down as he watched the door. Sure enough, two men wearing dark suits came hurrying in, their eyes going everywhere at once, obviously hoping to spot him.

They conferred for a moment at the cart corral and then

split up—one heading for the pharmacy department, the other heading for the back of the store.

Donnie slipped out of the booth and ducked into the men's department where he picked up a green and black ball cap, a green jacket, and a black wool neck scarf. He darted over to the cashier, paid for everything, and put it all on. Then he wandered back over to the men's department and kept an eye out for his escort as he waited for JJ.

But it wasn't JJ who showed up a few minutes later. It was his father-in-law, sporting a big smile and a wide-eyed look that said Mack was having the time of his life playing spy. "Car is parked at the curb. Out the door, go right." They exchanged car keys.

"Be careful," Mack hissed as Donnie started off. Shaking his head and smiling, Donnie left the store, jumped into Mack's car, and drove away.

His vigilance didn't ease up after leaving Wal-Mart. He kept a sharp eye out to make sure he hadn't picked up another tail, but he finally rolled the tension out of his shoulders as he pulled off the highway fifteen minutes later.

Judge Williamson was in court when he arrived, so after telling his assistant that he needed to see the judge, Donnie slipped into the back of the courtroom to wait.

Judge Williamson was in his midsixties, but with the bright smile and good bone structure, not to mention the full head of thick hair that resisted gray everywhere but his temples, he didn't look more than fifty. He had a reputation for being a hard-liner, taking crime very seriously, and those who committed those crimes were usually sentenced harshly if they were unfortunate enough to appear in his courtroom.

Finally, court was adjourned for the day, and Judge

Williamson left the room. Donnie hurried out of the courtroom and down the hall to the judge's chambers. With any luck, he'd have his warrant and be on his way home before five.

◆　◆　◆

Jane peered down at the lead report in her hand, her reading glasses perched at the end of her nose. After Mack had returned home all excited about helping Donnie escape his tail, she'd gotten the bug to help by doing something more than cooking, cleaning, and taking care of the children.

She'd set Cody in his battery-operated swing, gave him a little stuffed animal, and parked him next to the kitchen table so she could keep an eye on him while helping JJ and Zoe go through the leads.

It was tedious, boring work with moments of humor as the occasional lead would be so outrageous, it was shared around the table for a little bout of laughter. But even those were coming few and far between.

She glanced over at Zoe and then dropped her eyes. She wasn't sure what it was about the woman who made her nervous. She seemed nice enough. Okay, maybe she did know what was bothering her, and she might as well just get it off her chest.

"So, Zoe. I understand that you know about things happening before they actually happen?" Jane locked eyes with Zoe's and waited.

"I'm not sure what you mean. I don't know about things before they happen in any kind of detail. Sometimes the Lord lets me know that something bad is about to happen to someone, and He has me pray for them, but I don't know who or what."

"And just how does the Lord let you know? I mean, does He just whisper in your ear or give you a vision?" There was an edge to her voice she didn't try to soften.

Zoe picked up on it—Jane could see it in her eyes—but she didn't become flustered. Instead, Zoe almost appeared to wrap herself in a blanket of calm peace that irritated Jane. And then Zoe's gaze seemed to pierce right through Jane—as if Zoe could see Jane's soul. As if she could see the discomfort there.

"When your girls were young, did you ever have that sudden feeling that one of them was in trouble or hurt or needed you; and you went to check on them, and sure enough, there was a problem?"

Jane nodded reluctantly, feeling as though she were being drawn into a subtle trap of her own making. She looked for some indication of hostility, but the expression in Zoe's clear green eyes was warm and understanding.

"How did you know your child needed you?"

Jane thought for a moment. "Instinct, I suppose. I don't know. Maybe a mother's bond with her child."

"It works the same way with me. An instinct breathed into me by the Holy Spirit. The heavenly Father's bond with His child. I don't hear voices on the wind or anything weird or spooky like that. It's just a sudden knowing, that's all."

Jane could feel the guilt all the way down to the tips of her Birkenstocks. "I'm sorry. I didn't mean to make it sound like I thought you were a witch or something."

"You had your doubts, but that's okay. I'm not offended. We are all raised with certain views and understandings, and when someone comes along with a belief or a worldview that challenges ours, we can become a little defensive."

"I'll say," JJ muttered from across the table.

Zoe smiled at him and then turned back to Jane. "As long as we both love the same Jesus and are saved by the same blood shed on Calvary, and as long as we worship the same Father, Lord, and Creator, and as long we both read the same Word, we are sisters.

"One thing I've learned about the Lord in my relatively short walk with Him is that He loves to challenge our comfort zones from time to time and force us to see Him from a different perspective. Doesn't mean we're going to abandon our theology or suddenly run off and join some weird cult. It just means God is bigger than our conceptions, and He likes to remind us of that sometimes."

Jane dropped her hands to her lap and linked her fingers together as she transferred her thoughts to words. "I suppose you did challenge me. I have a problem with people running around saying that God told them this and God told them that. I never hear God talking to me like that."

"Sure you do. You just don't phrase it the way some people do. Just because someone said that God talked to them doesn't mean that it was some audible voice or a whisper in the ear. He speaks through His Word. He speaks through what we call instinct. He speaks through our pastors and family and friends. He isn't limited. His Word says His sheep know His voice, which means He speaks to us. It's up to us to hear with our spirits and our hearts and understand the many ways He communicates."

"Oh." She emitted a little, embarrassed laugh. "I see what you're saying. I apologize."

"Nothing to apologize for. You had questions in your mind, and those deserved answers."

Jane was saved from any further discomfort by the doorbell. She jumped gratefully to her feet. "I'll get it."

◆　　◆　　◆

As Jane left to answer the door, JJ rose from the table and headed for the pitcher of iced tea on the counter. "You know what scares me?"

"What's that?"

"What you just said there. . .it actually made sense to me."

Zoe laughed. "Watch out, Josiah. You're starting to sound like a Christian."

"Now why doesn't that scare me the way it used to?"

Jane returned to the room, Jack Fleming on her heels. "Hey. What's going on?"

"Jack! We thought you couldn't join us." JJ shook Jack's hand and then returned to his seat, sipping his tea, his attention remaining on Jack.

Jack shrugged out of his coat and thanked Jane when she took it from him to hang up. He pulled out a chair next to JJ and sat down. "I told Mann I had to go out and follow up some lead. Luckily he was real busy at the time and wasn't paying close attention."

"Well, we're certainly glad you're here. Is anything happening there we should know about?"

Jack shook his head. "Everyone is running around like puppies at feeding time, tripping all over each other, and themselves, too. Mann seems to have a handle on it all, but I don't think anyone else does."

The basement door opened, and Kitty stepped through, her hands full of glasses and plates. She froze, her eyes going wide as they jerked from Jack to JJ to Zoe and back to Jack.

"It's okay, Kitty," JJ reassured her.

Even so, she sidled over to the sink and set everything down carefully, shooting glances at Jack over her shoulder as if expecting him to jump up and handcuff her at any moment.

"She's here?" Jack stared at her. "Everyone's ripping the area apart and looking for her, and she's here?" He turned to JJ. "Please tell me you didn't help her escape."

"No, we didn't help her escape. And you haven't seen her."

Jack threw both hands up. "I haven't seen her." Then he laughed. "Oh, this is rich. No one would ever expect to find her here, that's for sure."

"That's the idea." Zoe lifted her glass. "Want something?"

Jack shook his head. "Thanks, but no. So what is she doing here?"

"Helping us bring down a very important criminal." JJ looked over at Kitty. "Come on. Sit. Join us. Jack won't bite. I promise."

Kitty didn't seem too sure as she eased over next to Zoe and slid into a chair.

Jack stared at her for a moment and then shook his head. "You do realize that when all this is over, they are going to want to question you from now until the cows come home, and then some?"

Kitty shrugged. "Like I care what they want."

JJ smiled, holding back the urge to give her a little high-five slap on the hand. Instead, he turned everyone's focus back to Jack. "So is Mann saying anything at all about Donnie or Lisbeth?"

"He hasn't buried you, if that's what you think. He has Neil Lagasse digging into Rick's past in hopes of finding something that might lead to Lisbeth's whereabouts. Corbett has orders that as soon as leads come in from around the area, they are to be either faxed over or brought over. He's got four agents up in the Braddock Heights area talking to people to see if anyone saw Rick or that van in the area on Wednesday night."

"Then why is he shutting us out of this?" Zoe asked.

"I wish I had an answer for you, but I don't." Jack looked around. "Where is Donnie anyway? His car is out front, so I thought he was here."

"He'll be back anytime. Actually, I expected him back before now. He's just out on an errand."

Jack leaned back in his chair, his mouth twitching with a suppressed smile. "I see. Not sure if you can trust me, either?"

"It's not that," JJ assured him. "It's just that the less you know, the less you'll have to answer for later."

"You've got a line on this, don't you?" He slapped his thigh. "Son of a gun, you guys are good. Then again, I always knew Donnie had a nose for the truth unlike any partner I've ever had."

"You know nothing, okay?"

Jack leaned forward. "I don't yet, but let me tell you this. . . regardless of what I may have to answer for later, I'm in this with you all the way. Donnie is my partner, and I have a lot of respect for him. I want his wife found alive, and I want the man responsible for ordering her abduction in custody."

"Good." Donnie stepped into the room and tossed a folded document down in front of JJ. "Glad to have you with us, Jack. How did you give Mann the slip?"

JJ knew what it was, but he picked it up and read it anyway. Sure enough, Donnie had come through. They had a warrant for General Rupert.

"Told him I had a lead I had to go check out." Jack stood up and slapped Donnie on the arm.

JJ folded the warrant and set it aside. He was starting to get worried for Lisbeth. She'd been in the ground nearing on twenty hours. From what Kitty told him about the pipe Rick installed, it was only about an inch-and-a-half PVC. Not nearly wide enough. By now, she was not only cold, hungry, and afraid, she was slowly running out of air. Carbon dioxide was slowly building up, and the oxygen levels were dropping. She'd be getting sleepy and lethargic. Then she would begin to slowly suffocate. And this was the part of the torture Rick had been planning on. He hadn't cut her oxygen levels off completely. No, he was stretching this out for her so she'd suffer that much longer.

It was a good thing he was already dead because JJ wanted to inflict just enough pain on the man to make him wish he were dead.

chapter 16

JJ turned to Donnie. "Who do you know in the press who can cover Rupert's arrest and make sure they get it on camera? Once he goes into custody, I don't want someone thinking they can make all this disappear and slip him out the back door."

Donnie whipped out his cell phone. "I know just the man. Works for Fox and he's good. Let me call him."

JJ ran everything through his mind again, double-checking every detail. His concern now was stopping the bombing of the plane in the morning. With any luck, Rupert would cooperate once he was in custody and give up whoever was going to do the actual bombing.

His thoughts abruptly shifted when Zoe came back into the room, buttoning her coat. "Where are you going?"

"With you." She pulled her gloves out of the pockets. "You're just going to arrest the general, not run into the middle of a bank robbery, so don't give me that look."

"You'd be better off staying here and going through leads." JJ looked to Jack and Donnie for a little backup.

Jack cleared his throat. "She might come in handy if the general's wife doesn't take any of this kindly."

Donnie didn't say anything, just kept his eyes downcast while patting his pockets like he was looking for his keys. *The coward.* JJ knew when he was beat, and this was another one of those times.

"Fine, but I don't want you anywhere near the general when we arrest him."

"No problem," Zoe responded, patting his cheek lightly. "You he-men take care of the rough stuff while we women keep the hearth warm for you."

"That's not what this is about."

"This is exactly what it's always about. You hate for me to be anywhere near danger, and you do everything you can to keep me away from the action."

JJ hissed as he cradled her face in his hands. "I want you to be safe. Does that make me a bad guy? I happen to care whether you end up hurt or killed."

"No." Zoe smiled up at him, and he felt it right down to his toes. "It's one of the things I love about you, but it's still aggravating when you treat me like some fragile piece of glass that might get broken in the scuffle. I'm a big girl, and I've gone a few rounds in this business."

"And nearly been killed a few times," he reminded her.

"But I'm still here, aren't I?"

"Kids. Kids." Donnie waved the warrant in front of them. "Can we argue about this later?"

"We're not arguing," Zoe assured him. "We do this all the time. Something of a ritual."

"Well, let's cut it short or finish it in the car."

◆ ◆ ◆

Special Agent in Charge Jim Mann paced his office, stopping from time to time to stare out the window. Not that there was much to see out there except more buildings and a parking lot, but he wouldn't have noticed if a parade of elephants was marching by.

Everything was crashing in, and if he didn't handle this with the utmost delicacy, it could explode in his face. It was one of the few times in his life that he felt as though he were walking a tightrope without a net. And the wind had just picked up, swaying the tightrope beneath him.

He'd be lucky to get through this with everything intact.

There was no doubt in his mind that Bevere suspected he knew more than he was telling, but hopefully, he'd neutralized Bevere sufficiently.

One never knew with Bevere. He was one of the best agents Mann had ever come across. It wasn't easy to get any-thing past him, but even if Bevere did suspect something, he was too devoted to go behind his boss's back. One thing he could always count on. . .Bevere's sense of honor.

He regretted Lisbeth's death. She hadn't deserved death, and especially not the one she got, but some things are more important than the loss of one civilian. And this was one of those cases.

Money, greed, power, and politics. Combined, it was a force that could level everything in its path. And this was one of those times.

Shoving his hands down into his pockets, he heaved a heavy sigh. *Ah, Rupert, what a mess you've gotten us into.*

◆ ◆ ◆

JJ knew from the vague look in Zoe's eyes that she was praying and no longer aware of him at all. He turned his attention back to the road, swallowing what he was about to say, giving her the silence she needed.

Lord, this is me. You know I'm not particularly good at this yet, but I did want to ask You to protect Lisbeth until we find her and help us get to her in time. She's a real nice lady, and her family really needs her.

He broke his prayer off as Jack and Donnie, driving the car in front of them, moved into the right lane and prepared to exit. JJ flipped on the blinker.

Earlier, Jane had asked him a simple question before leading them all into prayer. "Are you a Christian, JJ?" At the time, he'd merely nodded and bowed his head. Now the question tugged at his heart.

JJ looked in the rearview mirror, the side mirrors, and the rearview again, and then eased into the right lane. Was he? He went to church, but he knew that didn't make him a Christian. He believed in God, but that didn't make him one either. So, what would? He'd finally come to see that no matter how good a man he thought himself to be, he still had sin. Anger, hate, bitterness. It might not rival murder, but it was still sin. And if he was a sinner, then he needed Jesus to take over and change him. So, yeah. He was. He wanted to be. And that was as stunning a revelation as realizing that he wanted to spend the rest of his life with Zoe.

JJ followed Donnie as he made a left at the end of the exit ramp.

"Okay, when we get there, you stay in the car and make

sure no one else shows up and takes us by surprise. Hopefully, we'll be taking Rupert by surprise, and it will go down quick and easy."

JJ glanced over at Zoe, surprised that she wasn't jumping in with the usual outrage and indignation at being told to stay behind.

"Okay, Zoe?"

"Sure. You have handcuffs, right?" Zoe turned in her seat. "In all this rush, I didn't think to make sure anyone brought a pair."

"We have them."

She merely nodded, but there was a twinkle in her eyes that worried him.

"Zoe, I'm really serious this time. I want you to stay in the car."

"I hear you." She gave him a pat on the arm that did nothing to alleviate his worry. The woman attracted danger like a kid attracted dirt.

"I know you hear me. That's not the question."

The woman practically rolled her eyes at him. "I said I would remain with the car, and I will remain with the car. I'm not going to go rushing in and put myself in danger. I'll leave that to you he-man law enforcement junkies."

"That's not—"

Laughing, she reached over across the console and kissed his cheek. "You are too easy, Josiah."

◆　　◆　　◆

The general's Williamsburg home was nestled on a quiet residential street along with numerous other pricey homes on one- and two-acre lots. The two-story stone colonial was graced with a wide porch, a circular driveway, and landscaping as dignified as the house it framed.

JJ checked his weapon after shutting off the engine. As he opened his car door, he looked over at Zoe. Surprise. She was actually staying put. "You okay?"

Her smile told him that she understood the depths of his question. "I just feel the need to pray for Lisbeth. You don't need me, and she does."

JJ nodded and climbed out of the car. He, Donnie, and Jack stepped up to the front door and rang the bell. A few minutes later, a stately woman in silk and pearls opened the door. "Yes?"

Donnie flashed his badge. "We need to speak to General Rupert."

"Oh! Of course. Jim Mann must have sent you. He called just a bit ago. Please. Come in."

Donnie looked over at JJ and Jack as they stepped into the house and the door was closed behind them. JJ didn't need an interpreter. Mann had called the general. The question now was, were they expected? Had Mann found out about the war-rant somehow?

The woman, who introduced herself as Martha Rupert, led them into the study where the general was on the phone. "Roger, these gentlemen are here to see you." She then disap-peared from the room, closing the door behind her.

General Rupert stared at them as he listened to whomever he was talking to. Finally he said, "Let me call you back." He hung up the phone.

"Can I help you gentlemen?"

Donnie held up his badge again. "Donnie Bevere, FBI.

And with me are Jack Fleming, FBI, and Lieutenant Johnson, a detective from the police department. I have a warrant here for your arrest."

JJ wanted to flinch at the way Donnie didn't bother to mention *which* police department.

Rupert's face slowly turned red as he stood up. "I don't know who you think you are, but you obviously don't know who I am."

"General Roger Rupert. And like my partner said, we have a warrant here for your arrest." Jack pulled out the handcuffs as he recited the charges.

"Stop right there." Rupert pointed his finger at Jack. "You can't just come in here and arrest me for anything! I'll have your badge by midnight. I'm calling Jim Mann. You do know who he is, don't you?"

"It won't do you any good, General. The warrant is signed by the judge. This is all legal and airtight. Your friendship with Mann won't be any help to you." Donnie placed both hands on the edge of the desk and leaned forward, his eyes alight with temper. "Now tell me where my wife is."

Rupert lifted his chin, arrogantly staring them all down. "I have no idea what you're talking about. I'm calling my attorney. I'll have you out of this house in a matter of minutes."

As he picked up the phone, Jack reached down and yanked the wire out of the wall. "Oops."

"Tell me where my wife is, or so help me, you're going to need a doctor before you ever need an attorney."

Seeing Donnie's face flushed with anger, JJ quietly placed a hand on his shoulder. "Look, Rupert. We know all about your little side business with the weapons. And while that will send you away for a very long time, there's a woman out there who's going to die if we don't find her. Now. Where is Lisbeth Bevere buried?"

Rupert's arrogance shimmered around him as he stared JJ down. "I have no idea what—"

Jack grabbed Rupert by the front of his lapels and yanked him forward. "You hired Harrelson to kill her."

Rupert, nearly standing on his toes an inch from Jack's face, reached up and dislodged Jack's hands. Then he brushed his lapels straight and stepped back. "You people have no idea what you're stepping in the middle of. You're going to ruin everything."

JJ shook his head. "He's not going to tell us anything. Let's take him in. Maybe a few hours in a cell with Bubba will loosen his tongue."

"Sounds good to me." Jack jingled the handcuffs. "Shall we?"

Rupert squared his shoulders. "At least let me walk out of my own home with dignity. I will come peaceably. I'm sure this misunderstanding will be straightened out when we get to Mann's office."

Jack stepped forward. "I'll need to check you for weapons."

Rupert's lip curled in distaste, but he held his arms out and let Jack pat him down.

Jack nodded to Donnie and backed up, giving the general room to walk around him to the door.

"I'll need my coat," Rupert said as they headed for the front door. "And to tell my wife I have to go out for a little while."

His wife saved him the trouble of looking for her by appearing in the foyer as he was putting on his coat. "Going out, Roger?"

"Yes. I shouldn't be too late." He kissed her on the cheek and walked out the front door.

Outside, Zoe was standing at the car, leaning against the front fender, talking on her cell phone. She hung up as they approached her. "That was—"

Suddenly, Rupert reached out and grabbed Zoe, wrapping one arm around her neck and hauling her around in front of him, as he pulled a small pistol out from his coat pocket and aimed it at Donnie, Jack, and JJ. "Don't. I don't think you want this lovely young lady to lose her life."

JJ felt the shimmer of fear creeping up his spine and settling between his shoulders. "Don't do it, Rupert," he said quietly. "Don't make me have to kill you like a rabid dog."

Headlights flashed across the scene being played out like strobes across a dance floor. A van stopped with tires screeching, and two men jumped out, one holding a camera on his shoulder. Immediately, the light on top of the camera came on, flooding the area with brilliant illumination. Rupert flinched as it hit him in the eyes.

"You are now on live television, General." Jack tipped his head in the van's direction. "Smile for the camera."

The general bared his teeth, but it was no smile. "You fools! Do you realize what you've done?"

"Stopped a U.S. general from selling any more of our weapons to the terrorists to use against us," Donnie replied.

"And what do you think keeps this country's economy going? War! Munitions, planes, tanks, uniforms, food. All produced in factories manned by American citizens and sold by American companies."

"It wasn't the country's economy you were concerned with, General. We found the bank accounts in the islands. You were making a real nice chunk of money off this little *economic* venture of yours." Jack jerked his head at Zoe. "Let her go,

General. There's no way out of this for you."

Instead of releasing Zoe, he started dragging her backwards around the car, obviously intending to just drive away.

"Don't you understand? They're cutting our budgets and transferring our power to this new national intelligence director, weakening our military. This was the only way! If terrorists attack us, if people die, then they'll want war." His passion had him lifting Zoe to her toes as she struggled to breathe.

JJ clenched his fists, stifling the urge to jump on the general and beat him senseless. He glanced over at the reporter who was standing next to his cameraman. No help there with a distraction.

"You can't run, General! Everyone will be looking for you. There's no place you can hide."

"Oh, you are so wrong, Agent Fleming. You are so wrong."

JJ saw the flicker of red light skipping across the general's head, but before his brain could jump from concern for Zoe to identifying the red light, it was over. The blast sent General Rupert sideways, taking Zoe with him.

JJ lurched forward, managing a jump and roll over the hood of the car that he figured he'd regret later. He landed on his feet right next to Zoe. He reached down, grabbed her arm, and yanked her to her feet, immediately placing himself between the general and the woman he loved.

"I think he's dead," Zoe whispered roughly.

JJ stared at the blood seeping from the wound in the general's head and then slowly turned and pulled Zoe into his arms. "Are you okay?"

"Yeah. I figure I'll have some sore muscles tomorrow, but right now, the adrenaline is pumping too hard for me to feel anything." She wrapped her arms around him. "Who shot him?"

JJ looked back over his shoulder, staring in the direction the bullet came from. "I don't know."

chapter 17

Thursday, February 16

Fox News may have had the first jump on the other news outlets, but by the time the ambulance arrived, so had numerous other news trucks. Jack's cell phone rang while he and Donnie were talking to reporters. He stepped back into the shadows to answer it and disappeared behind a news truck. Now, finished with the reporters, Donnie and JJ were perched on the hood of JJ's Jeep, waiting for the last of the trucks to pull away so they could get out of the general's driveway.

Zoe leaned against the Jeep. Out there somewhere, Kitty was on the run. There was no doubt in her mind that Kitty had been the one who shot General Rupert. JJ had found a single shell casing on the ground. When they ran the ballistics check, something told her that it would match the ballistics on the murdered judges.

Where will you go now, Kitty?

Zoe whirled around. "The airport."

The two men looked over at her, but it was JJ who said, "What?"

"In less than five hours, that plane is going to land at

Andrews. A truckload of munitions will disappear. Kitty is on her way there to stop it."

Donnie stared at her for a moment. "What in heaven's name makes you think Kitty is on her way to anywhere?"

She pushed off the vehicle and strode over to them. "When you came out of the house with the general, Jane called to tell me that Kitty had disappeared moments after we left. I think it was Kitty who shot Rupert. And now she's on her way to the airport."

"Where's Jack?" JJ asked.

"Over there. Talking on his cell phone with Mann. Seems Mann saw Rupert's death. In living color. He isn't too happy."

Donnie slid off the hood of the Jeep. "We have to stop the bombing of that plane, and we have to stop the loading of those weapons on the other plane."

"If the terrorists saw the news like Mann did, what do you think they're going to do?" JJ asked Donnie.

"I can't say that I'm any kind of expert on terrorists, but I'd have to believe that they now wonder how much we know. As for what they're going to do—that's a good question. If they're going to hit the plane, they must want the men on that plane dead."

Zoe stepped into the conversation. "The plane with the terrorists was never the issue. It was the weapons being loaded onto that other military transport. Blowing up the plane was just a diversion. If they're smart, they're going after those weapons now, while we're sitting around planning to intercept them in the morning."

Jack came around the news truck, his face red. "Well, that was pleasant." He narrowed his eyes, looking at each of them in turn. "What's wrong?"

Donnie shook his head. "We're talking about the plan to hijack that shipment of arms in the morning. Zoe seems to think they may try to hijack tonight, to beat us to the punch."

"Mann seems to disagree. He just told me we blew his operation wide open, and he's not happy about it. He wanted the names of the other men involved in the operation, and he wanted to catch them in the act."

JJ huffed, zipping his jacket. "You believe him?"

"Not entirely. I'm more inclined to agree with you. They aren't going to let those weapons go. They're paid for. They'll go after them as quickly as possible, hoping to be long gone before that plane arrives from Gitmo."

"I'm just concerned about Kitty," Zoe said, bringing the two men back to the previous conversation. "She's going to be walking into this thing all alone. I don't know that she can handle it. She's going to be expecting one thing, and heaven knows what she'll find when she gets there."

"How does she expect to get access onto an air force base?"

Zoe rolled her eyes, folding her arms across her chest. "It's late at night; it's dark; you're a young man standing long hours on guard duty. Along comes a pretty little redhead with car trouble. Or a sprained ankle. Or—"

JJ threw a hand up. "Okay. We got it. Women are resourceful and devious."

Zoe laughed, wrapping her arms around his waist and hugging him. "We'll discuss the devious comment another time."

Jack arched an eyebrow, smirking. "Better you than me, pal."

"She's harmless. Talks big." JJ kissed the top of her head just as she punched him in the stomach. He laughed again, playfully doubling over. "Like I said. Harmless."

"I was playing nice. You won't be so lucky next time."

"No. We need to stop those weapons from being taken by terrorists. If Mann isn't going to step in and do it, then we have to." Donnie started waving at the news trucks to move faster.

As soon as Donnie came jogging back up the driveway, Jack pulled out his car keys. "I'm thinking we might call someone at the Pentagon. Tell them what's been going on. I'm sure they all know about Rupert by now. Maybe they'll clear the way for us at Andrews. . .cut through some of the military's red tape."

Donnie snagged the keys out of Jack's hand. "How about General Irby? He's Air Force, and he always appeared to be a fairly stand-up guy."

"I'm not sure he's still at the Pentagon. I vaguely remember something about him being transferred to Wright-Patterson."

"It's worth trying though." He turned to JJ. "Just follow us."

Jack grabbed his keys back. "You call. I'll drive."

It took Donnie a couple of calls before he finally reached General Irby. He then quickly briefed him on the situation. Indeed, he had heard about Rupert but didn't know all the details. Once he heard them, he assured Donnie he would call Andrews and put them on alert and let them know Donnie was on his way.

"And, General? One last favor. There's a young woman, a redhead, by the name of Kathryn Borders. She's with us but has gone ahead to scope the situation out. If she's picked up, could you let them know she's with us and not to arrest her?"

He hung up the phone. "Okay. Let's go."

◆　◆　◆

Kitty slowly scanned the airfield with her binoculars, but in spite of the landing and security lights, she was too far away, and it was too dark for her to see anything helpful.

In one of those hangars, a plane was being loaded with weapons that had been stolen, and the military personnel loading the plane probably didn't even know it. On the surface, everything would look normal. Manifests signed by all the right people would direct these weapons along normal channels, until at some point they would simply disappear in thin air.

She knew what was in those crates. Surface-to-air missiles that would be used to bring down commercial airplanes.

No way was she going to let that happen.

Okay, God. If You're up there, I could use some help here. I can't believe that the God I heard about in that church would want a plane full of everyday people on their way from one place to another to simply be blown out of the sky because of the greed of a few, and the fanatical, twisted views of a few more.

She eyed the security fence. Barbed wire, electricity, motion sensors. She was going to have to get on the base another way. Like through the front gate.

Sliding down off the hood of her car, she climbed in, tossing the binoculars on the passenger seat. Waiting to turn her lights on till she reached the main road, she backed up and drove off.

Once on the main road, she headed for the front gate. Tapping her fingernails on the steering wheel, her mind raced. If she walked in, she'd have to leave her rifle behind. There was no way to hide something that big. She had Archie's .44 with the scope, but she'd have to hope no one thought to search her.

As the main gate came into view, she eased Mack's car to

the side of the road, cutting the lights. Climbing out of the car, she leaned against the door, staring at the front gate.

Headlights suddenly hit her. She lifted her hand to block the glare in her eyes. It was a canvas-covered military truck, and it slowed down as it drew abreast of her. A young soldier leaned out the passenger window, grinning from ear to ear. "Hey, good-looking. You need help?"

Several more trucks pulled up behind him, patiently waiting.

She smiled up at him, tossing back a lock of hair. "My car broke down, but I've already called for a friend of mine to come pick me up. Thanks anyway, soldier boy."

He looked disappointed but shrugged and rolled up his window, and they began to pull away. Kitty reached in the back window and grabbed the rifle case. Then as the last truck started to roll past, she pulled the case out, ran up behind the truck, and grabbed on, jumping up on the rear bumper.

Taking a deep breath, she tossed the gun case into the back and rolled in after it, praying it wasn't going to be full of soldiers.

◆   ◆   ◆

General Carl Irby took the steps up into the plane two at a time. As soon as he was inside the plane, he nodded at the sergeant waiting at the top.

Carl Irby considered himself a patriot. With a lifetime of military service behind him, he'd seen men die and lives destroyed fighting wars that were supposed to be in defense of liberty and the country he loved.

Buckling himself in, he leaned back.

He wasn't quite so naïve anymore. He knew that some- times it was in defense of home and hearth. And sometimes it was all about political games and power strokes. He didn't have anything against power or politics, but he did have something against men who made themselves rich off the lives of young men who never realized they were just pawns on a chessboard of wealth.

He glanced out the window as the plane slowly lifted off into the night and the lights of the base behind him disap- peared in the distance.

When he saw General Rupert holding that young woman at gunpoint and then heard the news report about his involve- ment in stealing military weapons to sell to terrorists, he was stunned.

Now he was just angry.

He pulled out his phone and dialed the Pentagon. "General Irby here. Were you able to divert that flight to Pope? Yes, this is a matter of national security! I told you people that earlier. Now get that flight diverted. I do not want it landing at Andrews. You clear them to land at Pope, and you hold them there until further notice."

He snapped his phone closed. Military red tape. It could strangle you sometimes.

Unfortunately, this was going to hit the press like a firestorm—there was no getting around that. The military would get a major black eye out of this, but at least the operation would be shut down.

He leaned his head back and closed his eyes. Trusting Bevere and Fleming was easy. He'd met them five years earlier when his daughter had disappeared from her college dorm. The outcome hadn't been a good one, but Bevere and

Fleming had been relentless, finally bringing the young man to justice.

And then they attended his Christine's funeral.

If they needed his help, they would get it. Even if it meant leaving his warm bed and flying all the way to the Pentagon via Andrews Air Force Base in the middle of the night.

◆　◆　◆

Neil Lagasse sat staring at the television. Not that there was anything on it. After watching the eleven o'clock news and seeing the footage on General Rupert, he had turned it off. Ever since then, he'd been sitting there in the dark, just staring and thinking.

This was what his former partner had been involved in. Military weapons, terrorists, assassinations, national security, murder of innocent citizens.

It was mind-boggling.

And what made it all worse was that Mann didn't seem to be on top of any of this.

It had been Bevere and his friends who had grabbed the tail of the tiger and ridden it out, uncovering the operation, exposing and taking down the general, and risking their lives to do it. All without the help of the very people who should have been leading the operation. He reached under the sofa and pulled out the pack of cigarettes he had hidden there. Tapping the pack, he slid one out. After all these weeks of not smoking, he was finally going to break down and have one. If ever there was a time he needed one, it was now.

He'd no sooner lit it and taken the first puff, when Carmen seemed to appear out of nowhere, moving silently across the room, tying her robe. She stared at the cigarette in his mouth but didn't say anything. Instead, she curled up on the sofa next to him.

"Must be bad."

"It is. You saw the news." He took another hit and tapped the ashtray with the end of the cigarette. "I'm thinking about leaving the FBI."

Her eyes widened. She reached out and touched his arm. "Why? Because of Rick?"

"Rick, yes. And Mann. Do you know Bevere and Fleming had to take this on all by themselves? If they hadn't, Rick would still be out there assassinating people, and that General Rupert would still be stealing weapons and selling them to the terrorists. What does that say about us?" With jerky movements, he brought the cigarette to his lips again, inhaled, and then stubbed the cigarette out.

"It says that there was a problem with Rick and maybe with Mann, but what about everyone else? There are a lot of good people in the agency trying to do their best to bring criminals to justice. And you're one of them, Neil. I don't care what it is, whether it's local police or state police or the military or the FBI or the CIA—there are going to be bad apples in the mix, but it's the good ones, the dedicated ones, who keep things in balance."

Neil reached down and took her hand, curling his fingers in hers. "I should have been there tonight, backing Bevere up. We just didn't know what he was doing. He couldn't trust any of us enough to tell us and ask us for help."

"His partner was there for him, right?"

"Fleming? Yeah. He was there. Along with a private investigator and a police detective from upstate."

"Don't quit, Neil. Don't give the bad guys the satisfaction of thinking they ran another good man out. And if there's any way you can talk to Bevere, don't let him quit either."

Neil leaned his head back and closed his eyes. "I can't believe my own partner was in this up to his neck and I never saw it."

Carmen curled closer against him, resting her head on his shoulder. "And why would you think to look at your partner twice? He'd been with the agency longer than you. No one suspected him of being a rogue agent. No one. Don't beat yourself up over this, honey."

He was silent for awhile, lost in his thoughts, his thumb mindlessly caressing his wife's hand.

"Neil? You're a good agent. Rick double-crossed you, but he's the only one who ever has, and the only reason he could was because he was your partner. Don't quit."

He sighed heavily, lifted his head, and looked down at her. "Do you ever worry about something happening to you like it did to Lisbeth Bevere?"

"Sometimes. But not really. I can't live my life worrying about something that might or might not happen."

"How come you stopped bugging me to go to church with you?"

She raised his hand to her lips and kissed it. "Because I was *bugging* you."

Neil chuckled. "Not so much, really. You want me to go with you this Sunday?"

"Yes. I think that would be wonderful."

Contentedly, Carmen nestled into his arms. He held her as his mind drifted. There was still one loose end to tie up, and maybe he was the man to do it. He started this investigation.

Now he was going to finish it.

Assar el-Hajid.

◆　◆　◆

Donnie spotted Kitty's car sitting on the side of the road and eased up behind it. Fatigue pulled at him, slowing his movements. The few catnaps he'd managed, blanketed with the details of the case and pillowed with worry over Lisbeth, had been woefully inadequate. He rubbed his face, trying to wipe away the need to close his eyes and sleep for a month.

"I'll check it," JJ told him, opening the passenger door and climbing out.

JJ circled the car and then returned. "No sign of her."

"She's probably already managed to get on base." Donnie put the car in drive and pulled back out on the road. He spotted the front gate of the base and pulled up to the gate.

A soldier stepped out of the booth and approached Donnie's window. "Can I help you, sir?"

Donnie held up his badge. "General Irby was supposed to call ahead and clear us. Bevere and Fleming from the FBI. Also Lieutenant Johnson, detective with the Monroe County police, and Zoe Shefford with Cordette Investigations."

The soldier checked his clipboard and nodded. "Yes, sir. You have been cleared. You're expected at the colonel's office." He pointed and gave directions. "Someone will be waiting to escort you to the colonel."

"Thanks." Donnie waited until the gate was lifted and then drove through. "Now. Where is Kitty?"

"Knowing her, she's already down by whatever hangar is holding those weapons, waiting to stop them from being loaded on that plane," Zoe said.

Jack leaned over the seat. "Let's hope we get there before she starts shooting up the place."

◆ ◆ ◆

Kitty slipped out of the truck as soon as it slowed down inside the base. Dropping to the ground, she darted into the shadows and slipped behind the building. The place was huge. Buildings everywhere. How in heaven's name was she supposed to find the right hangar?

She set the gun case down and opened it. She took the rifle out and slid the strap over her shoulder. Then she closed the case and stood up. It would be far easier moving in the shadows without carrying that big case. Now she just needed to hide the case. It wouldn't do for someone to stumble across it and figure out it didn't belong here on the base, setting off alarms.

She found a stack of fifty-gallon drums and slid it behind them, hoping no one planned on moving them before she returned.

If she returned.

Taking a deep breath, she stepped on the fear that was slowly climbing up her spine. What in heaven's name ever made her think she could pull this off?

Because there was no one else to do it.

Moving from building to building, she worked her way down from one hangar to another, peeking in windows, checking the locks on doors.

Occasionally, a jeep would drive by, and she would duck down into the shadows, holding her breath; but so far, she hadn't been detected.

As she was getting ready to dart over to the next hangar, she saw lights going on two hangars down. Then another jeep pulled up, parking next to the one that was already there.

Bingo. Activity meant possibility.

Skipping the next hangar, she quickly made her way toward the activity. *I'm coming for you suckers. Beware.*

But they didn't seem aware at all as a radio came on and music began to blare.

Kitty bent over, running up to the hangar, staying low until she was under one of the windows. Then she slowly straightened up and glanced inside. Six men, all in uniform, were joking around, laughing, and loading long boxes onto a truck.

She ducked back down. A truck? They were supposed to be going out on a plane. They must have heard about Rupert and quickly changed their plans.

Were all the men inside in on it, or were some of them just innocent soldiers loading up what they thought to be a legitimate shipment?

She didn't want to kill innocent men.

But how was she going to know which ones were which?

Raising her head, she peeked in the window again, watching each man carefully, trying to see if one of them appeared guilty or nervous. A stupid thing to hope for, but it was better than rushing in and shooting everyone, good and bad.

The sound of truck engines interrupted her observations. Ducking down, she darted over to one of the jeeps and slid down. The truck pulled up, and two men jumped out, rushing into the building.

Kitty lifted her head a little and saw the men were wearing MP badges. Ah, the cavalry had arrived. Someone had clued the military in on this little operation. As soon as the door closed behind them, she jogged back over to the window.

Pressed flat against the building, she took a deep breath and then turned her head to look in.

The MPs were giving orders to cease the loading of the truck. Several of the soldiers seemed confused, but more than willing to take a break until the matter was cleared up.

But two men didn't seem too happy. They started arguing with the MPs. The MPs argued back.

Kitty didn't like the way this was going at all. Running down the length of the building, she checked every door and window until she found a window unlocked. She looked inside. It was a small office. She raised the window and climbed in.

Making her way to the door, she tried to hear what the men were saying. She was still too far away to hear clearly, but the arguing was still going on.

Easing the door open, she slipped into the hangar. Moving quietly from one form of cover to another, she slowly made her way toward the truck.

And then she heard a shot ring out.

Moving faster, she darted behind a mechanic's toolbox. Taking another deep breath to steady her nerves, she raised her head.

One of the MPs was on the ground. The other had his weapon out and was pointing at the two men in uniform, but he was trying to talk his way through it, clearly outgunned. The other soldiers had taken cover, hiding somewhere in the area.

Kitty slipped the strap over her head and brought the rifle around. She lifted it and slowly brought the scope into focus on one of the soldiers waving a gun at the MP.

The cold press of metal against her temple made her freeze. "Just take your finger off the trigger and slowly lower that weapon."

Swallowing hard, Kitty did as she was told, trying to see through her peripheral vision who held the gun. All she saw was camouflage. No help.

The man reached out and took the rifle from her, setting it aside. "Who are you?"

"Just a lonely girl looking for a little action."

The barrel of his gun tapped her temple hard enough to make her flinch. "I'm not in the mood to play, lady. Now who are you?"

"Kitty. I was Rick Harrelson's partner."

"I don't know any Rick Harrelson."

"He was also known as Archie Kemp."

The pressure on her temple eased a bit. "Well, now I know who you are, but I still don't know why you're here."

"The original plan got shot all to hell by those FBI agents. I came to help set things right."

"Uh-huh. And you're doing this why?"

"The money was paid. The job wasn't finished. Some of us take pride in our work and honor our commitments."

The gun was removed from her temple just a split second before he grabbed her arm and spun her around.

She stared up at her captor. He was a tall, stocky man with hard eyes and light hair, a tight-lipped mouth and a loose-limbed stance. Military. Well-trained military. A trained killer, paid for by taxpayer dollars.

His eyes drifted from her head down to her feet and back up again. "Archie had good taste. I'll give him that."

She lifted her chin, more than a little annoyed. "I take it

you're the one in charge of this portion of the operation?"

"And just what do you know about the operation?"

"Just that there's a shipment supposed to go out of here."

"Uh-huh. And who were you aiming to shoot a moment ago? One of my men, perhaps?"

"You know. . ." She folded her arms across her chest. "I hate to point out the obvious, but it looked like your men were about to be arrested."

He had the slow, menacing smile of a shark and eyes just as cold and empty. She had known fear at the hands of Archie from time to time, but she had never feared him the way she feared this man at this moment.

For the first time in her life, she knew she was looking death in the face.

"You got some spunk in you, I'll give you that. Not much on smarts, but you got spunk." He spun her around by the shoulder and pushed her forward with enough force to make her stumble.

The scene in front of her had changed dramatically. The MP had been joined by four other men in camouflage and were now holding the soldiers at gunpoint.

Oh no. She had been about to shoot the wrong men. The MPs were not the good guys.

chapter 18

Donnie folded and unfolded his arms. He rocked his foot. He blew out heavy sighs. And still the colonel hadn't called them into his office.

They had been escorted into the outer office and offered seats while waiting.

And waiting.

And waiting.

Donnie glanced at his watch. "This is ridiculous. What is going on?"

JJ, who had been checking out whatever he could find lying faceup on the secretary's desk, looked up. "Feels like another stall to me."

The office door swung open, and two soldiers strode purposefully through the outer office and disappeared down the hall, their footsteps echoing long after they were out of sight.

"Agent Bevere?"

Donnie jumped to his feet as the colonel appeared in the door. "Colonel." He reached out and shook hands with him.

"I ordered MPs sent down to the hangar to hold that

shipment, but we appear to have lost contact with our men. I'm heading down there myself, if you'd care to come along."

"Absolutely!" Donnie grabbed his coat, as did JJ, Zoe, and Jack.

They all slipped into their coats as they followed the colonel outside where several jeeps stood waiting with engines running and armed soldiers standing by.

The colonel jumped into the first jeep, and Donnie slid in behind him. As soon as everyone was seated, the jeeps took off down the street toward the airport.

Within minutes they were pulling up in front of the hangar. Several jeeps were parked out front. All was quiet.

The colonel nodded to several of his men, and they pulled their weapons, rushing into the building. Less than two minutes later, one of the men returned.

"We have four dead inside, sir, including one of the MPs. No sign of the shipment."

"Call the front gate. I want this base shut down now!"

Donnie, Jack, JJ, and Zoe were escorted back to the colonel's office to sit and wait a little more. Now it was Zoe pacing impatiently. "I'm worried about Kitty. Something bad went down in that hangar. What if she were caught up in it? She could be dead inside that hangar, and I don't think they'd tell us."

Jack stood up. "Why are we sitting around in here anyway? We were supposed to be given access to the base."

"This is a military installation. They don't take kindly to outsiders running around interfering with their business," JJ informed him. "I don't like it any better than you do, but that's the way it is."

The door opened, and a general came striding in, his

expression thunderous at best. Donnie rushed to his feet. "General Irby."

The general's expression lightened a bit, but not much. He shook hands with Donnie. "I'm truly sorry for this mess, Bevere. It wasn't supposed to happen this way."

"What *is* going on?"

"Not taking the situation as seriously as I explained it was, the colonel felt it didn't warrant more than sending a couple of MPs over to check it out. The MPs never made it there. They were found murdered in the motor pool. Obviously, the men we're looking for have taken their uniforms. They then killed some of the men who were loading the truck."

Donnie closed his eyes for a second and then looked back at the general. "So, now what?"

"They closed the base down. Everyone is on full alert. If they're still on the base, we'll find them."

"And if they're not?"

"They'll notify outside authorities."

"I *am* outside authorities." Donnie shoved his hands deep in his pockets, fiddling with the loose change. "What about Kitty? Any word?"

"One young soldier said he saw the truck pull out of the hangar and there was a woman with them. In civilian clothing. I'm assuming that's your Kitty."

"They got her." Zoe pressed a hand to her lips.

"What about the plane coming in?" Jack asked.

"Diverted to Pope."

Jack nodded. "One less thing to worry about. Now we just have to find that truck."

"I think we need to assume they got off the base and alert the Maryland State Police to put out an APB." Donnie began to pace. "We can't afford to spend hours looking on the base while they're crossing state lines into Delaware or Virginia to whereabouts unknown."

General Irby leaned back against the desk, crossing his feet at the ankles. "I'm sorry about this, Don. I tried to express the magnitude of the situation, but unfortunately, while egos are great for battle, they don't fare well when you tell them that something illegal is going on under their noses and on their watch."

"I understand, General. You did your best."

A young soldier came running in. He stopped and saluted the general.

"General Irby, sir. The colonel asked me to tell you that we have the men you're looking for. They've taken refuge in the motor pool building. We have additional men dispatched to the scene."

The general pushed himself off the desk. "Let's go, Don."

◆ ◆ ◆

Kitty glared as the soldier tied her ankles a little tighter than was necessary, clearly happy to do it. He grinned as he picked her up by the elbow, jerking her to her feet. "I think that should hold you, don't you?"

Then he tossed her over his shoulder and dropped her into the back of the truck. With a flick of his hand, he dropped the canvas cover over the tailgate, and she was enclosed in darkness.

When the truck first started sputtering, she was ready to shout hallelujah. The men had immediately headed for the motor pool to get another truck but hadn't made it any farther than that.

Now they were barricading themselves in the building, ready to shoot it out while some of the men transferred the crates to a new truck.

And she was no help at all to the men outside. If anything, she was going to become a major liability. The man with the cold eyes was going to use her as a hostage to get off the base.

Fat chance she was going to help him. If she could get her gag off, she planned on telling those soldiers out there to shoot her if they had to but not to let this creep get away.

That was, if she got her gag off in time, of course.

Wiggling and squirming, she managed to move from the rear of the truck's bed to the front, but didn't find anything in the journey to help her.

"Okay, get the girl, and let's get ready to go."

She didn't make it.

The canvas came up, and hands reached in, grabbed her ankles, and pulled her roughly across the bed of the truck. "Going somewhere, honey?"

Kitty gave him a look that should have told him she wished him dead, but he merely laughed.

Tossing her over his shoulder, he carried her to the new truck. Shark eyes was waiting. "Cut the ankles. I need her to walk."

The soldier did as he was told, wielding the knife a little too close to her flesh as he did. He wanted to nick her, and she knew it, but she refused to wince or flinch.

Then shark eyes grabbed her and yanked her forward. "Play it smart, and you may live to tell your grandchildren about this."

Fat chance, you chum scavenger. I'm not that stupid.

Shark eyes hauled her toward the door. He placed her in

front of him and eased the door open. Spotlights had been set up everywhere, making it look more like noon than three in the morning.

"Colonel! You don't need to lose any more of your men. Pull them back and let us go. You try anything, and we have a civilian in here who's going to go first, and I don't think she really wants that."

Wrong, fish face. Better I die than you live.

"I can't do that, Matterson. You have to let the girl go and give this madness up. You'll never get off this base with those weapons."

Yeah, scum sucker. Chew on that.

"We're driving out of here, Colonel. I just hate to see more of your men die in the process. We have missile launchers in here. Imagine the damage they're going to do to your base."

Can I make you eat one of them? You know, like that shark in the movie. Kaboom.

Shark eyes looked over his shoulder. "Ike. . .get ready to roll out of here. Bobby, unload one of those launchers and load it."

Yo, Lord. Are You seeing this? Could You, like, step in here any time now and help us out?

"Last chance, Colonel. Back away."

"Don't do it, Matterson. You can't win this."

"Sorry to hear you say that, Colonel. Just be careful when you're shooting. I don't think any of you want to hit the pretty lady in the front seat."

Shark pulled her back away from the door and hauled her over to the truck. "Get up in there."

She tipped her head and looked at him with as much sarcasm as she could. *With my hands tied? What am I supposed to do, fly up and in?*

Hissing with frustration, he picked her up and fairly tossed her into the seat. Immediately, she scrambled to get upright on the seat. He climbed up next to her.

"You might want to duck when we leave here, but don't. I want them to remember you're here before they start shooting."

She cut him another hard glance. He merely laughed at her. "You do have guts, lady."

Okay, Jesus. I guess this might be a real good time to tell You that I hope You'll forgive me for all the stupid and wrong stuff I've done in my life. I appreciate You dying for my sins, and I just wish I'd gotten the chance to know You. I think You'd be a really cool guy to hang out with. If You ever visit hell, will You look me up?

He leaned out the window and yelled back to his men. "Ready?"

When he had the affirmatives he needed, he put the truck in gear. "Brace yourself. This might hurt."

She wanted to close her eyes, but she also wanted to see it coming. She wanted to know if Donnie and Zoe and JJ were out there, and if they were, she wanted them to see her go bravely, not hunkered down like some coward. She wanted their respect. Even if it was only for a few moments.

The truck lurched forward, tearing the bay door off its hinges, squealing wheels as it fought for traction, and sending up a cloud of smoke as rubber burned.

She heard shots being fired. Felt the truck swerving. Saw lights. Smelled the bite of gunpowder.

Then something popped, and the truck started weaving, tilting nastily to the left. Someone had shot out the tires. Smart soldiers. Good boys.

But then there was a blinding flash. Kitty turned her head

when the truck stopped as if it had hit an invisible wall, jerking her forward. She slammed into the windshield. Then the truck flipped.

She registered the fear in her gut.

And then tasted the pain.

◆　◆　◆

Zoe jammed her hand over her mouth to stifle the scream as the colonel gave the order to fire on the truck as it came screaming out of the bay. Tires exploded as bullets ripped through the rubber.

A man with a missile launcher tumbled out of the back of the truck, hitting the ground and rolling.

Someone fired something explosive in front of the truck. It stopped suddenly, shuddered violently, and then flipped head over taillights, before landing to slide across the asphalt, metal screeching.

And then there was the most awful silence.

"Why did they do that? How could they!" Zoe clenched her fists, ready to do battle with the colonel.

JJ put his arms around her and pulled her close. "I'm sorry, baby."

She tipped her head back, stared up at him, tears running unchecked. "How could he do that? Kitty was in that truck. He knew that. I would have thought there was another way."

He brushed the tears away. "They couldn't afford to have those weapons leave here."

Zoe buried her face in his shoulder. "I know, but at least Kitty's okay."

She let him lead her a little distance away and help her

sit down in one of the jeeps. "I'm going to go talk to Donnie. Will you be okay here until I get back?"

She nodded, her mind already moving away. Bowing her head, she drifted into silent prayer, folding herself into the arms of her heavenly Father.

It was nearly half an hour later before JJ and Donnie returned with Jack tailing behind, all of them with heavy faces.

JJ leaned into the jeep and cupped her face with his hands. "I'm sorry, baby. She was killed instantly. If it's any consolation, she wasn't shot. She wasn't buckled in, and her hands were tied. She had no way to brace for the impact."

Zoe nodded. "I know."

She saw the confusion in his eyes. "But you said she was okay."

"She is, JJ. She's with the Lord."

chapter 19

Neil had every file he could find on el-Hajid stacked on his desk. He'd been going over them, line by line, since six that morning. His eyes hurt. His head ached. His mind was swimming in details.

Not much was known about el-Hajid's past. He was rumored to be a Saudi nationalist, but that couldn't be confirmed. According to the records, he was thirty-four, black hair, black beard, dark brown eyes, and stood five-foot-ten.

He was on everyone's watch list, and no one knew where he was.

When Neil finally came across Rick's files on el-Hajid, he found some very interesting information. El-Hajid had some connection to a mosque in Fredericksburg. This little fact had been buried in Rick's notes, jotted in a margin, and easily overlooked. Seems the man had been holding out on him in more ways than one.

El-Hajid's brother-in-law attended this mosque and was well-known to the Muslim community in the area.

It was worth checking out.

Then he found a business card tucked in an envelope in the file. He studied it for a moment. Then he smiled.

Gotcha.

◆　◆　◆

Sitting on the sofa, JJ tucked the phone under his chin, reached for his coffee, and resisted the urge to laugh. Chief Harris was going on and on, ranting about not having his calls answered or returned. About JJ running around arresting generals. About seeing his picture plastered on the front page of the newspaper and running on all the national newscasts. Being touted as a national hero. He wasn't happy with JJ, to say the least.

Sipping his coffee, he was tempted to just set the phone down and walk away.

Zoe walked through the room with Cody in her arms. He watched her disappear into the kitchen. What would it be like if this were their home and he was sitting on their sofa while she carried their child into the kitchen to get him a bottle?

Whoa.

Stunned, he dropped the phone. Somewhere, in the back of his mind, he could hear Harris screaming, but the ringing in his ears was too loud to make out what Harris was saying.

Married? Kids? Home? Family?

He picked up the phone, put it to his ear. "Chief. I have to go now." He closed the phone and stared into space.

He could see it. Maybe. Coming home to Zoe every night. Not such a hardship. Having a family with her? Maybe a daughter with that blond hair and those big green eyes. She'd have him wrapped about as tight as Mandy had Donnie wrapped, that's for sure. The kids crawling all over Zip. Yeah, like the dog would find that a hardship. The dog was a sucker for kids.

"What are you thinking about so hard?" Zoe sat down in the chair, holding the bottle for Cody.

"Not much."

"Everything okay with Chief Harris?"

"Who? Oh. Yeah. Fine."

She cast him a curious glance and then turned her attention back to the baby in her arms. "He's just upset that the world is applauding the man he suspended for possibly being a bad boy."

"Administrative leave."

"Whatever. The point is, it makes him look bad. He says the cop is suspect, but the world is declaring him a hero. Can we say *ouch*?"

JJ laughed. He set his coffee down. "Have you ever thought about having kids?"

Zoe shrugged. "Sure. Sometimes I have. I never thought I'd ever want any though."

"Why not?"

"Because of Amy. Because of all the children I had to try and find, and found murdered. But since I've come to know the Lord, I'm not afraid of the evil anymore."

He watched her lift the baby to her shoulder and rock him gently, patting him on the back.

When his cell phone rang again, he tore his gaze away to look at the caller ID. It was Matt. He flipped the phone open. "Hey, Matt."

"Do you have any idea what's going on here? You're the hometown hero. Harris is fit to be tied. One of the reporters from CNN asked him why he put an American hero on administrative leave for doing his job. Don't be surprised if the mayor rolls out the red carpet when you get back and gives you the key to the city."

"I hope not. I'll be happy to just have the charges dropped against me, and my job reinstated."

"That'll come through tomorrow. Mark my words. Already the uncle of that boy is backpedaling like crazy."

JJ felt a certain degree of pleasure in hearing that. He propped his feet up on the coffee table and let his gaze drift back over to Zoe who was now making cooing noises at the baby. "Anything from IAD?"

"Nada word. Like I said, no one is willing to look like they're persecuting the hometown hero."

"I am not a hero. How did all this get started, anyway?"

"With you ferreting out General Rupert's treachery and arresting him. There's a great shot in one paper of you doing this flying, rolling leap over the hood of the car to tackle Rupert."

JJ rolled his eyes. "I wasn't tackling Rupert. I was trying to get to Zoe."

"Either way, you looked like hero material, partner."

"Tell my hip that. I can barely walk today."

Matt laughed. "Ah, the price we pay for fame. So when are you coming home? The town wants me to find out so we can plan the parade."

"A month, at least. And even if I come home in a couple of days, I'm sneaking in under cover of night."

Matt chuckled again, clearing enjoying himself at JJ's expense. "Later, JJ."

Closing the phone, JJ leaned back. "I'm the hometown

hero. They ran that picture of me doing that flying leap over the hood of the car and said I was tackling Rupert."

"Works for me." Zoe looked up at him. "I'll never tell them the truth."

"I will! I'm no hero, and I don't want to be touted as one."

Zoe looked up at him from under her lashes, her lips curved in a dangerous smile. "Shame. I have a thing for home-town heroes."

Donnie stumbled into the room, looking as if he'd barely managed an hour of sleep. Considering they hadn't gotten back from Andrews until nearly five and it was just a little after eight, that was probably about all he did get. JJ had managed to get about two and a half before Zoe had woken him up to start going over leads again.

"Coffee," Donnie mumbled.

"It's made," Zoe replied, easing to her feet. "Here, hold your son a moment, and I'll get you some breakfast."

Donnie took Cody and eased down into the chair Zoe had just vacated. He looked over at JJ. "You feel as bad as you look?"

"Probably. We're not as young as we used to be, Donnie. This running around all night, going days without much sleep, leaping over cars in a single bound. It wears on the body a little."

Donnie managed a weak smile as he lifted Cody to his shoulder. "Jack call?"

"Yeah." JJ rolled his shoulders, trying to ease the stiffness from sleeping on the sofa. He really missed his bed. "They went through Rupert's files all night but found no mention of Lisbeth or where Harrelson might have taken her."

Donnie let out a hiss of frustration. "I should have been there."

"You needed a couple hours of sleep, and you couldn't have done any more than Jack did." Zoe set a mug of coffee down in front of him.

Jane came shuffling down the steps, tying her robe, her hair in curlers. "I can't believe I overslept. I'm so sorry. I had planned to be up before everyone else."

"We're good," Zoe assured her with a warm smile. "I was about to start breakfast for these guys."

Jane waved her off. "I'll get it. Mack is in the shower. He'll be down in a bit." She disappeared into the kitchen, and within seconds, they heard the clank and bang of pans being hauled out of the cabinet.

"You want me to take the baby?" Zoe asked Donnie.

Donnie shook his head as he carefully eased to his feet. "He's asleep, the lucky little guy. I'll just put him in his crib. Be right back."

Zoe curled up in the corner of the sofa and picked up the stack of leads she was going through before the baby had interrupted her. "El-Hajid. We need to find him. He was a big part of this weapons sale. And even when we find Lisbeth, this doesn't end until we have him."

JJ snorted softly. "I'll say. He was the buyer."

"That was Neil's case," Donnie added, coming down the stairs. "Lagasse? He and Rick were supposed to be tracking him. Seems el-Hajid got away right under their noses. I'll bet you anything that Neil would give his right arm to nail el-Hajid."

"So he would already have a file on el-Hajid." Zoe glanced up at Donnie.

"Oh yes. I'm sure." A smile slowly curled on Donnie's lips as he pulled out his cell phone. "I think I'll give Neil a call.

Wonder if he still wants my file on Archie Kemp? I'm willing to trade."

"Hold on, folks." Zoe stood up, a lead sheet in her trembling hands. "A young boy called in. He said Lisbeth is buried in the woods near his house. She told him to call the police and tell them to tell her husband she's alive and to come dig her up. She's in the woods near Hamilton Avenue Park near an old shoe factory. Look for a tree fort."

Zoe pressed a fist against her stomach. "Oh no."

"What?" Donnie nearly jumped her.

"She's cold, and she says it's getting hard to breathe. Hurry and help her, or she's gonna die."

JJ jerked to his feet so fast he knocked into the coffee table, sending his coffee flying. "That's it. Donnie, that's the one. We found Lisbeth!"

◆　◆　◆

El-Hajid was furious. There would be no shipment. The money was gone. The weapons were gone. And he had men waiting for those SAMs.

Staring at the television, he clenched and unclenched his fists as they went on and on about this hero Donnie Bevere and his friends.

Hero? These people did not understand what it was to be a hero. To devote everything to the cause. These weak Americans with their insipid smiles and their overwhelming arrogance.

The attack on their trade centers and their Pentagon meant little to them. They went on with their lives as if it would never happen again.

How wrong they were. How surprised they would be. They would wring their hands and weep in sorrow as blood ran in the streets. They would learn to fear. They would learn that this jihad was not something to dismiss or scorn. They would discover that they were not so strong, so invisible.

He spit. They were nothing but infidels. Immoral, weak, pleasure-seeking infidels.

He looked over at the man sitting on the floor assembling a bomb to be strapped on a martyr. "Ahmed. We have need of a martyr. This agent of the FBI, Bevere. . .he and all that he loves must die."

Ahmed bowed his head. "Praise be to Allah, and so it shall be."

◆　◆　◆

Neil hung up the phone, his eyes on the notepad in front of him as he jotted down notes to himself. El-Hajid was known to use the alias Mohammed Musab. In spite of being on watch lists and in spite of being wanted in England for bombing a train, how did this terrorist manage to even get into this country?

Suspicions were that he came in across the border with the help of the La Mara Salvatrucha, a ruthless gang from El Salvador known as MS-13. It fit. The gang, with members from El Salvador, Ecuador, Guatemala, Mexico, and Honduras, was known for trafficking military weapons. It was their main criminal enterprise, along with the usual drugs, murder, and robbery.

He mindlessly rubbed his jaw. MS-13 was known to be operating in Alexandria.

His phone rang once. Twice. Three times. Finally, he managed to pull away from the emerging train of thought and picked up the phone. "Lagasse."

"Jack Fleming."

Neil leaned back in his chair. "How are you, Jack?"

"Good. You?"

"Hanging tough. Glad you called."

"Oh?"

Neil leaned forward, propping his elbow on the desk and letting his forehead come to rest on his fist. His voice dropped to almost a whisper. "I want el-Hajid."

"So do we."

"When and where?"

"Donnie's place. At two."

"I'll be there." Neil hung up the phone, smiling. Then picked it up again and called a snitch he knew in Alexandria. It was a long shot, but worth taking. If el-Hajid was in Alexandria, it might be that Julio knew about it. Not much went on down there that Julio didn't hear about somehow. And there was no love lost between Julio's gang and the MS-13.

"Julio? Lagasse. Any word on the street about a man named el-Hajid? He runs with the MS-13."

"Muslim dude? Wears a black turban?"

"That's him."

"Yeah, dude. He's around. How much you payin' for the address?"

◆　◆　◆

"We need shovels, water, blankets, and cell phones. We're going to need an ambulance standing by." JJ gathered up all the call sheets and stacked them out of the way.

"I'll get the blankets and fill up jugs of water," Jane offered with a little wave. Then she hurried off upstairs to gather the blankets.

Mack strolled into the kitchen. "What's going on?"

"We think we found Lisbeth." Donnie placed a hand on his father-in-law's arm. "Go out to my shed. I need both of my shovels."

Mack nodded and hurried out the back door.

Zoe's cell phone rang. She walked away to answer it.

Jane rushed back in with a stack of blankets and handed them to JJ. "You're not sure the lead is valid?"

"There's no guarantee. I know it sounds legit, but I'm not counting on anything at the moment."

"It's valid," Zoe interjected, closing her cell phone. "That was Dan. Rick's brother owned some property in Braddock Heights that Rick inherited but never changed the deed over into his name. Wanna guess where it is?"

"Near an old shoe factory."

Zoe pointed her finger at JJ. "Right on the money. Forty-seven Franklin Street."

"Lisbeth? They didn't come. You want me to call again?"

Lisbeth didn't bother answering Justin anymore. It just took much effort. She knew he was as disappointed as she was that nearly a day had passed since he'd called the police and no one had shown up.

They hadn't believed him. He'd risked so much for her, and it had come to nothing. The poor child had spent most of the night with her, trying to keep her talking.

Her eyes drifted closed, and she didn't even fight the urge to sleep. *My Lord and my God, take care of my family. I didn't want to die, but I'm too tired to fight anymore. If this is what You want, then so be it. Take me. Just take care of those I love, and don't let them grieve long for me. Help Donnie raise our children in Your Word and in Your love. Don't let him blame You for any of this, and I know him well enough to know he'll want to.*

She felt her stomach cramp again, and she lovingly placed her hand over her abdomen. *I'm sorry, little one. I tried to give you life. But you'll be with Jesus now, and that's even better than the life I would have given you.*

Tears streamed down as she gritted her teeth against the pain as her baby struggled against the death that came to claim it. She wanted to scream but didn't even have the energy to do that.

"Lisbeth!" Justin sounded frantic now as she let the minutes pass without answering him. He probably thought she was already gone. Poor child. If only she could have spoken to Donnie one more time, she would have told him to take care of Justin. Heaven knew Justin had tried to take care of her. Fruit snacks, cereal, nuts. He had little to offer but gave all he could for a woman he didn't even know.

Hour after hour, the child had been sitting there on the cold ground, keeping watch, talking to her, trying to keep her hopes up.

"Lisbeth, please! Just a little longer. They'll come. They will."

She wanted to answer him. She really did. And in her mind, she reached out and pulled him into a hug. *You did good, Justin. You did good. Thank you for not letting me die alone and afraid.*

"Lisbeth!" He was screaming now, but she could no longer answer him except in her fading thoughts.

Thank you, Justin. Tell my family they were the last thing on my mind.

◆　◆　◆

Donnie felt it. It was like a sudden ripping in his heart. She was dying. "No!" he gasped, nearly running off the road as he fought to hold on to his wife.

"What's the matter?" Mack jerked in his seat, all concern and worry.

"She's leaving us. I can feel it. I don't know how or why, but I just know." He stepped on the accelerator a little more, taking his speed to more than twenty miles over the limit.

Please, Lord. Keep her holding on a little longer. We're on our way.

Donnie kept his eyes on the road as he wove through traffic, fighting the urge to scream at drivers to get out of his way. Even with the strobes on his dash going, rush hour traffic fought him every step of the way.

Hold on, Lisbeth. I'm coming. Please hold on a little longer. Don't give up yet.

◆　◆　◆

Jane rocked Cody as he stared up at her, sucking on his bottle. There was no worry in his eyes. No concern puckering his brow. He was cheerfully oblivious to the crisis around him. "Sweet boy. How lucky you are right now."

She remembered holding Lisbeth like this once. How long

ago that had been. At the time, she'd just been a young mother herself, worried that she might not do everything right, make mistakes, have regrets. She soon learned that every parent goes through that.

But looking back, she had no regrets. Lisbeth and Maureen were both happy, well-adjusted women, both devoted to their faith, both woman of strong morals. How badly could she have done raising them?

She could feel her daughter slipping away, as if she were slowly untying those slender threads that connected them in heart and soul. Swiping at the tears, she lifted her eyes to the ceiling. "Don't take her away from us yet. Please, Lord. Give her the strength to hold on. Breathe life into her a little longer. Help Donnie and Mack get to her in time."

Cody whimpered, and she looked down. The bottle had slipped away, frustrating Cody who was trying to get it back in his mouth. She repositioned it, and he settled back down, content once again.

Hold on, Lisbeth. Your children need you.

Neil motioned to the SWAT team behind him to move in slowly. Julio had been right on with his tip. Neil, posing as a deliveryman, had verified that el-Hajid was in the second-floor apartment.

Weapon raised to the ceiling, Neil eased up the wall, taking his position on one side of the apartment door. He pointed, and three men hurried into position on the other side of the door.

He reached out and knocked on the door. "FBI. Open up."

He heard the scrambling around inside and jerked his head at the two men waiting with the battering ram. "Take it down."

The nice thing about old, cheap apartments was that the doors come down fast. And easy. Within seconds, Neil was through the doorway, gun sweeping the living room. One man was halfway out the window. The other waiting impatiently to go out behind him. When they saw all the guns pointed at them, they went still, staring at Neil.

"Back in here. And don't make me shoot you."

El-Hajid eased back a little, but the little man halfway out the window must have decided he could make it. As he dived through, Neil fired, hitting the man in the thigh. The man screamed and went down, writhing on the fire escape. One of Neil's men pulled him back in while Neil cuffed el-Hajid.

"Sorry, el-Hajid. You won't be causing any more trouble for us."

El-Hajid smiled. And then spit in Neil's face. "You Christian pig. You will see trouble. It is too late to stop it. And when it is done, you will know that you may stop me, but you will not stop my brothers from finishing what has been started."

Neil wiped the spittle from his face. "Stop what, el-Hajid? You planning on bringing down another airplane? Or maybe it's a power plant this time, huh?"

El-Hajid merely smiled. "Infidel."

"Yeah, well, el-Hajid, that's the thing about infidels. We just take it real personal when you come here to our country and kill innocent people. We're funny that way. Of course, we're not too thrilled with the way you kill your own people either, but you're just a bunch of soulless murderers anyway."

"Sir?"

Neil looked away from el-Hajid to focus on the man speaking to him. "Yes?"

"Someone's been making a bomb back here, but the bomb's gone."

Neil looked back at el-Hajid.

El-Hajid grinned broadly. "Boom."

chapter 20

D onnie pulled up in front of the address Zoe had given him. "And you thought being an FBI agent was glamorous."

It was just a vacant lot. A house might have stood on the property at one time, but now it was just a place for the neighborhood to drop off the junk the trash company wouldn't pick up curbside. Tires, refrigerators, stoves, mattresses, boxes, car parts—they lay partially covered by tall weeds and snow.

He climbed out of his car, popped open the trunk, and started pulling out the shovels and handing them to Mack.

JJ pulled his Jeep up behind Donnie's car and cut the engine. A few seconds later, he and Zoe climbed out.

"Be careful where you step," Donnie told everyone as he closed the trunk. "Heaven knows what you'll be walking over."

Donnie glanced up at the sky. The sun was deep behind cloud cover, adding a gray cast to an already miserable terrain. With the temperatures hovering in the midforties, it was a little too warm to snow, so that meant rain. "We need to move fast. I want to find her before this weather turns on us."

They set off in single file, everyone looking for the shoe factory or a tree fort. Into the woods they went, ducking under branches, stepping over trash and fallen logs, and sidestepping through thick brush.

"There's the shoe factory," Zoe piped up about five minutes later, pointing west. "Now we look for a tree fort, right?"

"That's what the kid said," Mack replied.

Zoe started forward and then tripped, falling into Mack. He reached out and grabbed her, dropping his shovel. She clung to him a moment, and with a shaky laugh said, "Sorry. I didn't see whatever it was I tripped on."

Mack steadied her on her feet and then reached for the fallen shovel. "No problem. You're sure you're okay?"

"I'm fine. No damage done."

Donnie held up his hand. "Shhh."

A voice cried out. Young. Male.

"Did you hear that?" Donnie's face lit up.

"Yes!" Mack started forward in the direction of the scream.

They came across the little boy kneeling on the ground in a rush of hope and questions.

"She stopped talking to me," the boy told them.

Donnie knelt down. "We'll get her out. I'm Donnie Bevere. What's your name?"

"Justin."

Donnie put his hand on Justin's shoulder. "Thank you for calling, Justin. I'm just sorry it took them so long to pass your message on to us."

"Lisbeth! Honey? We're here. We're going to get you out. You hold on, okay? We're here." Donnie thrust his shovel in the ground. "Zoe, call for an ambulance."

She already had her cell phone out. "On it."

Justin stood, backing away from the grave as Mack and JJ joined Donnie with the digging.

Hope rose and fell as Donnie worked feverishly. He was almost there, but she wasn't talking back. *Please don't let us be too late, Lord.*

Zoe closed her phone. "The ambulance is on the way. Justin and I are going to walk back so that we can lead them in."

Donnie nodded. "Good idea."

The three men kept digging, with Donnie talking to Lisbeth the whole time. He didn't know if she heard him or not, but he wasn't going to think the worst. He refused. God had brought them this far. It couldn't be too late. It just couldn't.

Donnie heard the siren getting closer and closer.

"I've hit something," Mack said. He poked down with his shovel and hit solid wood. "Okay, let's clear this off and open it up.

In spite of aching muscles and fatigue brought on by endless days of stress and lack of sleep, Donnie felt a surge of energy as they removed the last shovelfuls of dirt. Finally, he tossed the shovel aside and started brushing with his hands.

Then he reached down at one end with Mack at the other and lifted the lid.

The stench was the first thing that hit him. It was the familiar smell of blood and excrement that came with death. The memory of every time he'd walked in on a dead body—the sight, the smell, the horror of it—washed over him. But this time, it was his wife.

Then he saw her. She was so pale. So still. Everything in him exploded. He lifted his head and screamed out in denial—a scream so deep and so primal, a wolf standing over his dead mate would have understood.

Pain ripped through him. He staggered backwards, fighting to keep his knees from buckling. *Lisbeth.*

Mack grabbed him, wrapping his arms around him. Slowly, Donnie eased out of Mack's arms and reached down to lift his wife's limp body into his arms.

"Help me, Mack. Help me get her out of this."

Mack tossed out one of the blankets on the ground. He reached down and tucked his arms under her legs as Donnie lifted her from the neck and waist. Gently they laid her on the blanket. Donnie knelt there, her head in his lap, brushing her tangled hair with his fingers. "I'm here, baby. I'm here."

Blood? Why was there so much blood?

Had Rick hurt her before he put her in the coffin? Twin daggers of hot pain and cold rage ripped through him as he envisioned what she might have suffered.

Three men and a woman burst on the scene carrying a stretcher. Immediately, they surrounded Lisbeth, gently easing Donnie away as they checked Lisbeth for a heartbeat.

Donnie looked up and around. Justin stood there, arms closing in around himself, tears streaming down his face. "Where's Zoe?"

Justin looked over his shoulder and then turned back to Donnie. "She told me to bring these guys while she stayed to guide the police who were pulling up."

"We got a pulse. It's thready." The EMT grabbed the oxygen. "Drip. Now." He barked out as he slipped the oxygen mask on Lisbeth's face.

Alive? Donnie collapsed inward, his head falling slowly to rest on the ground as he sobbed with relief. She was alive. Barely. But alive.

He looked up. "I want her flown to Washington Trauma as soon as possible. Can you arrange that?"

The female EMT nodded and stood up, barking into the mic clipped to her shoulder.

"She's had a miscarriage," one of the EMTs mentioned to his coworkers.

Miscarriage? Donnie slowly climbed to his feet. She'd been pregnant. Locked in this coffin, slowly bleeding to death as she lost their child, and no one to hold her or comfort her.

They laid out the stretcher, lifted Lisbeth onto it, wrapped her in thermal blankets, and buckled her in. The police showed up, asking a million questions. Mack took over, gathering up the blankets and shovels, as Donnie walked beside the stretcher back to the ambulance, holding Lisbeth's hand.

When they reached the ambulance, the woman walked over to him. "We're taking her over to Frederick where a helicopter is waiting to airlift her down to Washington Trauma. Doctors are on board to care for her in transit."

Donnie nodded, numb to his core. "Can I ride with her?"

"I'm afraid not, sir. Against regulations."

Donnie pulled out his badge. "FBI. Does that make any difference?"

The woman looked over at the EMT who was clearly their leader. He nodded silently.

"Okay."

Donnie handed his keys to Mack. "Someone drive my car back."

"You call as soon as you know anything."

Donnie nodded and climbed into the back of the ambulance.

◆   ◆   ◆

Neil tried Jack's cell phone again. This time, someone answered. "Jack. Neil. I've been trying to get in touch with you."

"They found Lisbeth. She's alive, but barely. They're airlifting her to Washington Trauma. Donnie's with her."

Neil bowed his head with a heavy sigh of relief. "Thank God."

"I know we were supposed to meet at two, and I should have called, but—"

"No. That's why I'm calling you. We have el-Hajid."

"You have him! Good going. How'd you find him?"

Neil glanced up and through the observation window. El-Hajid was sitting handcuffed to his chair, staring back through the mirror with the secret smile on his face. The man knew something. But what?

"Just hard work." He turned away from the two-way mirror. "Look, el-Hajid has something up his sleeve, and it's making me nervous. We've been going at this guy for nearly two hours, and all he'll say is. . .*boom*."

"That's it?"

"That's it. He's got a bomb planted somewhere, and we have to find it. Fast."

◆   ◆   ◆

Donnie sat with his head buried in his hands. He looked up as JJ and Zoe entered the waiting room, and from the disappointment on his face, he must have been expecting the doctor.

"Any word?" Zoe asked, sitting down next to him and draping an arm over his shoulder.

He shook his head. "I don't know if she even knew yet. And now, on top of everything else, I have to tell her she's lost our baby."

"She's alive, Donnie. Focus on what's really important. There can be other babies. There can't be another Lisbeth."

"You're right," he replied softly. "I'm just so worried about her. How long was she without adequate oxygen? What if there's brain damage? What if she's in a coma and never comes out of it?"

"Stop it, Donnie. Quit looking for something bad. Lisbeth will be fine."

"She was alone in that box, Zoe. Losing the baby, slowly bleeding to death, and all alone. How terrifying that must have been for her. I can't even imagine."

"She wasn't alone." JJ knelt down in front of Donnie. "The Lord was with her."

Donnie stared at JJ and then nodded. "You're right. He was there. Keeping her safe until I could get there. And that child, slipping food down that pipe to help her. Do you know he gave her fruit snacks? She hates those things. But she ate them. Cereal. Nuts. And he talked to her. Kept her spirits up by talking to her."

"He's a little hero. Sent by the Lord to take care of Lisbeth."

❖   ❖   ❖

A doctor in green scrubs came through the double doors and looked around. "Mr. Bevere?"

Donnie hurried over. "I'm Mr. Bevere. How's my wife?"

"Stable, but I'm still going to classify her as critical. I'm moving her into ICU and keeping an eye on her. Tomorrow

I'll decide whether to downgrade her or not."

"Did she awaken?"

The doctor shook his head as he toyed with the stethoscope hanging around his neck. "I'm afraid not. But that's not a bad thing right now. It's giving her body a chance to heal. If she doesn't start to come out of it a little in twenty-four hours, we'll start to worry."

"Can I see her?"

"Just for a few minutes. We're getting ready to move her into a room. I'll let you see her for five minutes. Then I would suggest that you go home and get some rest. You won't be able to see her until after nine tomorrow morning."

Donnie looked over his shoulder at the group. JJ nodded. "Go. We'll wait here for you. Give her our love."

Donnie gave them a weak smile and then quickly disappeared through the double doors with the doctor.

"She'll be okay." Zoe leaned her head against JJ's shoulder. "But it was close."

"For some reason, the Lord likes to cut it close. Have you ever noticed that? Matthews had you within a hairbreadth of death before Donnie got that shot off. And when you were trapped in the van underwater with Tappan." He shook his head.

Zoe was going to respond, but she caught sight of Jack running down the hall toward them.

"How's Lisbeth?"

"Critical, but she'll be okay," Zoe told him.

"They caught el-Hajid, but it looks like he's planted a bomb somewhere. I've got to get back to the office. Tell Donnie what's going on?"

JJ nodded. "We will."

◆ ◆ ◆

Donnie dragged the chair up next to his wife and sat down. Monitors kept pace with her heart and blood pressure, while oxygen streamed into her system through little plastic air tubes at her nose.

He took her hand in his. She was still pale, but her color was far better than it had been. There were dark circles under her eyes, and her hair was matted and stringy around her face. He'd never seen anything so beautiful in his life.

"Hey, baby. I have missed you so much."

Lisbeth slowly opened her eyes, and her lips curved ever so slightly in a painful smile. "Hi."

"I didn't wake you, did I?"

"No," she whispered. "You look worse than I feel."

"I was so terrified, Lisbeth."

"You forgot to pray and trust God again, didn't you?"

Donnie pressed her hand to his lips. "I didn't want to face life without you."

"You would have been fine." She lifted a finger and lightly traced his mouth.

"I don't know how you could be so sure."

"Because I prayed and asked the Lord to make sure you were okay without me."

Tears swelled, and he didn't even bother wiping them away as they streaked down his face. She moved her hand over and captured a tear with her fingertip.

"I lost the baby."

Donnie nodded. "Yes. Did you know you were pregnant?"

"Yes."

"Why didn't you tell me?"

"I was planning to surprise you on your birthday with the news."

"I'm so sorry, Lisbeth. There can be other babies if you want."

She started crying. "We can talk about that later. I need you to help Justin."

Donnie wrapped his hand around hers. "Justin? Help him how?"

"He's—" She winced as she moved, going perfectly still until the pain passed. Then she slowly relaxed back into her pillows. "He's all alone. His grandmother is in the hospital. His mother has abandoned him. He's been taking care of me, but there's no one to take care of him."

"You want me to call the authorities?"

"No," she whispered, and he could tell she was about to fall asleep again. "I promised him. Go get him. Take care of him until his grandmother is out of the hospital. He's terrified he'll end up in some foster home."

Her eyes drifted closed. He lifted her hand and kissed her palm. "I'll go get him for you."

◆　◆　◆

Jack poured a cup of coffee. It smelled like it had been made sometime that morning and cooking for eight hours. Nothing he wasn't used to. He added plenty of cream as Neil added sugar to his. "Well, it can't be the plane from Gitmo. It's already landed and was swept for explosives. It's clean. The weapons are safe. Rupert's dead. That doesn't leave us much to go on. Could be a government building. Courthouse."

Neil rubbed his knuckles over his chin as he looked back

over his shoulder. "We alerted the courthouse. D.C. police have been notified, but do you have any idea how long it would take to search every monument and government building?"

Jack raised an eyebrow as he took the sugar from Neil and poured it liberally into his coffee. "White House?"

"Notified."

Jack walked back to the conference room with Neil, sipping at the coffee. It was worse than he thought. "Who made this garbage?"

"I did."

"Figures." Jack pulled out a chair and sank down into it. "Okay, what else do we have?"

Neil walked over to the whiteboard where he'd been making notes. "I've got men taking el-Hajid's apartment apart; but so far, they haven't found anything, or they'd have called."

Jack leaned back in his chair, staring at the board. "Boom. That's all he said?"

"That's it."

Boom. El-Hajid was going to blow something up. But what? What was left besides revenge? The weapons were safe. The sellers locked up. And the military was arresting all their personnel involved. It was over.

He jerked up out of his chair and began to pace. "All the loose ends have been tied up. What could el-Hajid gain by blowing something up at this point?"

"A few deaths. Hundreds. Thousands. Who knows? Regardless of how many, it's going to be bad. El-Hajid is a terrorist. He's as mad as a hatter. You know how terrorists operate."

"I sure do. They either plant bombs, or they con some poor misguided young fool to walk a bomb into a building and blow himself up."

As the double doors opened and Donnie stepped through, all attention was turned on Donnie's pale, drawn face.

Zoe stepped forward, wrapping Donnie in a warm hug. "How is she?"

"It was hard seeing her like that, but she's alive. She's alive, and she'll heal, and she'll come home."

Zoe stepped back out of his arms. "Absolutely."

"You were right, you know."

"About?"

"The Lord was faithful and well able. Look how He took care of her. With the help of a child, for heaven's sake. I heard those monitors recording her heartbeat, and it was solid and strong; and it was because the Lord protected her. He kept her alive for me."

Donnie swiped at the tears in his eyes, not looking the least bit embarrassed to be seen crying.

Zoe squeezed his hand. "Your heavenly Father means what He says and says what He means."

Donnie's mouth twitched with a smile. "I need to call Mack and Jane and let them know how Lisbeth is."

"Aren't you going to head home?" JJ asked.

"She wants me to go back and get Justin. Seems he's all alone right now."

Zoe picked up their coats off a chair. "Then let's go."

Donnie took his coat and then her hand. "You've done more than I could have ever asked or expected from friends. Now go back to my house and get some sleep. I can go get the boy."

JJ shrugged his coat on. "I got a better idea. You and I go

get the boy. Zoe can go back to the house, let everyone know that Lisbeth is fine, and get some sleep."

Zoe raised her hand. "Anyone care what I want to do?"

JJ wrapped his arms around her waist and pulled her close. He kissed her nose. "Of course, darling. What would you prefer to do?"

"I'm going back to Donnie's and get some sleep. Wake me up when you get back." She reached up and kissed his nose.

◆　◆　◆

Lisbeth was aware of the bleeps and chirps of the machines before realizing she was awake again. Blinking a couple of times, she slowly opened her eyes, registering that while there was some discomfort, the shooting pain she'd felt earlier was gone.

Just like her baby.

And while she usually didn't indulge in good crying jags, it seemed like a really good time for one. But just as the tears welled up, she became aware of the fact that she was not alone.

Turning her head slowly to the right, she cautiously studied the stranger sitting in the shadows with an armload of yellow roses. She didn't know the man, but she recognized the pain in his eyes.

"Hello, Lisbeth. My name is Jim Mann. I'm your husband's supervisor."

She gave him a smile as he offered her the flowers. "They're beautiful. Thank you."

He pulled his chair a little closer to the bed. "I'm very glad to see you doing so well. You gave everyone quite a scare. Especially Donnie."

"Well, I have to admit. . .I was a little scared myself."

"I can imagine you were." He stared down at his hands. "I came here to see you for two reasons. One, to see how you were doing and to pay my respects. And two, I wanted to talk to you about Donnie."

Lisbeth set the flowers on the table. "About Donnie?"

"A great deal went down while you were. . .before you were rescued. It was pretty complicated. I had to do some things. . .make some decisions I would have preferred not to make. Your husband is not happy with me, and I can't say that I blame him. Not at all. But Donnie is one of the best men I've got, and I don't want him to quit the agency over this."

"Quit?" Lisbeth couldn't believe what she was hearing. Why would Donnie ever consider leaving his job? He loved it. "I don't understand. He hasn't said anything to me about quitting."

"Well, I'm sure that right now, he's not bringing it up because he wants you to rest and get well. And maybe he won't consider quitting. All I'm asking is that if he does speak of quitting, you'll try to convince him to stick with it. Transfer to another office if he has to, but don't leave the agency."

Lisbeth studied him for a moment. "Why don't you tell me what went on."

He shook his head. "It doesn't matter in the long run. It was a difficult situation. Donnie did what he had to do. And I did what I thought was best for everyone involved."

He slapped his thighs and then rose to his feet. "I've taken up enough of your time. It was nice meeting you, Mrs. Bevere. I hope we have the chance to meet again."

"I'm sure we will," she told him as she watched him put on his overcoat. "And thank you again for the flowers."

After he left, she reached out and touched one of the roses. That man was up to his neck in regrets. What in the world had he done? And why was Donnie thinking of leaving the FBI because of it?

It must have been something horrendous. Donnie loved his job. Not much would make him even consider leaving.

She stared at the door. *What did you do, Jim Mann?*

chapter 21

J ustin stared at the last of the cereal. It wasn't even half a bowlful. He really, really wanted his grandma to come home and cook a meal for him. Maybe macaroni and cheese and meat loaf. Or chicken and dumplings.

When he heard the knock at the front door, he set his cereal bowl down and prepared to go hide.

"Justin? It's Mr. Bevere. Lisbeth sent me to check on you."

Lisbeth sent him? He ran to the front door and peeked out the window. Sure enough, it was just Mr. Bevere. He unlocked the door and pulled it open. "Hi."

"Hi, Justin. Go get your shoes and coat."

Immediately, Justin backed up. "Why?"

"We're going to see your grandmother at the hospital. You do want to see her, don't you?"

He broke out in a grin. "Really?"

"Really. Now go get your shoes and coat."

He did more than that. Shoes, socks, clean shirt, washed his face, and brushed his teeth. Then he presented himself to Donnie for inspection. "You look spiffy."

"What's spiffy?" he asked as they headed for the car.

"You look very good. Your grandmother is going to be very proud of you."

Justin climbed into the backseat. Donnie leaned in to buckle his seat belt. "I can do it, Mr. Bevere."

"Sorry. Habit. My daughter still needs help with it. You remember Detective Johnson, don't you?"

"Yes. Hi."

JJ nodded with a warm smile. "Hi again, Justin."

On the way to the hospital, they drove up what Donnie referred to as "The Golden Mile" where it seemed to be just one restaurant after another. "Hungry?"

Justin nodded, his nose pressed to the window. Pizza Hut, Burger King, Taco Bell, Denny's, Ground Round, Chi-Chi's, The Outback, The Red Horse.

"What would you like for dinner? Pick something."

The choices just went on and on, and Justin wanted everything.

He finally settled on McDonald's and had a hamburger with French fries and a milk shake. Justin couldn't remember ever eating anything so good in his life.

"That's only because you're hungry," Donnie told him.

When they got to the hospital, JJ stayed in the car to nap, he said. Donnie stopped in the gift shop and helped Justin pick out a little flower arrangement for his grandmother with a big balloon that said GET WELL SOON. Proudly, Justin carried it up in the elevator and into his grandmother's room.

She burst into tears when she saw him, and the flowers were nearly crushed as he ran to her and was swallowed up in her hug.

After the tears were wiped away and Donnie saved the

flowers, Justin perched on the side of the bed and enthusiasti-
cally explained about his adventures. When he got to the part
about thinking Lisbeth was going to die, his grandmother had
to reach for tissues.

"I'm so sorry, Justin. I didn't know I was gonna be in the
hospital so long. I should never have told you to stay alone
like that."

"I was fine," he insisted and then jumped back and told her
more about Lisbeth. "It was on the TV and everything. Well,
not me. Lisbeth promised to keep me a secret, and she did."

"But he was a hero," Donnie told her, and Justin swelled.
A hero. Wow. An FBI guy was calling him a hero. How cool.
Wait till he told Ty about this.

"When do you expect to be released?" Donnie asked her.

"They said Monday or Tuesday if I don't have no more of
them episodes with my heart. I wanna thank you for bringing
Justin to see me. I've missed him, but when I try to call the
house, he don't answer the phone."

Justin felt his heart drop. "But you told me to never answer
the phone when you weren't there."

"I know, baby. That was my fault. Never mind about that
now. You're fine, and you did real good; and I'm real prouda
you taking care of that nice lady the way you did. That was
real brave of you."

"If you don't mind, Lisbeth and I would be honored to
have Justin come stay with us until you're released." Donnie
smiled down at him. "Lisbeth is going to be coming home
from the hospital in a day or two, and I know she wants to
fuss over Justin here a little more."

Justin was thinking how cool that would be when his
grandmother shook her head. "We can't go imposin' on you

nice people like that. I appreciate it and all, but—"

Justin's heart dropped to his feet.

"It's not an imposition. It would be our pleasure. We owe your grandson a great deal, and this would be such a little thing to do. Let him come stay with us. I'll give you our phone number, and you can call him every day and talk to him. I'll bring him back when you're released.

"I also want you to know I talked to your doctors, and you're going to need to take it easy for a while. So I talked to an agency, and they're going to send a woman over every day to take care of cooking and cleaning and running errands for you for the six weeks the doctor recommended."

His grandmother opened her mouth to say something, but Donnie cut her off again. "No. Don't refuse. It's all paid for. Just accept with our gratitude."

Justin didn't like seeing his grandmother cry, but at least she didn't look unhappy. "It's too much."

"It's not enough. This is one of those times when I wish I made a lot of money so I could help you and Justin even more."

She waved him off. "It ain't the money that makes life worth living. It's the people you meet along the way."

Justin curled up in his grandmother's arms, content for the first time in over a week.

chapter 22

Saturday, February 18

J ustin stretched out on the soft carpet, watching television
with Mandy in her room. The room, all pink and white and
frilly, was too girlie for him, but he loved it.

Mandy had a bed with curtains over it, a dresser with a
mirror, bookshelves full of books, games, and movies, and a
desk with her own television and DVD player. How cool was
that? And all the movies. *Aladdin, Nemo, Brother Bear, Peter
Pan*, and *Home on the Range*. She even had *Shark Tales*.

She also had stupid stuff like *Cinderella* and *Winnie the
Pooh*, but she was practically a baby, so he guessed it was okay.

It had been his turn to pick the movie, so they were
watching *The Incredible Journey*. He really loved that dog,
Chance, and wished he had a dog. If he ever got a dog, he
wanted it to be really cool, like Chance. But then Shadow was
pretty cool, too.

"You found my mommy, didn't you?"

"Yeah."

She tilted her head and stared over at him, eyes wide.
"Daddy told my grandma that you were very brave."

Joy flooded him as he rocked back on the soft pink carpet. "I guess."

"Were you very scared?"

He shrugged, trying to decide just how much to admit. "Sometimes."

Mandy jumped up. "Did I show you my playhouse?"

"No."

She ran over to the window and climbed up in the window seat. "Come see. My daddy built it for me, and my mommy and I painted it."

Justin walked over and sat down next to her. He looked out the window. It looked just like a real house, only smaller, with a door and windows and a chimney, and it was painted all blue and pink. "That's pretty cool. Do you have furniture in it?"

"Not right now. Daddy puts it all away in the garage when it turns winter, but when winter is over, I have chairs and a table and dishes and everything."

"Wow."

"Do you have a playhouse?"

Justin stared down at the little playhouse. "I'm a boy. I have a tree fort."

"Really?" Mandy sounded very impressed.

"Yeah, it's up in a tree. You have to climb up a ladder to get to it."

"Really?"

Justin nodded as his attention drifted to the man out beyond the yard, staring at the house. Something about the man made him feel creepy. Just like the man in the woods had.

"Who's that?" he asked Mandy.

She looked out the window. Shrugged. "Don't know. Hey!

Wanna play with my trucks?"

"Trucks?" Now she was talking.

Mandy climbed down off the window seat. "Yeah, me and Daddy have these 'mote 'trol trucks. Wanna see?"

"Yeah."

He followed her down to the basement, forgetting all about the man watching the house.

◆　◆　◆

Lisbeth was sitting up, dressed and ready to go, when Donnie and Zoe entered her hospital room. Her doctor was frowning, signing forms on a clipboard. "I would still prefer you to stay another day or two for observation. You went through quite an ordeal."

"I can rest better at home," Lisbeth insisted.

"Will there be anyone there to take care of you?" he asked, spearing her with a look over the top of his glasses.

"My husband, my mother." She ticked off her fingers. "My dad, my friends."

His frown never budged. "I'm still not happy about this, but here you go. This is your release form, your scripts for meds if you need them, and these are your meal restrictions. I want to see you back in my office in ten days, and your OB-GYN wants to see you next week."

Lisbeth nodded, handing everything to Donnie. "I under-stand. I'll be a good little girl, I promise, Doctor."

After exchanging quick pleasantries with Donnie, the doctor left. "Get me out of here."

Donnie laughed. "That's my girl." He leaned over and kissed her. "We're waiting for the wheelchair."

Lisbeth shook her head, easing off the bed. "And I'm not going out of here in a wheelchair. I'm quite capable of walking."

She managed three steps before she felt a little light-headed. She grabbed Donnie's arm. "But rules are rules, aren't they?"

He helped her sit down in a chair. "Stubborn woman."

The nurse finally brought the wheelchair. Lisbeth sat in it, loaded down with flowers.

JJ was waiting curbside for them, doors open. He leaned down and gave Lisbeth a kiss as he took the flowers out of her arms. "Hey, beautiful. Your chariot awaits."

As Lisbeth was easing into the backseat, assisted by Donnie, she happened to look over at Zoe. Zoe was staring at a man walking into the hospital, and her face was white.

Zoe grabbed JJ's hand. "That man."

"What man?"

"A man just went into the hospital. JJ, I'm telling you, he had a bomb strapped to his chest. When he reached for the door, his coat opened just enough for me to see it."

JJ tossed Zoe the car keys. "Get Lisbeth out of here." Then he took off in a run for the hospital doors.

Donnie quickly tucked Lisbeth into the car while Zoe jumped into the front seat. Something on her husband's face as he kissed her made her heart leap in her chest.

Then he was gone, and Zoe was driving away from the hospital.

"Where are we going? Are we leaving them behind?"

Zoe shook her head. "I'm just going to drive a block or two away and wait. JJ will call me when he and Donnie get the guy in custody."

Despite the touch of nonchalance in Zoe's words and

manner, Lisbeth could see the wariness shadowed in her eyes. "I'm not fragile, Zoe. And I'm not ignorant of the fact that we've all been front and center in a terrorist's plot to acquire weapons, and now a terrorist just happens to target the same hospital I was in. Coincidence? I think not."

Zoe pulled into an office building parking lot and backed into a space. They could both see the top floors of the hospital as they waited.

Zoe cut the engine and turned in her seat to face Lisbeth. "I'm not trying to protect you or pretend it isn't serious. It just doesn't do either of us any good to jump to conclusions. Do I think the man was going after you? Yes. I do. And I thank God that you insisted on being released early."

"But there's a hospital full of people who could be hurt because I'm not there."

Zoe shook her head, glancing back at the hospital. "First of all, you're not there. He's not going to waste his life if you aren't going to die in the process. As soon as he finds out you're not there, he'll abort and come up with another plan. So those people are now safer without you there."

Lisbeth tore her eyes from Zoe and stared up at the hospital. "Help Donnie and JJ capture this maniac, Lord."

◆ ◆ ◆

As soon as the elevator door opened, JJ and Donnie lunged forward, two hospital security guards right behind them. They took off in a full run down the hall. Nurses scattered out of their way, and when someone saw the gun in Donnie's hand, she screamed.

They turned the corner into the north wing. Lisbeth's room

was in sight. The suicide bomber came out of the room. He saw Donnie and JJ, turned, and ran down an opposite hall.

JJ could hear the security guard behind him calling for backup.

They turned the corner, only to discover the man had disappeared.

One security guard pointed. "The stairs!"

They were on the run again. Flinging open the door, they took the steps in leaps and bounds, trying to cover as much ground as they could. Even so, the bomber was nowhere in sight. Either he hadn't taken the stairs at all, or he'd gotten off one floor below and taken the elevator.

They continued to search for another ten minutes to no avail. JJ finally pulled Donnie aside. "Leave this to them. I think we need to consider something else."

"Which is?"

"Lisbeth isn't the target. You are."

"But they couldn't know I would be in visiting at that particular time."

JJ just stared at him, willing him to find the answer himself because he didn't want to say it.

Donnie paled. "Oh no." He whipped out his cell phone, running for the hospital doors.

JJ emerged from the lobby right behind Donnie. While Donnie was calling his house, JJ was dialing Zoe's cell phone. "Come get us. No, he got away. We'll talk when you get here." He disconnected the call.

Donnie was pacing. "Come on. Come on."

"Problem?"

Donnie disconnected the call and dialed again. "I'm getting a busy signal. Which means Mandy probably knocked the phone off the hook in the bedroom again."

JJ watched as Donnie stomped his foot, disconnected the call, and tried dialing again. "I should have seen this coming. My name and picture have been all over the news. No way could el-Hajid let this pass. These guys are all about retaliation and intimidation." He disconnected the call. "Still busy."

"We're going to need help, Donnie. We can't handle them alone, and we can't run."

Donnie ran his fingers through his hair. "That means trusting Mann."

"I'm sure he'll come through on this."

Donnie looked at JJ, uncertainty flickering in his eyes. "I suppose it's worth a try, but so help me, if he lets us down again. . ."

"He won't," JJ assured him. "There's Zoe. Let's go."

JJ opened the driver's door. "I'm driving."

Zoe climbed over the console and into the passenger seat as Donnie slid in beside Lisbeth in the backseat. JJ tossed his cell phone to Lisbeth. "Call your house. Let us know when someone answers."

"What's going on?" Zoe asked.

"We're just concerned about everyone at the house."

"Jim? Bevere. We got a problem. A suicide bomber just tried to pay a visit to Lisbeth at the hospital. I want my family protected, do you hear me? It's going to take us nearly an hour to get home with traffic. How fast can you get help to my house?"

JJ pushed the Jeep through traffic without regard to speed limit. Weaving in and out of city traffic, he headed for the Wilson Bridge. He was never going to complain about Monroe County traffic ever again.

Donnie disconnected his call. "He'll meet us at the house."

"The line is still busy," Lisbeth cried out softly. "What if it's busy because. . ."

"Don't, Lisbeth. Don't even think like that." Donnie wrapped his arms around his wife.

Zoe glanced over her shoulder. "The Lord has brought you this far. Don't go losing hope now."

◆　◆　◆

Mack lifted Cody out of the swing as he addressed his wife. "Why don't we go downstairs? The kids are in the family room, and who knows what those two will get into."

Jane wiped her hands on the dish towel and draped it over the edge of the sink. "That sounds like a good idea. I'm just going to get my knitting."

Mack carried Cody downstairs and was going to put him on the floor, but Mandy and Justin were running remote control cars from one end of the room to the other. With his luck and their driving skills, Cody would end up the casualty of a hit and run.

He set Cody in the playpen in the corner instead, settled down on the sofa, and turned on the television. Jane joined him a few minutes later, curling her feet up under her to keep them out of the way of the trucks.

"Coward," he told her, grinning.

Slipped her glasses on, took her needles in hand, and didn't even give him a second glance. She started knitting. "I'm no fool."

Maureen came bouncing down the steps. "Okay, Lisbeth's room is all ready for her. I put fresh linens on her bed, cleaned her bathroom, and lit one of those wonderful aromatic candles. Lavender. Very relaxing. Everything is dusted and vacuumed and put away."

Jane kept her eyes on her knitting. "Thank you so much for doing that. I was going to get to it earlier but got caught up with all the cooking."

Maureen dropped down on the sofa between her parents. "What are we watching?"

"From Here to Eternity," Mack answered.

"Again? How many times have you seen that movie?" She reached for the remote.

He grabbed the remote and tucked it under his thigh. "As long as they keep running it, I'll keep watching it."

Mack felt the rumble before he heard it. There was no time to do anything but scream, "Get down!"

He turned and leaped over to the playpen as the room exploded in a deafening roar and disappeared in a shroud of smoke.

chapter 23

Donnie leaned over JJ's shoulder, pointing to the sky. "Look!"

JJ sped up, going around the corner so fast the Jeep fishtailed a little, squealing wheels in the process.

Lisbeth started weeping quietly, burying her face in her hands. Zoe propped her elbow on the edge of the window, covered her eyes, and went quiet. Donnie knew she was praying.

"God, no," Donnie whispered. "Please, Lord, not our house."

Fire trucks jammed the cul-de-sac. JJ, unable to get close to the house, pulled over to the curb. Everyone except Lisbeth jumped out and began to run toward what remained of the house.

Smoke billowed into the air as flames leaped high into the air. Neighbors gathered in groups, watching Donnie's house crumble. Firemen rushed from house to truck to pumper to hydrant. The fire chief yelled orders; men jumped to obey. Police worked on taking statements from anyone who might have seen anything before the explosion, and working crowd control.

Jim Mann stood on the fringe of the activity, staring at the house in disbelief. Four agents mingled around him, talking on cell phones.

Donnie rushed up to him. "Tell me you got everyone out."

Mann shook his head. "I'm sorry, Donnie. The house exploded just as we were coming around the corner. We came as soon as you called us, but we were still too late."

Donnie turned and rushed over to the fire chief. "My family is in there!"

The chief nodded. "Only the front and right side of the house is engaged. We have men working in the back. They have heard someone yelling for help in the rubble. We're trying to get the fire out so we can get in there and rescue the survivors."

The word *survivors* rang in his ears, echoed through his brain, and jabbed at his heart. Who had survived?

JJ put a hand on his shoulder. "What do we know?"

"They know there are survivors. They're trying to get to them."

"You want me to go tell Lisbeth?"

Donnie nodded. "I need to be here."

"I understand."

Zoe linked her arm in his. "I'll stay with you."

Donnie barely heard her. He just stared at the house. El-Hajid had succeeded.

"I can't do this anymore," he murmured. And hearing himself say it gave his words life. He walked over to Mann. "I quit. I'll have my resignation on your desk within the week. I won't be back."

"Don't do this, Donnie. Never make a decision like this in the heat of a crisis. Wait. This is exactly what el-Hajid wants. Don't let him win."

"He's already won."

Donnie circled the house, and when he reached the back-yard, saw Mandy's little playhouse. It had caught fire, but one of the firefighters had doused it. Part of the roof was gone, but it could easily be rebuilt.

If there were a Mandy to rebuild it for. The thought jammed his throat like bile.

"Donnie?" Zoe caught up to him. "What are you going to do?"

He shrugged, shook his head, and didn't know for sure. "I just need to be here when they find. . ."

Who? Who would they find? Mack. Jane. Mandy. Justin. Cody. Maureen. Who would survive? And who would they bury?

The question burned like acid through his veins, but he couldn't respond to it. Numb, he stood there and watched as the firemen worked at pulling lumber and siding and bricks away from where the basement door had once been.

It seemed like hours passed as he stood there watching them clear debris and enter the basement of the house. JJ and Zoe flanked him now, but he still hadn't said anything to them. He couldn't. What was there to say?

Lisbeth stood in front of him, leaning back into him, with his arms wrapped around her, holding her close. She was as silent in her fear as he was. They could only stand there and pray. And the prayers had become so repetitive, they had ceased long ago.

Finally, one of the firefighters emerged with a small body draped in his arms. "I have a little boy here. He's alive."

Justin. Justin made it. As quickly as they had found him, he must have been in the basement playing at the time of the explosion. Mandy was probably with him.

He and Lisbeth moved closer as they placed Justin on a stretcher and quickly put an oxygen mask on him. The boy never opened his eyes.

Another firefighter emerged, a woman slung over his shoulders. EMTs ran over to help lay her out on the ground until another stretcher was brought around.

Lisbeth stiffened. "Maureen."

"I've got a pulse," someone yelled out.

Lisbeth sagged against him. "Mandy? Cody? Where are they, Donnie?"

They both knew he had no answer for her, so he remained silent.

It was nearly five minutes before another body was brought out. Lisbeth grabbed his hand. It was Mandy. And she was screaming her head off.

Choking a laugh, Lisbeth pushed forward and grabbed their daughter out of the fireman's arms. "It's okay, baby. It's okay. Mommy and Daddy are here."

Lisbeth sank to her knees, rocking Mandy while EMTs tried to check her for injuries. She had a cut on her head, scratches on her arms, and what appeared to be a light burn on one leg.

Donnie knelt there, wanting to smother them both in his arms and fighting the feeling, knowing the medical team needed to treat his daughter's injuries.

Then the fireman who had brought out Maureen emerged again, this time carrying Jane. She was barely conscious, but clearly alive. Donnie hurried over and grabbed her hand as they placed her on a stretcher. "It's okay, Jane. We're here."

"Mack?" she whispered softly. "He had the baby."

"They'll bring him out in a minute. You just rest."

She closed her eyes.

Donnie stood up and watched for the next fireman, his heart crying out to God, half in gratitude that so far, everyone had survived, half begging for the life of the two who still had not been found.

When another firefighter emerged, he was screaming. Flames licked up the back of his coat as he sheltered something in his arms.

Cody.

Donnie ran forward. Another firefighter was spraying his buddy, putting out the flames while another took Cody from his arms.

Donnie reached out and touched his son's cheek. Cody looked up at him and smiled.

Donnie's heart shook in his chest.

"He seems to be just fine," the firefighter said as he handed the baby over to one of the medical team.

Then Lisbeth was there, taking the baby away from the EMT, weeping openly, cradling Cody in her arms.

Donnie turned in time to hear the firefighter explaining.

"The beams came through. There's one more in there. A man. He was protecting the baby with his body. He told us to bring out the child first. We were almost out when the whole ceiling came down. I don't know if we can get back in there to get him."

Mack.

Oh, Mack.

Donnie knew tears were streaking down his face, but he couldn't feel them; and he didn't care who saw them.

"You have to try," he told one of the firefighters.

But the firefighter's response was cut off when the house suddenly crashed in on itself.

Donnie swayed. Felt someone's hands on him.

And then felt nothing at all.

◆　◆　◆

Zoe looked up as JJ waved a cup of coffee under her nose. "We have to stop meeting like this."

The hospital waiting room was half full and fairly noisy. She had just tuned it all out, retreating to a place of solitude and peace. Prayer.

JJ snorted, dropping down into the seat beside her. "Truth, woman."

"It's hard to believe, isn't it? I keep thinking that any minute now, I'll wake up and find that this was just a bad dream."

JJ reached over and gently stroked her back. "I know the feeling. Look, I know you're the one who's usually pointing out the positive while I'm busy focusing on the negative, but I'm going to switch places with you for a minute. Only one person died in that explosion. It could have been all of them."

Zoe couldn't help smiling over at him, then dropping her head against his arm, snuggling closer. "You always manage to surprise me, Josiah Johnson. You're right. It could have been far, far worse. It's a miracle everyone else got out, not only alive, but with relatively minor injuries."

"Miracle?" JJ kissed her temple. "Maybe. And maybe it was because the bomb was placed on the wrong side of the house. If everyone had been upstairs or in the kitchen, they wouldn't have had a chance."

"And you don't think that maybe it was a miracle the bomb was placed where it was and everyone had gone downstairs?"

"I don't know, baby." He ran his hand down her arm. "I'll go along with the fact that it was a miracle everyone was downstairs at the time of the explosion. How's that?"

Tired, hungry, and content to have his arms around her, Zoe closed her eyes and leaned in closer to JJ. When she felt him stiffen, she opened her eyes. Donnie was coming down the hall toward them.

She straightened, setting her coffee down on the chair beside her, and stood up. When Donnie drew close, she opened her arms, and he walked into her hug. "Thanks, I needed that."

"How is everyone?"

"Good," he replied, nodding his head, emotion swirling in his eyes. "Everyone's being released. Jane's hurt, but hers is more emotional than physical."

Donnie took a deep breath. "Jack is on his way. He's loaning me his van. I'm taking everyone to a hotel tonight, and then tomorrow, we'll drive to Mack's. . .Jane's place in Ohio."

Zoe reached out and touched his arm. "That's a good idea. She needs to be home, with all her family around her."

Donnie nodded again. "And it'll be better for the kids. I called Justin's grandmother, and she made arrangements to be released tomorrow. I'll take Justin home on the way out of town."

"And after? What are *you* going to do?" JJ asked.

With a shrug, Donnie dropped his eyes. "I don't know. It's too soon to say. I have a lot of thinking to do." He looked up. "What about you guys?"

"Well," JJ replied. "I don't think you need us anymore, so we'll head home and clean up the mess we left behind."

Donnie's lips twisted in a sober smile. "I can't thank either one of you enough. I don't think I could have made it through all this without your help."

Zoe reached up and gave him another hug. "We love you, Donnie Bevere."

"Yeah, well." He blushed. "Right back at ya."

After JJ and Donnie shook hands, Zoe and JJ stood and watched Donnie walk back down the hall, his shoulders slumped.

"Do you think he'll be all right?" JJ asked.

Zoe linked her fingers in his. "He'll never be the same, but he'll be all right. The Lord never wastes anything in our lives to bring us closer to Him."

"I'm not going to pretend to understand that," JJ admitted as they finally turned and headed for the elevator. "I guess it's one of those things I'll just come to figure out in time."

Zoe smiled inwardly. *Yeah. You will.* She reached out and pushed the button for the elevator. "So when do we have to be back here for the lunch at the White House?"

"I think they said two to three weeks. They're going to let us know."

"Looking forward to it?" she asked as the elevator doors opened and they stepped inside.

JJ pushed the button for the lobby. "It has a certain appeal."

Laughing, Zoe stepped over and wrapped her arms around his waist. "And what is that?"

"Food. I'm starved."

chapter 24

Monday, February 20

Zoe opened the door to the salon and stepped in. Instead of the usual light rock music, a lively jazz tune was playing. She stepped up to the receptionist. The last time Zoe had been in the salon, the girl's hair had been tipped in red. Today it was tipped in purple.

The girl smiled up at Zoe. "Hi, you're here to see Daria, right?"

"Yes. Is she busy?"

The girl shook her head. "She's not taking appointments."

"Well, she is now. Can you let her know she has a customer?" Zoe made her way back to Daria's station and sat down in the chair. She spun it around and waited for Daria to come out of the office.

Daria came out a minute later, the confusion on her face clearing into a welcoming grin. "Zoe! You're back!"

Zoe stood up and embraced Daria. "Got back early yesterday morning and then slept most of the day away. You look great." She reached up and fingered Daria's spiked hair. "You colored it lighter. I like it."

"Thanks. So you need a trim?"

"More than that. I want you to cut it all off."

Daria's jaw dropped, and she took a step backward. "What? You can't be serious."

"I'm extremely serious. I want you to cut it."

"Zoe." Daria's tone was that of a mother trying to deal with an unreasonable child. "You have hair most women would die for. You've been growing it forever." She narrowed her eyes. "Does JJ know you're cutting it off?"

"It's none of JJ's business, and I need to cut it off."

"Need?"

Zoe sat down. "Do you remember meeting a young girl at the hospital. Erin?"

"Sure. We snarled at each other for a couple of days, and I wasn't home twenty-four hours before I was back over there visiting her. She's a terrific kid."

"And because of cancer, she's bald. I contacted Locks of Love. They'll take my donation of hair and make a wig for Erin."

Daria's eyes filled with tears. "That is the most incredible thing I've ever heard. Wow."

"It's just hair, Daria. It'll grow back."

Daria swiped at her tears and then waved airily. "You'll never grow it this long again. Trust me." She took a deep breath. "Okay. I'll do it. Go back and get it shampooed while I sharpen my scissors."

Five minutes later, Daria tied Zoe's hair just below the shoulder. Then she took her scissors. "You're sure?"

"I'm sure," Zoe replied. And she was. Her mom had told her the hats were selling faster than Erin could make them, but selling them meant she had less of them to wear. She had so much hair, and Erin had none. It was the perfect solution.

Daria hesitated as she put the scissors at the cut line.

"Do it," Zoe insisted.

With another deep breath, Daria cut the hair off and then lifted it up so Zoe could see it. The whole salon saw it, and there were numerous *oohs* and *aahs*.

Zoe reached up and touched her head. She shook it. "It's so much lighter."

With a laugh, Daria handed Zoe the ponytail of hair. "I'm sure it is. Now hush, and let the master work on your hair. I want a style that is going to knock JJ's socks off."

◆　◆　◆

JJ was fidgeting. He knew it, but he couldn't stop it. All around him, conversation hummed low and steady. Waiters moved quickly, but efficiently, from table to table. The linen was crisp and clean, the crystal sparkled, the silver gleamed, and the smell coming from the kitchen was making his mouth water.

He glanced at his watch. Where was she? He had chosen the restaurant; she had insisted on meeting him here. The least she could do was—

His thoughts fled as he caught sight of her weaving her way through the restaurant toward him. Slowly, he stood up. She was wearing black. A calf-length black dress with long sleeves and a full skirt. Okay, he had never seen her in black, but that wasn't what was making his jaw drop.

She'd cut her hair!

It barely swept her shoulders, sleek and straight, framing her face, lifting her cheekbones, and widening her eyes. She was stunning.

He had always thought her beautiful. She was far beyond that tonight.

"JJ?"

The look in her eyes said she was nervously waiting for some response, but he couldn't seem to make his mouth work.

With eyes darting all around her, she slid into her chair and picked up her napkin.

"You cut it," he finally managed to say.

She reached up and touched it. "Yes."

"You look. . ."

When he hesitated, searching for the right word, she looked up at him. "I look what?"

"Beyond stunning."

Then she smiled. Her eyes lit up with pleasure. "Thank you."

JJ realized he was still standing and drawing attention to himself. Or maybe they were all staring at Zoe. He couldn't blame them. He quickly folded himself into his chair. "Wow."

She emitted a light laugh. "I guess that's a good reaction. I cut it and donated the hair to Locks of Love. They're going to make a wig for Erin."

"That's a wonderful thing for you to have done, Zoe."

She shrugged, shaking out her napkin and laying it in her lap. "I was tired of all that hair anyway. I had to keep it tied up all the time, or I'd sit down on it. It took forever to wash and dry. This will be better."

"It looks great."

The waiter slipped up to the table. "Can I get you anything to drink?"

Zoe picked up her menu. "Just water with lemon, please."

"Iced tea," JJ added.

The waiter nodded and slipped away.

Zoe lowered her menu. "So how was your first day back on the job?"

"It was good. I spent most of the day catching up on current cases and everything that happened while I was away. Matt said to say hi."

"Tell him I said hi right back. Did Harris question you about everything that happened in Washington?"

JJ rolled his eyes. "Endlessly. I couldn't decide if he was angry that I drew so much attention to myself, or if he was thrilled that one of his men has drawn national attention for doing something good."

"He should be proud of you. It reflects well on him."

JJ studied the menu, his hand drifting down to his pocket. It was still there.

"JJ?"

He jumped, startled. "What?"

"I asked you what you were going to order."

"Oh. I haven't made up my mind."

She eyed him warily before slowly dragging her eyes back to the menu. The waiter returned with their drinks and then took their order.

Zoe ordered the salmon, and he ordered a steak. They made small talk over their salads about pending cases at the station. Then their meals arrived, and they chatted about Zoe taking the day off from work, getting her hair cut, and visiting with Erin at the hospital.

"It sounds like Daria is getting back to her old self," JJ said, pushing his plate away.

"She is. I think Erin is helping in that. I didn't realize at the time that they would end up being so good for each other."

"Speaking of good for each other—"

"Can I get either of you coffee?" The waiter suddenly appeared, picking up their dishes.

"No, thanks," JJ said. "I've had enough of that stuff for a few days."

Zoe laughed. "No doubt. I think we lived on it for the week." She looked up at the waiter. "None for me either. Thanks."

The waiter nodded and cleared the table. As soon as he had left, Zoe turned back to JJ. "You were saying."

"If one more person interrupts me, I'm going to pull my gun."

Zoe's brows furrowed, and she tilted her head. "What?"

"I've been trying to say this to you for over a week, and it seems like every time I start, someone interrupts us." He reached into his pocket. "What I'm trying to say is—"

"Dessert?" the waiter asked.

JJ clamped his mouth shut. Zoe laughed, but she was the one to shake her head and say, "That's all for tonight, thanks. Just the check."

The waiter nodded and disappeared again. JJ took a deep breath. "He'll be back in thirty seconds."

Zoe leaned forward, her eyes sparkling with humor. "Then you better say it fast."

Reaching into his pocket, he pulled out the little box and handed it to her. "Will you marry me?"

Zoe stared at the ring. Then she lifted her eyes to JJ. They were filled with tears. "You're asking me to marry you?"

"I think that's what I'm doing. Let me see. Declaration of love, diamond ring, romantic dinner. Yep. I do think that's what this is." A thought suddenly occurred to him. A horrifying thought. "You aren't going to make me get down on one knee right here in front of everyone, are you?"

Zoe shook her head as she gently lifted the ring from the box. She wiped at the tears with one hand while holding the ring out to him with her left hand. It was trembling. "You better put it on. I don't think I can."

He took the ring and then her hand, slipping the ring onto her finger. "I guess that's a yes."

She laughed that little laugh that always made delightful little shimmers echo in his heart. Light, bright, and pure Zoe.

chapter 25

Zoe critically studied her image in the full-length mirror. She was wearing an emerald green silk shirt, matching calf-length floral skirt, heeled boots, and a cashmere scarf in the same pale pink reflected in the skirt.

Tugging on her bottom lip, she wondered if it was right for a White House luncheon.

She fluffed her hair, once again enjoying how light and airy it felt. The barest touch of blush on her cheeks and a touch of mascara. This was as good as it was going to get.

There was knock on her hotel room door. She pulled it open.

JJ stared wide-eyed. "You look beautiful."

Zoe whirled around so JJ could admire the whole package. "Yeah?"

"Very. You know those secret service guys who never show any emotion?"

"Yes?"

JJ grinned. "They'll be showing emotion today. Jealousy that I'm the man you're with."

She went up on her toes to kiss him for that. Then she stood back to admire JJ. They had gone shopping the day before, and he was wearing a new suit in olive green that Zoe told him made his eye color pop. He'd blushed but bought the suit. To go with the suit, she'd talked him into a darker green shirt and tie. Then she saw his feet and frowned.

"Cowboy boots?"

"Trust me," he told her.

"Well, you look wonderful. Is Donnie ready?"

"We're waiting on you, gorgeous."

She was looking forward to seeing Donnie and Lisbeth. The Bevere family had arrived in Washington late, so there had been no opportunity for a get-together the night before.

She and JJ had been unable to get away to Ohio for Mack's funeral, but they had sent a donation to the Locks of Love organization in his memory.

When the elevator doors opened to the lobby, Zoe stepped out, looking around for Donnie and Lisbeth. She spotted them, as well as Jack, standing near the front doors.

Lisbeth spotted her first, coming forward to embrace her and make a fuss over her hair. Then she spotted the engagement ring on her finger.

"Donnie! They're engaged."

Donnie congratulated them both, smacking JJ on the back. "And you didn't come to me for any help. I'm proud of you."

"Have you set the date?" Lisbeth asked as they stepped outside and into the limo waiting for them.

"Not yet," Zoe told her as she settled herself in. "I'm talking six months; he's talking six weeks."

That drew laughter from everyone.

◆   ◆   ◆

Zoe took JJ's hand and held on to it as they were led through the maze of halls echoing with memories and seeped in history. JJ's eyes were unusually huge as he stared at the sparkling crystal chandeliers and the rich woods glistening with lemon oil and loving care.

She could relate to his awe. It was magnificent. Huge oil paintings, lush draperies, expensive fabrics, thick carpets, and priceless antiques. Up the wide, sweeping staircase and down the endless hall of portraits. It made you inclined to speak in whispers.

Once in the West Wing, they were led into a conference room and asked to wait.

"If this were all there was, it would be enough," Zoe said, sinking down into a soft leather chair.

Lisbeth sat down slowly, perching on the edge of her seat as if afraid she'd break it. "I am so nervous, my hands are like ice."

But the girls weren't the only ones affected by their surroundings. JJ was fidgeting with his tie. Donnie was pacing. Jack couldn't seem to find a comfortable position to sit in.

Finally, the doors opened, and one of the aides strode in, carrying a clipboard. Everyone stood up. "Okay, I'm going to be taking you to the Oval Office where you will meet with the president for fifteen minutes. Then the press will be admitted for a photo op. That will last ten minutes. From there, you will proceed over to the Blue Room where the press will have an opportunity to ask questions. We would like you to keep your answers as brief as possible. If anyone asks you something you don't feel comfortable answering, simply say: 'No comment.'"

The rules and protocol went on for another five minutes, and then they were finally taken up to the Oval Office.

It seemed to take forever to finally get into the Oval Office, and then it seemed as if it was over in seconds and they were standing in front of the press taking questions.

Lunch was less formal and just as rushed. The president was interrupted four times by someone whispering in his ear, and as soon as he was finished eating, he stood to leave. "I'm sorry for leaving you like this, but I have a meeting in five." They stood up as he went around the table and shook hands with everyone. "I'm very proud of you all. What you did was very courageous."

He spoke a moment with each of them, thanking them again for going above and beyond to protect the national security, and then two aides swept him out, both talking at once, followed by two secret service agents.

The aide attached to them insisted that the president wanted them to relax and take their time with lunch, but it was as if when the president left, he took all the life in the room with him.

"He is far more charismatic in person than he is on television," Jack said as soon as they were back in the limo and headed home.

"How he does it, I'll never know. It seemed like there were fifty things coming at him all the time. I'd be pulling my hair out."

"That's why all presidents go gray during the first four years." Zoe laughed and leaned her head back. She was exhausted. She turned her head and looked over at Donnie. "You've been awfully quiet. What's going on in that mind of yours?"

Donnie blinked, as if jarred from his thoughts. "You know when the undersecretary of Homeland Security took me aside to talk to me before lunch?"

"Yes."

"He offered me a job with his office. Information Analysis and Infrastructure Protection. Isn't that a mouthful?"

Zoe couldn't tell if Donnie was pleased or not. "Are you thinking about taking it?"

"Maybe." He pulled at his tie and unbuttoned the top button of his shirt. Then he shook his head. "No. I'm happy with the FBI. I think I'll stay with them."

Lisbeth laid her head on his shoulder. "We're going to rebuild and go on."

JJ wrapped his arm around Zoe. "And we're going to build."

"You're going to stay with the police force?" Donnie asked him.

"For now. Five years down the road, who knows?"

"He'll still be there," Zoe said. "And I'll be working part-time for Dan."

JJ slanted his eyes in her direction. "And is this just a nice guess, or are you getting that feeling of yours again?"

Her lips curved in a sly smile. "You'll just have to wait and see, won't you?"

He lifted her hand to his lips. "You're not going to make my life easy, are you?"

"Never."

JJ kissed her hand. "Thank goodness. No. Wait. Thank You, Lord."

JJ leaned over and opened the bar. "Anyone want something? We have Pepsi, Sprite, water, juice, and iced tea."

"Pepsi," Zoe said.

Jack was fiddling with his tie. "Nothing."

"Nothing for me," Donnie replied.

Lisbeth ordered water.

There were a pop and a hiss as JJ opened Zoe's soda and poured some into a clear plastic cup. He handed it to her. "Don't spill it."

She gave him one of those looks that made him smile. He handed Lisbeth her water and paused in front of Zoe to give her a quick kiss before settling back in his seat with his iced tea.

He raised his bottle of iced tea. "To love, to family, and to friends. May God always bless us with plenty of all three."

A Word from the Author:

For more information on Locks of Love and their Wigs for Kids Cancer Program, please contact:

Locks of Love
2925 10th Avenue North
Suite 102
Lake Worth, FL 33461
561-963-1677

To find a participating salon in your area, visit them online at:
http://www.locksoflove.org

About the Author

Wanda L. Dyson is a Christian counselor, author, and speaker. She has released two novels, *Abduction* and *Obsession*, to critical acclaim. The mother of an autistic child, Wanda lives on a farm with her quarter horses and Australian shepherds. For more information on Wanda and her books, visit her Web site at: www.WandaDyson.com.